Harley's Return

Wait For Me

Ride With Harley Series Book 3

Cassandra Parker

Parker, Cassandra (2018-09-30). Harley's Return. Cassandra Parker. E-book Edition.

Parker, Cassandra (2018-09-30). Harley's Return. Cassandra Parker. Paper bac Edition.

Dedication

This book is dedicated to John Goadsby aka Goldy McJohn for his endless hours of musical enjoyment. R.I P. Goldy, original founding member of Steppenwolf. Sonja Goadsby, the heart of Goldy McJohn, for her kind and generous spirit.

Goldy, you might be gone from the physical plane, but your spirit soars onward in the heavens. Every time we hear the thunder, it is you playing your Lowry organ and rocking out 'Heavy Metal Thunder.' When the rain tinkles up and down the scales, it is you playing 'Tenderness.' The sound of a Harley-Davidson motorcycle roaring down the asphalt highway is you ripping up 'Born to be Wild.' When we look into the night sky and see the winking of a star, it is you looking down from the heavens. Stay free, stay wild my friend. Most of all, you are watching over your fans and your heart, Sonja.

Sonja, Goldy isn't gone for good. You will meet again when the time is right.

Tina Schneider at The Ohio State University-Lima Campus. Your help in researching historical information on WOSL radio is greatly appreciated.

R. Harley, my angel, this one's for you wherever you might be in the heavens. This is our story as it might have been.

Acknowledgments

Jennifer Reginato for her editing and encouragement without which this book would never have been completed. She kicked my butt when I wanted to throw in the towel.

To Kim Williams for her proofreading and endless hours reading aloud while I followed along in print.

Amber whose enthusiasm and encouragement helped me over the rough spots.

Anne Mangas Smith whose poetry got me through rough times after the loss of R. Harley all those years ago.

To Carsten Degenhardt whose insights, encouragement and friendship I cherish.

To Gloria Siddoway for her invaluable opinions and enthusiasm.

To the wonderful staff at Piatt Castles for providing historical information.

To Amanda, Monica, and Donna, you know who you are. For encouragement and support.

Chapter One

1977 Star Wars opened in cinemas. Roots, a mini tv series was aired. The Concord cut transatlantic flying time. Elvis Presley died at age 42. Roman Polanski is arrested and charged with sexual misconduct. The New York City Black Out lasted twenty-five hours.

Mari

"Mari," Harley's voice sounded weak. He had been hospitalized for months. As time passed, he seemed to lose more strength and vitality. He was so thin; a mere shell of the man I knew. He looked like a skeleton, so much weight had dropped from his frame. Even his muscles appeared flaccid.

A large lump formed in my throat. Harley was so pale and haggard it tore my heart asunder. I looked around the hospital room. All the medical equipment, the IV pole, the narrow bed, the bland colors, the room was nothing like the Harley I had come to know and love. It was so sterile and had a medicine stench. I remember thinking all this agony must have a reason, but what; I didn't know. I would gladly trade places with him; he meant the world to me. It hurt to see him like this.

"My parents want to take me back east. They said Columbia or Walter Reed hospitals would give me a better chance of beating this Rhabdomyoscarcoma. They also mentioned MD Anderson in Houston, Texas. They specialize in cancer treatment." His voice was raspy; weary.

Rhabdomyoscarcoma is also known as RMS. Even the name sounded terrible. It is a very aggressive malignant form of soft tissue cancer that generally affects children and young adults. Harley had the most aggressive form known as Anaplastic Rhabdomyoscarcoma. Back in 1977, the survival and cure rate was not high. Once the cancer has spread, less than twenty percent of its' victims survive.

"What do you want to do?" I perched on the side of his bed and rested my hand on his. I spooned some pudding into his mouth and gently wiped his lips.

"It appears treatment might take a while with surgery, chemotherapy, radiation, and something called immunotherapy. I understand that this therapy is relatively new. It became available in 1975. Insurance won't cover it because the company considers it to be experimental. I would have to pay for it out of pocket."

"Is that what you want to do?" I fought to keep my tears at bay.

"It gives me the best chance of beating this cancer. Not much of a chance, mind you, only twenty percent. Mari, it's spread from my leg to my lungs and bone marrow," he sounded depressed and scared. "I don't want to do it, but it's my only option."

"If it doesn't work?" I asked softly, feeling as though my spirit was being ripped from my body. A dreadful sense that this might be one of the last times I saw Harley washed over me. I felt so terribly cold with fear.

"I want to die at my home in Lima surrounded by you, Garrett, and Thomas." His voice was barely above a whisper as he talked.

"Then that's what you should do." My heart was breaking hearing him talk as though he was going to lose this battle. I struggled to keep the tears in check.

"We'd have to postpone our wedding plans, possibly forever." A deep sadness overcame him, twisting his handsome face into a mask of emotional pain. "It'd be selfish of me to ask you to wait for me. I can't do that to you."

"I know." I whispered, "just don't let us go because I won't let you. Even if we never officially marry, I will always be yours, and you mine. I'll wait for you." I paused for a long time trying to find the right words.

"Harley, I want what is best for you. If you think this treatment will help you get well, then I'm all for it. I will wait for you for however long it takes, forever if necessary." I gently held his hand.

Even the slightest touch seemed to cause him pain. "You are my love for eternity. The first time I saw you, I never thought someone like you would be so kind, generous, caring, and loving. What I saw was a biker dude, with a stubborn streak and a bit of a temper. But something in your eyes and your demeanor said I didn't see past the facade. I never thought I could love anyone as much as I do you."

He smiled and puckered his lips. I bent forward and gently kissed him. "You turned my life upside down, Harlan Christian Robert Davis. You made all my days bright and sunny. You helped me become a better person."

"Awe, shucks, ma'am." Pleasure spread across his face. "I fell in love with you the moment I saw you, Mari." His eyes never left my face as he spoke. "It was the day I woke up in the hospital after wrecking my Hog. I had a vision of you sitting by my bed telling me to come find you."

We spent the next few hours quietly. I gave Harley sips of ice water to soothe his parched throat. Tenderly I wiped the sweat from his brow, tucked blankets around him, and adjusted his pillows to make him more comfortable. When he said his back hurt, I helped him roll onto his side and gently massaged him. I placed many kisses on his lips, his hands, and his cheeks while murmuring, "I love you."

The door to the hospital room opened, and his parents strode inside.

"Mari," his father said dismissively. "Harlan, we've come to take you home. The hospital has completed the transfer papers for Columbia University Hospital in Manhattan. An ambulance is waiting to take you to the airport."

"Father," Harley struggled to sit up. I pressed the button on his bedside to raise the head of his bed. "I think MD Anderson in Houston is a better option. They specialize in cancer treatment."

"Columbia is a fine hospital. They keep abreast of all new medical treatments."

"Mister Davis, please excuse me for interrupting." I bristled at the authoritative tone of his voice. "This is Harley's life we're talking about. Don't you think he should have the final decision on where he gets treated?" I rested my hand on Harley's shoulder.

"Who do you think you are to address me so rudely?"

"She is my fiancée, Father. I'll not have you speaking to her this way." Harley gripped my hand while glaring at his father.

"I believe I know better than you, Mari, what is better for my son. You are young, and Harley has authority issues."

"If you mean, he doesn't like being bossed around, you're right. I'm just saying, it's his life. He should be the one to select what his options are." How dare he talk in such a dismissive manner about my beloved!

"I am his medical power of attorney. Harlan is too ill to make such an important decision."

"Since when, Father? I don't remember giving you that authority." He looked at me. "In fact, I distinctly remember asking Garrett to be my DPA."

"He isn't. I am. You were delirious when you made that selection and later changed it."

"Did I? I don't remember doing that."

A cadre of nurses and attendants entered the room. "Well, Harlan, everything is set. We're going to put you on a gurney and take you to the ambulance. We wish you the best and hope for a full recovery." The nurse said cheerfully.

With practiced ease, the attendants lifted Harley off the bed and placed him on the gurney while keeping the IV lines from tangling.

"Walk with me, Mari?" He looked so lost. "Hold my hand?"

"Of course, my love."

As he was wheeled down the hall, Harley's gaze never wavered from me. "Do not be sad for me. I've lived a full life made even better with you at my side." He softly squeezed my hand. "Nothing can ever separate us, not even death. I will be with you always."

"And I will do the same for you, my love. Whatever the fates bring, just wait for me."

As we reached the ambulance, he pulled my hand to his lips and kissed each finger. "I will always love you with all my heart and soul. I will always watch over you."

I felt dampness running down my face and reached up to touch the tears. When they started, I have no idea other than somewhere between Harley's room and the vehicle.

“If I should die, Mari, you will not be alone. I will be the leaf tumbling across your path on a windy day. I will be the stray hint of the sunshine that kisses your face on a cloudy day. I will be the moonshine smiling at you. When you are feeling scared or down, I will be the soft unseen touch on your shoulder, the scent of Old Spice and Irish Spring when no one is around, and the hint of a familiar voice calling your name.”

“I will love you forever my Steppenwolf loving prince. Or should I say a biker?” I leaned forward to place one last kiss on his lips before they took him away.

I stood in the ambulance bay watching as they took my heart away. I don’t know how long I remained there.

“Miss Mari?” Garrett walked toward me. “Master Harley requested I make sure you got home okay. Come with me.” He gently guided me down the sidewalk to where he had parked the limousine.

“After I take you home, I will be leaving Lima to join Master Harley at Columbia. You have my solemn word I will take care of him as best as possible during these trying times. I will do my best to make sure his wishes are honored.”

“I know you will do your best, Garrett. You are more of a father to him than Mister Davis ever was. He loves you.”

“Thank you, Miss Mari. I will keep you updated and try to find a way for you and Master Harley to talk.”

Garrett was true to his word. Every week he got my work schedule and arranged for Harley to call me. He made secret arrangements with the hospital to allow long distance calls with payments from Harley’s emergency savings. The calls often came after ten at night and were brief but filled with remembrances of our escapades. We laughed a lot during those telephone conversations.

“Hi, my love,” he greeted me. “How are you?”

“Missing you. Everyone at WOSL sends you greetings.” My heart felt laden with loneliness. How could this one man I’d barely known two years cause such bittersweet memories, by night and fill my every waking thought by day?

"I miss you too," he whispered.

"Peg says to tell you not to let the aliens cart you away in their flying saucer."

"You tell Peg they're not taking me anywhere. Tell her those probes up my butt, in my brain, and belly sure hurt." He chuckled,

"That Peg is a live wire!" Harley paused for several minutes, his voice dropped in pitch and became serious. "They say it's too early to say for certain, but I might be responding to treatment."

"That's good, Harley! Keep responding, and you'll be home in no time." That little bit of news lifted my spirits beyond measure.

It gave me hope. Hope for a future with the best, most endearing, generous, enchanting, and yet frustrating man I have the pleasure of knowing.

"The chemicals make me feel so sick, weak and tired. I wish it were all over and I was back home."

This was the first time I'd ever heard him complain. How awful the treatments must make him feel. "I wish you were too. Classes this term have been hard to concentrate on and the quarter just started!"

"And WOSL?"

"Is doing fine. We are officially on the air. We got the tower and the FCC permits. Everyone is excited." Just hearing his voice made me both happy and lonely.

"I dedicate a Steppenwolf song to you every show. Today's was 'Rock and Roll Song' from their 'Skullduggery' album. Tomorrow I'm playing 'Hippo Stomp,' to encourage you to stomp out that cancer. No matter how many times you slide down and stumble around, you get back up. After that, I'm putting on 'In Hope of a Garden' to remind you of the gardens and gazebo here at home."

"Thanks." I could hear the joy in his voice and the weariness.

"You sound tired. I better let you rest."

"I'm sorry, Mari," his voice wavered. "I am exhausted."

"That's okay, my love. You get some sleep. We'll talk again soon. I love you." I made a kissing noise.

"Love you too," he responded.

Chapter Two

1978 saw a craze for computer video games with the launch of Space Invaders. Atari led the pack with its cassette system. Gold hit a high of $200 an ounce. The first test-tube baby is born. Out on bail, Roman Polanski fled the US to France. 900 members of the 'People's Temple' under cult leader Jim Jones committed suicide in Guyana. The Susan B. Anthony dollar makes its appearance. Japanese vehicles now account for at least half of the car import market in the US. The first cellular phone is introduced in Illinois. Serial killer David Berkowitz, known as the 'Son of Sam,' is convicted of murder. Movies were booming with the release of Grease, Saturday Night Fever, and Close Encounters of the Third Kind.

Harley

January

I sat in the recliner. My heart was filled with happiness. Today was the day I was going home to Lima to rest and recuperate between treatment rounds. Due to my health, it was going to take me several days to get home. I was going to land in Cleveland to rest before continuing to Dayton where I would spend a night and then to Lima. I could go home for three blessed months. I would be surrounded by the people who truly cared about me.

Thomas, the WOSL gang, Garrett, and most of all Mari. Members of my local Church volunteered to accompany Garrett and me to the airport. Garrett must have contacted them.

"I can't wait to get home, Garrett."

"I'm sure you can't, Master Harley. It's been a long time. Everyone sends their love."

"I know. I'm glad you made the arrangements for me to talk with Mari. I miss her so much."

"As do I. She's a keeper, Master Harley."

"I know." I sat quietly kneading my lap blanket as I looked out the window.

Someone from church came by daily when my parents were at lunch or dinner. They shared the gospel with me. The Priesthood said prayers for faith and gave me blessings for strength, and healing. Garrett must have contacted them and explained my situation.

My parents entered the room. "You may leave now, Garrett," Father said dismissing him.

"Master Harley?" Garrett fussed with my lap blanket, making sure it was tucked under my legs.

"Have you eaten?" I asked him. Garrett was more of a parent to me than my mother and father. He was the one person I've always been able to count on. Him and now Mari. Without them and Thomas's constant chatter, I don't know what would happen to me. Garrett steered me in the right direction. Thomas made me laugh when I felt down. Mari, well Mari taught me that true love does exist. She made me understand that I could be loved whether or not I was rich. She got me. Even when I broke her heart, she stayed by me and fought for our relationship. How I long to see her beloved face and hold her in my arms.

"When you were sleeping." He smiled at me.

"I'd rather you stay."

"Then stay, I shall." He perched on the edge of my bed.

I had endured months of agonizing treatments that left me feeling debilitated and constantly nauseous. The doctors said I was well enough to travel. I couldn't wait to see Mari. Even though it was January, I had Christmas gifts to give her. Garrett had picked them out for me.

Mari.

Just thinking about her and my heart beat wildly. I can't wait to see her, hold her, and talk with her. She means the world to me.

Garrett had me add her to my accounts. I was glad I listened to him. She's been paying my household bills and distributed quarterly bonuses to my employees. With Garrett here attending to me, I'm sure she's been a tremendous help to him. I give thanks daily that she took me back after my trip to jerkdom last year.

A horrendous pain hit my chest. It radiated down my shoulders and across my back. It was a sharp clenching agony. What was going on? It was hard to breathe, and I quickly became light-headed. As my vision faded, I heard alarms go off. There was a scurry of activity.

Garrett rushed from my side calling out for a doctor. "We need a doctor in here!"

"We have a code blue!" Someone shouted. Carts rumbled into the room.

"Mister and Mistress Davis, you need to leave!" Shouted a nurse.

Blackness descended upon me.

Cold.

Searing pain.

So cold.

And the pain struck again. Then there was nothing.

I regained consciousness sometime later. The morning light had faded to night. Garrett was not there. I had been moved into intensive care.

My chest ached. I was hooked up to a ventilator. It was difficult to breathe even with the assistance of machines. I had suffered a coronary spasm. This meant the coronary arteries cramped cutting off the flow of blood. Since I had no previous heart problems, it was thought my treatments may have triggered the event.

I drifted in and out and lost track of time. I don't know how long it was before I awakened again. I squinted into the light creeping through the windows. Even those faint, wispy rays burned my eyes. Slowly, I let my vision get used to the brilliance. My memories were foggy at best.

Where was I? The last thing I remembered was being loaded into an ambulance to be flown to Columbia Hospital. Mari was standing beside the bay door looking frightened.

Slowly my memories crept back. The weekend get-together. My collapse. The ambulance. St. Rita's hospital in Lima, being transferred to Dayton. Months later being flown to Columbia. Telephone calls with Mari.

I looked around the room. Sterile. White walls, gray counter, sink, green clothes cabinet. A bedside tray with white flowers in a vase. I was in a hospital room. I was hooked up to a heart and an oxygen monitor. A clear tube ran from a bag into a vein with what I believed to be saline and possibly medicine.

I felt so weary.

So very, very weary.

Sleep overcame me as I closed my eyes.

Floating. I had the sensation of floating on a sea of foam.

I awakened to a light shining in the window. The sunlight had that cold look you only get in winter. A date on a chalkboard told me it was January 9th, the day I was supposed to arrive home. Well, obviously that wasn't happening.

I'd been gone from Lima for six months! Garrett was not in the room. I assumed he went to eat. Faint memories of telephone conversations with Mari came to mind. Mari. How I missed her.

Sleep claimed me once again.

Drifting.

I was drifting in a mist. Through the fog, I heard Mari sobbing. Why was she crying? I could see the faint outline of my home in Lima. She came running from the house into the driveway, repeatedly screaming, "NO!"

"Mari! What's wrong?" I called to her, but she did not respond.

Mari dropped to her knees on the pavement and shook her fists at the sky. "WHY MY HARLEY?"

"Mari, don't give up on me," I pleaded though no sound issued forth from my lips. "I am not gone. I'm just in another place. Wait for me, my love. Wait for me. We'll be together again."

"Why?" She sobbed. Her body shook, and her face was streaked with tears.

"Mari?" I whispered as she faded from sight.

I felt myself drifting away, up into the heavens.

"Mari, I love you." Darkness overcame me and with it came oblivion.

Chapter Three

Mari

January

Months passed, then came the call from Garrett telling me Harley would be coming home in two days. He gave me flight information and asked if I could be at Harley's home when they arrived. Those were the two longest days of my life. Finally, it was time. I raced over to the house and let myself in with the key Harley had given me. Even though I was scared out of my wits, I managed to light a blaze in the fireplace. I turned the furnace on so the rest of the house would be warm.

I even selected some Steppenwolf songs to play when he got home. Among them were 'Berry Rides Again,' 'Howlin' For My Darlin', 'I'm Going Up Stairs,' the rest of the 'Early Steppenwolf' and 'Monster' albums, 'Hour of the Wolf,' and the hit single, 'Born to Be Wild.'

During Garrett's absence, he had hired maids and groundskeepers to keep the place presentable. I often checked the place and picked up the mail. The important ones I told Garrett about and either forwarded them to him or handled them with his instructions such as paying for the maid and grounds service.

Thomas arrived, bringing Harley's favorite Chinese takeout meal. "I thought he might be hungry." He carried the bags to the kitchen. "They aren't here yet?" He asked.

"No," I replied miserably.

"I'll call the airport. Maybe the flight's been delayed." Thomas walked into the foyer and dialed. I could hear snippets of conversation.

"Well, okay. Thanks." Thomas came back into the living room scratching his chin. "The plane landed four hours ago. There was no record of Harley or Garrett being on that flight. Maybe they had to take a later flight. I'll call and check that out."

I felt a creeping sense of dread coming over me. I just knew the answer was not going to be pleasant.

Thomas returned, looking dismayed. “Garrett was on a flight that landed a half hour ago, but Harley wasn’t. I wonder what that means.”

“It means,” I fought to keep the tears and disappointment at bay. “He isn’t coming home.”

I wrapped my arms around me and paced the floor. My heart was filled with dread.

“But his parents said he was doing better, and the doctors were giving him a respite from treatments.”

“They lied,” I said flatly.

Thomas gently guided me back to the sofa.

“Come, sit beside me,” he whispered.

We sat silently on the couch in the living room. Both of us were so wrapped in our thoughts we didn’t hear the car approach the mansion.

“Miss Mari? Mister Thomas?” Garrett called out as he entered the foyer.

“Garrett!” We jumped up and ran to meet him.

“Where’s Harley?” Thomas demanded.

“What happened?” I asked.

“I’m sorry. Master Harley had a sudden relapse late last night. He passed away at eleven this morning. I was tied up with arrangements to transport him to a funeral home. I didn’t want to break the sad news over the telephone, so I took a later flight.” Garrett peered at us with red, puffy eyes.

Thomas abruptly sat on one of the ottomans lining the foyer walls. He stared vacantly at his hands. His fingers kept twining around, forming knots.

Time seemed to come to an abrupt stop. I could hear the ticking of the grandfather clock, the rhythm of the pendulum swinging back and forth was irritating. The crackling of the wood burning in the fireplace was obscenely loud.

I felt terribly cold as though I was standing inside an ice palace. I stood there taking in the scene as though I was frozen in place. Everything seemed to move in slow motion. Then suddenly time came rushing forward bringing with it a multitude of searing, heart-wrenching pain.

I ran from the house into the driveway, repeatedly screaming, “NO!”

I dropped to my knees on the pavement and shook my fists at the sky. “WHY MY HARLEY?”

I was oblivious to the icy cold weather. The wind picked up and whipped around me. Snow flurries swished around me. I took no real notice of it. The only thing that mattered was the ice surrounding my heart.

I lifted my face to the sky. “Why, God? Why my Harley? You can do miracles. Bring him back! PLEASE BRING MY HARLEY BACK!”

As if in answer to my pleas, I felt unseen eyes gazing at me. “Harley?” I whispered.

Was that a hint of a well-worn leather jacket I saw? Was there a black helmet in hand? A scent of Irish Spring and Old Spice wafted over me for a second. A misty figure formed surrounded by a hazy glow. For a few seconds, I saw him standing there gazing at me. The sensation of his presence slowly drifted away into the ether, and I was alone, so terribly devoid of feeling; alone.

“Why?” I sobbed. My entire body was wracked with my cries.

I have no memory of time passing, or of Garrett lifting me and carrying me back inside.

“Now, now Miss Mari. Master Harley would not want you to be so sad. Mormons believe you will be reunited with your loved one when the time is right. We also believe he can visit you. Do, you understand? Master Harley isn’t really gone. He’s just in another place.”

Garrett wrapped me in a blanket and settled me in front of the fire. Thomas had turned on the stereo. ‘Another’s Lifetime’ was playing softly.

Garrett brought me a cup of hot herbal tea. It was the only tea Harley drank; herbal. It was Chamomile with lemon and honey. “Drink this, Miss Mari.”

He lifted my face with the tip of his finger. “Master Harley would not want you to be so heartbroken.” He pulled the blanket tighter around me. “I will call your parents and explain you are staying with friends tonight.”

At some point, I was led from the living room into Harley's room where I curled into a ball on his bed. As I lay on the bed, I could see the backyard and gardens from the window. Garrett gently covered me with Harley's comforter as I remained motionless looking across the room and out the window to Harley's favorite place.

The gazebo looked lovely; painted in white with a light dusting of snow around it. It was peaceful. How I wished Harley was there with me now to enjoy the view. He would have loved it like he enjoyed the many simple things in life.

It almost felt as though he was sitting on his bike waiting for me to join him. Never again will I ever sit astride that machine with my arms around his waist as we roar down the road on another adventure. No more surprise nighttime picnics awaited me. I will never again look into his blue-gray eyes and see the wrinkles of merriment, or hear his deep laughter, feel his arms around me, or kiss his sweet lips.

I couldn't help the tears that streamed down my face. My heart was broken. I never believed I could come to love someone so completely and so quickly as I did Harley. From that first encounter in the Commons at the Ohio State University-Lima campus, my heart was doomed to fall in love with him.

Harley claims he saw me in a vision as far back as September 1969. He said he chased these visions across the country. I know we crossed paths five times before actually meeting at college. He was so persistent and went to great trouble to date me. I couldn't help but fall for him. After our first date, I learned what a great, kind and generous man he was. He was a true gentleman. Where most boys expected sex, Harley said physical intimacy was reserved for marriage.

Why is it the good guys always seem to be taken away, while the wicked survive? He had so much he wanted to do for others to lighten their burden just a little. Harley was always looking for a way to serve others; the less fortunate. He called it doing service. He once told me that in serving others you are serving and doing God's work. I wondered how he kept such strength in his faith when battling horrible odds. He never wavered in his belief in God.

How I loved him. I will love him forever. No one could ever replace him. He is my soul mate and the love of my life. No one can ever come close to him. My Harley is gone, snatched away by the cruelty of fate in the prime of his life.

Two days later I was able to go home. As I walked in the door, I saw my Dad sitting at the kitchen table reading the newspaper.

"Hi, Dad." I still felt numb and couldn't believe it had only been two days.

Garrett was leaving later that afternoon to attend the funeral services back east. I doubted I would ever see him again. During the past couple of nights, I heard his sobs when he thought everyone was asleep. Thomas had refused to leave either of us alone. I think we three just needed each other to get through those first days.

"Morning, Mari. I read that Harlan Davis passed away. He was your young man, wasn't he?" Dad looked up from the newspaper.

He had a cup of coffee in his hand. My father always seemed to be holding a coffee cup. I wondered how many he drank in a day. Such an inane thought to have, but there it was. How many cups of java did Dad consume in a single day?

I paused so long. Dad looked at me. Concern for me was apparent in his face.

I took a deep breath before answering, "Yes, Dad."

"I'm sorry to hear he passed. Was it sudden?" He stared intently at me. "You were very close."

"Yes, we were," I sobbed. "It was sudden to me, well, not really. Harley had been fighting cancer for almost eight months. Two months here and six at Columbia."

My Dad isn't very demonstrative, but that day he hugged me close until I stopped crying. "He must have been very special."

"He was, Dad. Very, very special." I hiccupped. "He was the most special man I ever met, and now he's gone."

Tears streamed down my face again. From where was all this wetness coming? I never knew a person could shed so many tears and not get dehydrated from loss of water and salt.

“Then be glad you had him even for such a short time.” Dad used his thumb to flick the tears away. He pulled me back into his embrace.

“Be glad of the time you had with him, Mari.” He whispered and lightly kissed the top of my head. “A love so profound comes around once in a lifetime.

“I am.” My Dad’s words brought a strange sensation of peace to my aching heart.

Chapter Four

Harley

February

In and out I went. I have no idea how long each episode lasted. I was vaguely aware of being tended to by nurses. Doctors came and went. Sometimes it felt like the bed was in motion, and I was being wheeled somewhere. Other times gentle hands turned me from side to side.

A warm damp cloth was wiped over my body. Fingers scrubbed my hair. Most times I felt like I was drifting in a sea of fog.

One day I opened my eyes to see a different hospital room, even the flowers had changed. They were pink carnations. The door was now on the left side. This room was a mirror opposite of the one I remembered. I looked around and noticed I was completely alone. Every other time I had regained consciousness Garrett or my parents were there. Never my sister, Elizabeth.

I looked around, familiarizing myself with this new location. How I longed to go home. I grasped the telephone and dialed Mari's trailer.

"This is the hospital operator."

"I'm trying to call Lima, Ohio." I gasped. My breathing was shallow.

"I'm sorry, long distance calls from that room are not possible."

"What? This is Columbia University Medical Center, the hospital, isn't it?"

"No, sir. This is the Cancer Institute of New York."

"Never heard of you."

"We're a private institute researching cancer treatment."

"I'm a guinea pig, you mean."

"We accept only the most critically ill."

"The terminal ones with nothing to lose." I closed my eyes.

"We prefer to call it changing lives and giving hope."

"Call it what you want. Can I make arrangements to pay for long distance calls separately?"

"I will send someone from the business office to make the arrangements."

"Thank you." I hoped my account information was still in my billfold. I closed my eyes and drifted to sleep.

Awhile later an orderly appeared with a wheelchair. I was lifted from my bed and taken to the business office. Once there, my wallet and a checkbook were taken from a safe and handed to me.

"There was a foreign checkbook found with your billfold. We decided it'd be safer kept locked up."

I looked at them. Inside my billfold were pictures of Mari, Garrett, and Thomas. I took them and tucked them into the pocket of the gown I wore. The checkbook was for my Swiss account.

With those checks, I arranged to have long distance telephone access set up in my room. The lady promised she would keep the arrangements secret. It would take a few weeks, but I'd be able to call Garrett if he was still at my home and Mari. All was not lost. With my spirits buoyed, I was returned to my room in time for physical therapy.

More treatments.

More therapy.

I drifted endlessly as each treatment and therapy left me drained of energy.

One day I woke from my stupor feeling better than I had in months. The sunlight dappled across the room giving it an uplifting rosy glow. I had been dreaming about Mari and Garrett.

Garrett. Where was Garrett? Maybe he stepped out for a bite to eat.

I felt confused. My memory was nothing like it had been. So many gaps exist now. It seemed Garrett should be here, but I vaguely recall something about him leaving or being terminated.

He wouldn't leave me here alone with my parents, so he must have been terminated.

I squinted and thought very hard. Finally, it came to me. Father had sent him packing after telling him I had died.

The door to my room popped open. My father walked in. He was sipping a cup of coffee.

"So, you're awake. Finally."

"Father, where is Garrett?" My voice sounded unusually weak.

"Garrett? You jest!" Father settled himself in a chair.

"No. Garrett's normally here when I wake up." I frowned. There was a hint of memory trying to break through, but try as I might I couldn't bring it out. Why did my memories come and go like the tides of the ocean?

"Garrett is gone. Finite. Left two months ago."

"Why?" Garrett would have never left me without good reason. I loved and depended on him too much. He always had my back when things got rough. He'd never desert me during my blackest hours of need.

"He was no longer needed after he made your final arrangements."

"Arrangements?"

"For your funeral. You took a downward turn just before you were to go back to Lima. The doctors thought you were dead. Garrett arranged for your funeral and then left. Silly man thought it'd be best to tell that girl in person. He came back three days later, but we'd already moved you here and had invoked privacy. No information could be given out. When he arrived at our home, the butler got me. I met him in the lobby and told him he was no longer needed. He said he wanted to attend the services. I told him we were done with that. I had the butler bring his bags down."

"You let him believe I had died?" I asked incredulously at how my father could be so dispassionate.

"He was no longer needed," Father shrugged. "We can take care of you here at this hospital. Now, you no longer have Garrett or that girl to distract you from fighting this cancer."

"How can I beat it? It had already spread six months ago." Shock at his callousness left me feeling numb.

"And yet, you are turning the battle around with each treatment. It's no longer in your liver, kidneys, or lungs. Aggressive therapy with chemicals, radiation, and surgery lay ahead. You need all your focus on yourself. Forget about your so-called friends, Garrett, and that girl. All they ever wanted was access to your money, which it looks like they got. Your funds are depleted. That girl wrote checks to various companies in your name. Really, Harley, she wrote checks to pay for lawn and maid service."

"Mari." I grated.

"Hmm?"

"Her name is Mari. And she would never steal from me. Garrett must have asked her to pay the household bills. I put her on my account."

For the first time, I was truly shocked at the hate coursing through me. I hated Father with everything I had in me. As for my funds, he didn't know about my emergency stash in Switzerland. I always kept enough back for my loved ones to live comfortably in the event I lost my main funds or accounts. That was a teaching Garrett had drilled into me since I was young. I always had to save back twenty percent of my allowance.

I struggled to sit up. The effort took all my strength, and I lay propped up on my elbows. "Get Garrett back."

"What?"

"I said, get Garrett back. I want him back."

"I'm afraid that's not possible."

"Why not?"

"I don't know where he is."

"You had no right! No right to let him go. He worked for me."

"On the contrary, we all thought you had died."

"Liar. You knew I wasn't dead. You had me moved to this hospital, this room, remember? You said so yourself."

"Don't get yourself all worked up. The orderlies will be here soon to take you to the operating room for the first of your surgeries to remove cancerous lesions in your leg."

"Father, I want you to please locate Garrett." My head was swimming with the news. How could Garrett be gone? Dismissed like a nobody after all his years of dedicated service?

“I told you that wasn’t possible. Garrett’s gone. I have no idea where he went.” Father sat with a smug expression on his face. He carefully trimmed under his nails. It was a practice I found disgusting to do in public.

“Have you checked my home in Lima?”

“There’s no need.” He waved a dismissive hand at me and picked up his Styrofoam cup. The coffee smelled strong; bitter.

“Can’t you please do that one thing for me after what I’ve done for you?”

“You?” Father set the cup down and picked up the newspaper. He folded it open to the business section.

“Yes, me.”

“What exactly have you done for me?” He glanced at his watch. “Where is your Mother? She should be here by now.”

Unbelievable!

“What I did for you? I’ll tell you since you seemed to have forgotten the financial straits you found yourself in a while back. I bailed you out financially and paid back the money you owed the mob. That’s what I did for you. You can’t even see fit to make one phone call to Lima for your deathly ill son. I now know you lied when you said you loved riding Harley-Davidson motorcycles. I don’t think you ever rode one. I bet the only thing you love about them is how much money my little customizing business brings in. Money that continued to funnel into the family coffers, if you will.”

“That is not true and is uncalled for!” He thundered.

“Prove it. Get Garrett back,” I grated. I felt my energy draining rapidly.

“Oh, all right. I’ll call your house when I get home.”

“Thank you.”

Mother rushed in. She had some bags in her hands. Shopping. “Harlan, I bought you some new sleepwear. Now you don’t have to dress in those horrid hospital gowns.”

“I’m sorry Mother, but I think I’m wearing the gown for a reason.”

“Truly? They want their patients parading around in ugly clothes? You’d think they’d want you to look your best. Especially, if you are in high society or a celebrity. No one wants to look like a stray dog. Lean forward, and I'll help you get dressed."

"No, Mother."

She reached around me and untied the strings. "Harlan!" She gasped. "Where is your underwear? You're...you're naked!" Her fingers flew to her lips, and her face turned scarlet. "No, no, this won't do! This won't do at all!"

"I'm fine, Mother. Really. I didn't wear any at the other hospital either." I started to lay back against my pillows when an orderly and two nurses came in.

The orderly pushed a gurney into the room. "I'm afraid you folks have to step outside." He maneuvered the bed into place. "Ready for surgery?" The orderly was a giant man and easily lifted me from my bed onto the gurney.

"I guess," I mumbled.

Chapter Five

Mari

March

Dear Harley,

I cannot believe you are actually gone. It's been almost two months now, and I still feel your presence everywhere I go. My heart is heavy. Gone is the light that you brought to me. Darkness has crept into my heart and my soul.

How can I continue without you by my side to love, cherish, and guide me? I wish I had disregarded your desire and taken pictures of you. They would have brought me such comfort to be able to gaze upon your ruggedly handsome face and remember.

Trying to live without you is the hardest thing I have ever done. I miss you so much. The way you smiled that lopsided grin at me makes me yearn for you even more. The twinkle in your eyes gave me so much comfort. Your gentle, caring love brought a glimmer of joy and hope into so many lives. I need so much to feel your arms around me helping me make it through this long, lonely time.

Lunch in the cafeteria is awkward at best. Maryanne, Peg and I sit at the same table, but we don't talk or laugh much. I notice each of us glancing at the vacant chair you used to occupy. It's as though we expect to see you sitting there and offering up one of your oddball comments and making us laugh so hard our stomachs hurt. But you aren't there, and the silence becomes deafening.

Going to biology class is hard too. Professor Schmidt looks to the seat you always occupied. He seems startled not to see you there. I think he misses your probing questions. He had to think about his responses to you.

Even Professor Jennings misses the lively discussions you started about the merits of different types of music. I recall the time he suggested you could teach a class on music history. His off-handed compliment made you blush a lovely dark red much to your discomfort and the amusement of the rest of us. You finally stuttered, "What can I say? I love music."

One of our assignments was to compose a musical number. We had to play it in class. On your day you brought your violin.

"Mister Davis, if you can play this, I'll give you an 'A' for the quarter." Professor Jennings smirked as he handed you a sheet he had composed.

You took that composition, got out your violin, and played it perfectly. Then you played your song. It was so hauntingly beautiful Professor Jennings sat stunned with his mouth open. After you finished, he applauded. "That was divine, Mister Davis. Simply divine."

Then it was my turn. I played the piece you helped me with. We both got an 'A' for the quarter but kept coming to class for the enjoyment of music discussions.

Tuesdays and Thursdays are the hardest. I keep expecting to see you lounging against the wall of the auditorium, or leaning against your Harley-Davidson with a burger bag dangling from the handles. I can picture you sitting on the hood of my Satellite with a Zaganos pizza box. Those nights are the worst because I leave class and reach the parking lot only to see my car alone. No motorcycle. No you.

Morning shows at WOSL are almost as bad. I keep waiting for you to call with a request for a Steppenwolf song such as 'Jupiter's Child' or 'Jeraboah,' or 'Skullduggery.' But, of course, the call never comes, and I leave the station with an icy grip surrounding my heart and yearning for you deep in my soul.

The memories that come to mind are bittersweet. I would trade them all for just one more hour, one more day of having you here. How I wish I could have one more week of loving you, and hearing you wax poetic about the things that brought you so much joy. I know that true love means never saying goodbye, but does it have to be so hard?

Harley, if you're in the heavens looking down at me, please share these memories I have of you. I never told you my thoughts and feelings about meeting you that day on the Commons. My first impression was that you were a stereotypical dangerous, reckless biker. If you remember, I had the same reaction when you spoke to me at the department store, Rink's, a year earlier. Then I looked into your face and your eyes. I saw the most handsome, sexy man I had ever seen in my life. You wore your sex appeal as though you were completely oblivious to the effect you had on women. I also noticed the gentle kindness in your eyes.

These impressions were completely at odds with each other. I was drawn to them, but hesitant of the biker image. When you asked me out you said it with such conviction, it was as if you knew I would eventually give in. Boy, were you persistent! I'm glad you were because I would not trade the ensuing two years for anything in the world. Well, almost anything. If I could, I would have changed the outcome and had you still with me.

I miss you so much, Harley, it is hard to go on; and yet, I must because you would have wanted me to. As I sit here writing to you, I'm listening to Steppenwolf's 'Just For Tonight.' It somehow fits the mood I'm in. Before that, I listened to 'Tenderness.' You were completely correct about the brilliance of Goldy McJohn's keyboard playing. I tuned out the lyrics and focused on the keyboards.

Such lovely music. I had never listened to Steppenwolf until you started calling in a request for one of their songs every day during my show. WOSL radio had only been in operation for a few months so we DJ's often brought in our own albums and singles. I had to go out and buy every single Steppenwolf album available just so I'd have the song you requested.

At first, I thought, "What is it with this guy and Steppenwolf?" I wondered how that love affair came to be. Then I started listening to the lyrics. Yeah, some were very taboo, but others were an accurate portrayal of our current state of affairs. Then I noticed the music. I loved the guitars until you pointed out the poignancy of the keyboard playing. Needless to say, I was hooked.

Do you remember what we did after attending the Steppenwolf concert? You were so sick after the show, it scared me. I held you most of the night while you slept fitfully. I've often wondered if that night was the first indication of the illness that robbed our future together.

The next morning you were fine and tickled at the meager gifts I had gotten you. I told you I loved you and you shouted it to everyone we passed. Such a little thing, three simple words is all it took to bring you happiness. Three words that meant the world to you and me.

Harley, you taught me to find joy in the simplest things from an inexpensive gift, to the falling of a leaf, the trickle of a stream, and the laughter of a child.

I remember the time you helped a homeless, out of work veteran of the Vietnam War. You bought him a meal and gave him a job. Then there was the time you prayed for a couple's daughter. You went around to the soup kitchens handing out warm coats, blankets, diapers, and toys. I remember you telling me how you helped make people's dreams come true by providing them with the assistance they needed to build a business, buy a home, get medical treatment, and a host of other things. Then there are donations to wildlife centers such as Wolf Park. Remember how we all worked on an environmentally friendly campsite at Tecumseh? At the time I didn't know you had protested the clear-cutting of forests in Oregon and Washington state. Did I ever tell you I did the same thing in Chehalis? Our little high school group stopped a major lumber company from deforesting our area.

Your simple gestures touched many lives. When news of your death got around, people brought flowers, handmade cards, and notes. Every one of them testified to how your kindness helped them through some dark times. Those acts of kindness are forever etched into my mind.

So much you gave to a world that frowned upon you. People looked at you with fear because you rode a motorcycle. Some pretended to love you because of your wealth. For a long time, it gave you a jaded view of life, but your religion and Garrett showed you a different way.

Harley, you taught me so much. I'm a better person from having you in my life. I was completely wrapped up in my own world. I never noticed others were in desperate straits. You opened my eyes to a world I didn't know existed. It was you who taught me to be compassionate and generous of spirit.

As you once said, "You don't know what they have gone through. A little kindness and a helping hand never hurt anyone."

You also taught me that love means never saying goodbye. I'm holding on to that, my love. I miss you so much, I have to believe that someday, somehow, we will be reunited whether in this life or the next. I can't imagine not seeing you again. I don't know how I can live if it means a lifetime without you. I can't forget your face as you were being taken to the waiting ambulance. Somehow, I knew you were leaving, and I would never see your countenance again.

You once told me to never grieve for you because you aren't really gone. If that's true, Harley, then why do I feel this giant void in my heart? My soul? You told me do not be sad. To call your name and you would be by my side to talk, laugh, and share all the things we did before. I can't, Harley. I'm not strong enough. You said you would be waiting for me, watching over me. I wish I could hear your voice, and smell your scent. I long to hold you, to see you, and feel your love wash over me, just one more time.

I would tell you all the things I thought we had a lifetime to talk about. I'd kiss you a thousand times deep, and laugh at all your pranks. I'd gaze into your beautiful eyes and tell you how handsome you are. And when you were down about your cousin or your parents, I'd wipe away the sadness.

I wish you were here and could put your hands over mine. I'm broken in two. If you were with me now, I could believe everything will be okay. I want so badly to see your face, to hear your voice as you take away my pain and tears. All I need is to hear you tell me everything is going to be okay, and I'll believe you. You opened so many doors for me. Your love taught me that even if everything isn't the way you think it should be, with your love it can be made right. I close my eyes at night and desperately hope to see you riding your Hog up to me in the morning sun.

Tears stream down from my eyes as I contemplate life without you. I was so shy and afraid to try new things. You thought I was crazy for climbing rocks. But, I wasn't. You made me unafraid of trying something different. You encouraged me to get my FCC license, to live life as though there was no tomorrow. How prophetic that turned out to be. You were always there when no one else knew the sorrows I was feeling. My strength, my heart, my love, you kept me safe even from myself.

I put down my pen as the tears coursing down my face make it impossible to see what I am writing. After several minutes, the crying has slowed, and I look at the knife in my hand. I have no memory of getting it or holding it pointed to my wrist, or it digging into my flesh.

As I sat there looking at the gleaming stainless steel close up, I thought about how it would feel to dig so deeply that veins would sever. What kind of pain would there be as my flesh became gouged, and blood poured from the wounds until only a single drop remained?

Such an act is the most selfish thing I could do. I understand how much hurt such an action brings to those who care about me. It is showing blatant disloyalty to you, who cherished life and fought so hard to win back your future. But, what I don't know is how to stop this all-consuming pain slicing through me.

My life, my heart, and my essence broke into a million pieces like the jagged shards of a mirror or Humpty Dumpty who fell off the wall. How do you pick up the pieces of a broken, dream-filled life?

I've always been taught that committing suicide will keep you from getting into heaven. But, I wonder if that's really true, or will it just stop the pain? This crushing, suffocating, killing pain never leaves my heart. I can't sleep, eat, or focus. All my energy is on wishing you were here with me.

I want so much to join you. I am so confused, Harley. You taught me in the Church of Jesus Christ of Latter-Day Saints President George Q. Cannon says, "Man did not create himself. He did not furnish his spirit with a human dwelling place. It is God who created man, both body and spirit. Man has no right, therefore, to destroy that which he had no agency creating. Those who do so are guilty of murder, self-murder it is true, but they are no more justified in killing themselves than in killing others."

You also said Church President Spencer W. Kimball said in 1976, "It is a terrible criminal act for a person to go out and shorten his life."

And yet, Elder Bruce R. McConkie expressed that "persons subjected to great stresses may lose control of themselves. These people may become mentally clouded to the point they are no longer accountable for their acts. Such is not to be condemned for taking their own lives. It should also be remembered that judgment is the Lord's. He knows the thoughts, intents, and abilities of men. In his infinite wisdom, he will make all things right in due course."

I thought about what you taught me, and I feel more confused. Does it mean suicide is wrong, but I could still be forgiven? Guide me, Harley.

I need so much to hear what I should do. Help me. I have nothing left inside. Nothing left to give. I love you. I want you, but you are no longer here for me to kiss or hold. You belong to God now. I just wish I could have had you a little bit longer. I wish you could be here just a few years, a couple of months, weeks, days, hours, or even minutes longer. I would tell you how much I care for you; how much I love you.

Just one more time I'd like to walk out of WOSL and see you leaning against the wall decked out in your well-worn leather jacket and boots, your faded denim and a helmet dangling from your hands. To feel your arms draped around me and see your goofy begging puppy grin once again. One more night sitting in my car listening to eight-track tapes of Steppenwolf while you talked about your life, your philosophy and asked me about mine. I wish I could have you with me just one more time.

I closed my eyes and felt the tears come once more.

My stereo was playing Skullduggery when the music died. Silence engulfed me so much it was preternatural. A cold such as I'd never felt before surrounded me. Goosebumps appeared on my arms. The light bulb overhead popped, flashed and fizzled into darkness.

I looked up from the floor where I was sitting and saw a bluish-white mist move from the stereo to the upper corner of my room where my door is. The mist transformed into brilliant white light. I felt your presence envelop me as I felt comforting arms encircle my waist. A whiff of your scent surrounded me.

"Harley?" I whispered.

"Hush, I'm right here," I heard Harley's voice croon.

"Harley, I miss you so much," I cried as tears coursed down my cheeks.

"I never went away. Do not do this, Mari. It's not your time. I will come for you. I am never far away. Wait for me."

I felt lips feather light against my cheeks kissing away my tears. Fingers gently brushed my hair from my face in that old familiar way of his.

"Just think of me when you see a rainbow. I am the cold, and soft wetness of a snowflake, the shadow you see standing under a tree. The ray of sunshine warming you is me wrapping you in a hug. Talk to me, laugh with me. Remember the times we shared with joy. Do not give up on me. Nothing has changed. I am not gone."

A deep sense of peace overcame me. I felt the thumping of his heart and his breath upon my cheek. I put the knife away.

Chapter Six

Harley

March

Surgery to remove tumors from my leg was successful. The physical therapy staff had me up and walking around my room within days. They were pleased with my progress. Unfortunately, my leg did not agree. As I walked from the window and around the corner of my bed, I felt a sharp, searing pain in my calf and it gave out. The therapist was quick to react and got me into my bed. The doctor was called, and while waiting for him to arrive, I was rushed to Radiology for X-Rays and an Ultrasound. The results indicated some muscles had either torn or become detached. This meant I needed another operation later to repair my muscles so I would be able to walk, albeit with a probable permanent limp. The corrective surgery was performed two days later.

The continuing treatments felt worse than my cancer. They made me so weak, nauseous, and dizzy. The cramps were nearly intolerable as they sent spasms up and down my leg. The doctor said it was normal to feel them since they had to perform grotesquely invasive surgery to remove multiple lesions in my calf and thigh.

I felt depressed. I didn't even have Mari to talk with. She, Garrett, and Thomas as well as the rest of the WOSL gang thought I was dead. I had only my parents. I believe Garrett informed Keisha, Jamal, Shauntelle, George, and Evangeline of my demise.

I had to listen to my father drone on and on about how my funds were depleted, and he was paying my insurance premiums and anything out of pocket. How quickly he had forgotten that it was me who bailed him out financially a little over a year ago.

The treatment left my memory less than intact. I had trouble with dates and numbers. Some days I simply couldn't recall Mari's telephone number, and on other days, I knew it like I knew my own face. I barely remembered the number to my own home. I just had to let the people that cared about me know I was alive. After thinking very hard, a phone number came to mind. I used the phone in my hospital room and called it.

"Hello? Davis residence. This is Garrett speaking."

How wonderful it was to hear his voice! "Garrett?" My voice was a mere fraction of its normal tone.

"Who is this?" He sounded wary.

"It's Harley," I whispered.

"Mister Harlan Davis is dead." The bluntness of his words shocked me. This did not sound like the Garrett I knew and loved.

"Mari." I struggled to tell him Mari needed him to help her get through this difficult period.

"What kind of sick monster are you?" He hung up.

At least I knew Garrett was still at our home in Lima. I lay back against my pillows. That little effort had sucked the strength from me.

Tomorrow I will try to reach Mari if I can remember her telephone number. If that failed, I could call WOSL and get a message to her that way. If I can get through to her that I'm not dead, surely, she can convince Garrett. How I miss her. Thinking I was dead must be horrible. I feel her sorrow.

I was lucky she stuck with me when I treated her so poorly. I still have no idea why I acted so nasty to her, except to say I listened to my father when I shouldn't have.

My thoughts turned back to that time shortly before and after our engagement. Before our engagement, I had let her wait for hours and then got angry with her about her concern for me. I stood her up for a date. Then I showed up at the restaurant where we were to have dinner with Thomas and Peg. I was with a group of bikers. My arm was draped around another girl. I was horrible to her and yet, a few days later I proposed and she accepted. She agreed to marry me when I had been such a louse. Admittedly, I am not normally like that, but somehow my father had gotten to me.

After we became engaged, I got stupid again with the same biker group. There's no excuse for what I did, and I will forever be sorry for causing Mari's heart to break.

I wiped at the tears threatening to pour from my eyes. The memory of the worst things I did to Garrett, Thomas, and most of all Mari came back to me with a vengeance. How they ever forgave me, I'll never know. I'm just grateful they stuck with me. I wish they were here with me now. They thought I was dead.

I reclined in the chair and allowed the memories to wash over me. I thought about the time I came so close to losing Garrett and Mari. Memories of the days I hurt them hit me with a clarity that had been absent from my mind for months. Instead of doing the right thing and making two of the most important people in my life happy, I gave them grief by choosing to run with a motorcycle club.

###

On a Tuesday in June, after I proposed marriage to Mari, I ran into Red's Motorcycle Club. It was mid-morning, and I had just finished meeting with my staff. The rest of my day was free until my evening date with Mari. The day was nice and sunny. Temperatures ranged between a pleasant seventy to seventy-eight degrees. It was a perfect day for riding my Hog. I chose to go for a ride down to Columbus and back. I planned to stop in the biker dive near there for a burger. After eating I would ride around Columbus for a bit before heading home.

The lot was packed with cycles from vintage Harley-Davidson 1952 side valve K model to the 1972 XR750. There were Kawasakis, Hondas, Suzukis, Yamahas, BMWs and every other brand you could imagine. It was biker heaven. I parked my Sportster tail to the back wall and front-end ready to leave. As I walked through the lot toward the entrance to the place I took great care not to bump any of the bikes.

Inside, the place was even more crowded than the lot made it appear. It was wall-to-wall bikers. I stood in the entry looking to see if there were any vacant seats.

"Harley!" A hand clasped my shoulder. "Good to see you, man." Red Hawk shouted. "Join us over there." He pointed to the left corner of the dive.

Once we got to the tables, he urged me to take a seat next to him.

"Snake, go order him a burger with the works and a beer."

"Water, if you don't mind," I said.

"Yeah, yeah. Forgot you don't drink beer." Red Hawk nodded at Snake.

Snake, a slim, extremely pale man with reptilian tattoos from his hands up his arms to his chin, nodded and headed to the counter. His blond hair was whiter than a plain t-shirt. He wore it in a Mohawk style with the long strands tied in a ponytail. I didn't trust him but felt he wouldn't do anything with the motorcycle club President sitting beside me.

"We're going on a run after we're done here. Want to join us?" Red Hawk asked.

"Where to?" I was curious, but wary, after all, they wore outlaw patches on their jackets.

Snake returned with my order. I dug in, relishing the zest of the burger and the cool lime taste of my water.

"Bellefontaine. We're going to a barbecue with a couple other clubs."

"Cool." I chewed thoughtfully. "I'll join you for a while."

"Hey Loner, I see you're wearing a broken wing on your colors. When'd you crash?" Patsy asked.

"Ate asphalt in a low side back in '69.' It was a fifty-five-inch Ironhead. Totaled it during a blackout. Had to have surgery to fix injuries."

"Dude! You dumped your bike?" Snake sneered.

"Not on purpose. I blacked out. All I know is what the reports said. From my positioning, it was a low side and probably dump."

"Dang!"

"What you ridin' now?" Patsy asked.

"Sixty-one-inch Harley Sportster XLCH Ironhead heavily modded. It's much larger than its class."

"How so?" Asked one of the guys who weren't at the dive the last time I was here.

"Larger tank, larger engine, blinkers, stuff like that."

"I been meanin' to ask, are you a RUB?" One of the guys asked as he tossed back a beer.

I frowned at the derogatory name. A RUB is a rich urban biker who buys and has installed superfluous accessories to look cool regardless of a decline in the machine's performance. I might be wealthy, but I do not have parts modded for coolness. Everything I've installed on my Hog increased its functional capabilities.

"No. I did all the mods myself."

The ride to Bellefontaine took under forty minutes with us traveling over the speed limit. We arrived at a building that looked like it had once been a warehouse. I was introduced as an associate of Red's Motorcycle Club.

"What'll ya have?" A member of Malice Runners MC asked.

He wore a red vest known as a cut or Kutte. The back had Malice Runners on the top rocker. Below that was a logo with a skull, devil horns, and slash marks to resemble running. The bottom rocker said Kenton, Ohio, their hometown. The front of his vest had some patches including 1%'er which meant the Malice Runners were an outlaw motorcycle club just like Red's Motorcycle Club. There was a 22 meaning he'd spent time in prison. This was followed by a Defender patch with a teardrop on the lower left side to indicate he was the club's enforcer or sergeant of arms and had killed for the club. There was an MRFFMR patch which meant Malice Runners Forever Forever Malice Runners. The remaining patches included GBNF, gone but not forgotten for club brothers who have died, and a 666 MR to indicate Satan-like Malice Runners.

In all, this guy was bad news. Serious bad news. I began to doubt my wisdom in being here. Sometimes when two or more clubs are nearby, they invite an unwanted visit from the local police. I did not need that, not with my business customizing police bikes. Nor did I need the other kind of uninvited guest where a rival club shows up looking to rumble. I decided to stay for about half an hour then make my excuses to leave.

I looked over the beverages in the iced barrel and was pleasantly surprised to find sodas mixed in with the beer. Sitting in the middle surrounded by assorted beers was a Vernors.

"Loner," Snake came over to me. "Boss wants to chat. I'll bring your poison when I get mine."

"Thanks. Get me a Vernors, will ya?"

"Got it."

I stopped by my Hog and put my helmet onto a saddle bag before ambling over to where Red Hawk was seated. He had his arm draped over the ample breasts of a brunette.

"Snake said you wanted to talk."

"Have a seat." He patted the space next to him.

"Rather stand a bit. Had a fairly long ride to Columbus and then here. Know what I mean?" The man didn't need to know long rides weren't unusual for me. I could ride an entire day without stopping except for fuel and restroom breaks.

"That's cool." He removed his hand from the girl and necked his beer. "Been thinking. I like you. You have my respect. You say you built your Hog for performance. From what I saw, I believe you. I want you to consider joining our club."

"Wow!" Oh boy! Just what I needed, an outlaw motorcycle club membership. The trick was going to be how to decline the invitation and remain on their good side.

"That's quite an honor, Red Hawk. I'd be proud to join, but I'm more of a free rider. Know what I mean? I prefer my own rules. I don't know if I could promise to follow club laws."

"You don't have to answer right now. I want you to consider the offer. For now, how about remaining an associate?"

"I can do that," I spoke slowly and deferentially. Red Hawk held all the cards. If he thought I was flipping him off, I could wind up just another body lying in a field or ditch somewhere.

"Thought so. Had a Kutte made for you." He beckoned Snake over.

Snake stepped to the table and placed an open Vernors in front of me. I eyed it suspiciously. I don't like having an opened drink handed to me unless it was by wait staff in a restaurant. Call me paranoid, but a man of my position and wealth had to be careful. From the expression on their faces, I knew this was a test about trust. The can felt cold as I took a swallow to their delight.

Snake handed me the Kutte. It was in the club colors. The top rocker said Red's Motorcycle Club. The logo was of a red hawk flying over a bike. The bottom rocker proclaimed Columbus, Ohio as their town. The patches on the front included a 1%'er, a lone rider, a low side showing a rider sliding low to the ground with his leg under the bike, and the last patch simply said RMC Associate for Red's Motorcycle Club Associate.

"Gee, thanks." I took the leather vest and examined it. The garment was well made.

"Only thing I ask," Red Hawk stated, "is that you wear our colors when you ride with us."

"No problem," I responded slowly as I removed my leather jacket and put the Kutte on. "I'll be right back."

I walked over to my Hog and put my jacket into a saddle bag.

"The food smells great," I reached into the barrel and fished out another Vernors.

The barbecue was fantastic. The President of the third club, Hellions Motorcycle Club, really knew his meats. There were beef and pork ribs, chicken, sausage links, hot dogs, and burgers with potato and three bean salad, and coleslaw.

"What's your favorite run?" I asked as I licked the sauce off my fingers.

"We like the Dragon out of Cincinnati. It has smooth cambered twists and turns. The turns are marked, so you know what to expect and can get into a rhythm." Jake, an older club member, said. "Still, it's a challenging run."

"Ever ride the Triple Neck out of Zanesville? It's just as much of a challenge as the Dragon, but there's no way to expect the turns. Many of them are unannounced. Keeps you on your toes."

"We haven't done that one." Red Hawk said, running his hand along his chin. "Don't know why. We'll have to schedule one."

"That would be great. Leave word at the burger joint with a few weeks' notice, and I'll ride with you." I rubbed my eyes as my vision suddenly clouded over. I was more tired than I thought I'd be after riding just under three hours since leaving Lima. I hoped I wasn't getting sick like I did on the trip to see Steppenwolf.

"Sounds like a plan."

"That's great. Now, if you'll excuse me, I need to get going. Have plans tonight." I rubbed my eyes as my vision blurred again. Had to be something in the first Vernors I had. I wondered what drug had been stirred into my drink.

As I stood to leave, we heard the loud roaring of a group of motorcycles coming down the road. In minutes the new group had turned toward our building.

"It's Satan's Hounds!" A member of the Malice Runners yelled.

Everyone rushed into a battle formation, pulling out knives, chains, brass knuckles, lead pipes, and guns. I could almost smell the testosterone in the air and feel the adrenaline pounding through my veins. The enemy club raced headlong into the fight, knocking people down with their bikes. We responded by hitting them with everything in our arsenal.

Red Hawk swung a chain, wrapping it around the SGA of Satan's Hounds and yanked him off his bike. A jab at the man's throat and he was limp. Red Hawk quickly cut off the SGA's identifying patch.

Snake smacked a pipe on the skull of another Satan's Hounds member. His swing cracked the guy's head open. I caught a sickening glimpse of bone and brains. I threw my knife into the side of a biker sneaking up on Patsy. After making certain the guy was still breathing, I removed his patches and tossed them to her.

Crip, the Vice President of Hellions Motorcycle Club, lashed his bullwhip wrapping the spiked end around a Satan's Hounds member. They retaliated by shooting him in the head. I saw two of Red's Motorcycle Club members go down along with several of our affiliates. Red and Snake grabbed the Kuttes, knives, and wallets off the dead members of our group. No personal belongings left behind meant it was harder to track any killings back to us. Motorcycle clubs, even rivals, are reluctant to finger others. Doing so meant they were present and retaliation was certain by the others. Death rained its fists down upon the groups.

I froze when a Malice Runner pointed a pistol at me. The bullet whizzed past missing me by inches. I pivoted in time to see a Satan's Hounds member clutch his chest and topple to the ground.

Blood poured freely. More guys were killed. I have never been involved in any kind of killing before, and now, here I was surrounded by death because I chose to go to a barbeque with the wrong people.

I was in serious trouble, and I didn't know how I was going to get out of this mess! At the very least I could be charged as an accomplice to murder even though I didn't kill anyone! Garrett was going to be furious. I didn't even want to think about how Mari would feel.

Someone in the neighboring area called the police. Upon hearing the sirens, we raced to our cycles and took off. My heart beat a rapid rhythm as adrenalin coursed through me. Red Hawk set our pace. We rode hard and fast. The speedometer on my Hog was pinned. My sled didn't feel right. It was clanking loudly, and steering took a lot of effort and strength, which I was losing fast. When we encountered traffic, we split lanes thereby quickly outdistancing the cops. Splitting lanes are legal in some states and not others. Simply put, it meant we rode down the center between two lanes.

As we neared Columbus, I began to feel woozy. I could feel blood on my chest. My Kutte and shirt were drenched. As we approached a building similar to the one in Bellefontaine I realized I might be in trouble health wise in addition to the legal ramifications of my day with Red's Motorcycle Club. At the moment, my health was most concerning. I had sustained an injury in the chest. The blood on my torso was mine. I could feel it gushing from the wound.

"Loner, you okay?" Snake asked. He reached out a hand and touched my Kutte. "Red Hawk! Loner's been slashed!"

"Let's get him inside."

The interior of the building had a garage area and an extremely large apartment. It was decorated in the club colors with posters and parts of motorcycles hanging from the wall. There were large vinyl couches, card tables, a refrigerator, oven, billiard tables, and a television set. I was in the clubhouse.

"Get his Kutte and shirt off," Red Hawk barked as he brought out a trunk filled with medical supplies.

I struggled to remove my Kutte without groaning. Patsy reached out and helped me out of it. She then removed my shirt.

"Looks kind of deep, Red Hawk. Might need stitches."

Red Hawk brought over rubbing alcohol, bandages, needles, and thread. Snake handed him some pills and a glass of water.

"Take these. They'll dull the pain. Patsy won't stitch you up while you're in pain." Red Hawk held the pills out to me.

I took them and placed them in my mouth. Then I sipped some water while keeping the pills tucked into my cheek. I didn't want to take something I didn't know.

"Open wide so I can make sure they went down."

Busted. I had no choice but to swallow. Hawk peered into my mouth. "He took 'em, Patsy."

"Red, you know the pigs are gonna visit us," Snake paced the floor. "What're we going to tell them?" He asked, worried.

"We went for a burger at our favorite joint and came back here to drink beer and play cards. They can't prove otherwise. We got the Kuttes, wallets, knives, and anything that can associate our fallen brothers with us."

"Start counting backward from one hundred," Patsy instructed as she grabbed a towel and soaked it with rubbing alcohol.

"One hundred, ninety-nine, ninety-eight," I mumbled. My speech sounded slurred. My eyelids felt droopy. Those pills sure worked fast.

The next thing I knew, I was laying on the couch. A bandage covered my torso. There was some spotty blood on it.

"What time is it?" I asked, struggling to sit up. "I need to head home."

"Seven," Patsy replied.

"Seven! I'm going to be late. I have to go." I tried to stand but the room went waltzing on me, and I sat back down.

"It's seven in the morning and time for another round of painkillers and antibiotic medication."

"Easy there, Loner." Red Hawk said. "You aren't goin' anywhere until Patsy says you can. She's a certified nurse, so you're in good hands." Red handed me a flannel shirt and blanket.

"Put this on. Can't have the cops seeing you decked out in bandages."

Seven in the morning! I had stood Mari up after promising I wouldn't do it again. Will she forgive me this time? I had a lunch scheduled with Thomas and will miss it too. I started to get up, but a wave of dizziness kept that from happening.

"Open up," Patsy pressed two painkillers into my mouth, followed by a drink of water.

As I rested my head on the couch, I heard pounding on the door. Red glanced around the room as Pasty put the medical supplies away. I pulled the blanket up, so it covered my face.

"Police! Open up!"

I heard the door creaking open. "Yes, officer?"

As the police entered the facility, I heard Red say, "Who? Him? He's sleeping off a drunk."

The police asked a few questions about Bellefontaine and the motorcycle club war. I heard Red tell them we had eaten burgers nearby, came back here to play cards and shoot some pool.

I have no idea how long the police remained. I felt myself drifting into slumberland. In no time, I was sleeping. When I woke up, it was night. Patsy brought me a bowl of chicken noodle soup and some saltines.

Immediately after eating came more painkillers. "How much longer do I need to take these?"

"Until you can get up pain-free. Probably through tomorrow."

"Tomorrow," I mumbled.

Thursday I was given my first solid food; Cream of Wheat. Yuck! For lunch, I had oatmeal and toast.

Dinner was scrambled eggs, toast, a salad, and a fruit cup. Friday morning, I ate eggs, toast, cantaloupe, bacon, and sausage. Lunch was soup and a sandwich. Dinner was a hamburger and fries. After dinner, I was given my Kutte and told I was well enough to ride home.

"You want an escort to make sure you get home okay?" Red Hawk asked as he mixed a packet into my water.

"Nah. I can get to Cincinnati just fine." Something told me I didn't want them to know I lived in Lima. "What are you putting into my water?"

"A mild painkiller so the ride home doesn't hurt," Red Hawk said as he stirred the contents.

"I don't need one." I carefully dressed and gingerly put the Kutte on.

"Yes, you do. Riding home on your sled isn't going to be pleasant." Red held the glass out.

I nodded and looked from Red Hawk to the glass. I was reluctant to drink it but knew I wouldn't be leaving if I didn't. I slowly drank the liquid and handed him the glass. I put on my Kutte. I'd rather wear my own jacket, but it was in my saddle bag on the Hog.

"We'll leave word at the burger joint when we've scheduled the Triple Neck run." Red Hawk clamped my shoulder in a friendly pat.

I nodded and headed to my bike. It had a lot of dings and dents on the frame, and it looked as though I'd ridden through a battlefield, which, in a sense, I had. Even my helmet was scuffed. I mounted my Hog and sat for several minutes. I vowed to myself never again will I ride with a club. I'd find some way to return the Kutte or not.

I kickstarted my Hog. It sounded even more ragged than I remembered. I was going to have to make major repairs or custom build a new one. I shook my head and rode off.

Chapter Seven

Mari

March

Dear Harley,

For some reason, my mind keeps wandering back to the days after our engagement. The Tuesday after you proposed, we were supposed to meet in the parking lot outside Galvin Hall, but you never showed up. I couldn't believe you had stood me up again, and so soon after we made up and promised to marry. Harley, you had promised never to skip out on a date again. When we first started dating, you once told me you never lied or made a promise you didn't intend to keep. I believed you. Therefore, I knew something must have kept you from coming. It might be family matters again, or the shop. I'd find out tomorrow.

You stood Thomas up on Wednesday and me again on Thursday. Friday morning, I drove to your shop and learned you had not been there since Tuesday. I just knew something bad had happened. I headed directly to your home. Garrett would know.

###

"Miss Mari," Garrett opened the door. "Have you seen or heard from Master Harley?" Worry creased his craggy face. He looked older somehow and very tired.

"No, I haven't. That's why I'm here. He stood me up Tuesday and Thursday night."

"And me on Wednesday for lunch," Thomas said as he walked up behind me.

"Okay, we need to put out some feelers. Thomas, you start calling folks he might know. I'll call WOSL and ask them to put an announcement on air asking anyone who knows his whereabouts to call the station. They'll call us," I said.

"And I will call the police and file a missing person's report. Enough time has passed now, they should take it," Garrett volunteered.

The next several hours were hectic as we organized searches and made telephone calls. The police came and took down a report.

"What kind of vehicle was he driving?

"A Harley-Davidson Sportster XLCH," Garrett and I answered at the same time.

"Motorcycle rider." The cop scratched his head. "Was he in a club or gang?"

"No!" We again spoke in unison.

"Why do you ask, officer?" Garrett questioned.

"Look, you know he is a respectable businessman, right?" Thomas chimed in.

"He owns Davis Motors for Pete's sake!" I raised my voice.

"And they build custom motorcycles," the officer commented, never looking up from his notepad.

"They also customize cars and trucks, and restore vintage vehicles, and perform routine vehicle maintenance and repairs. What's wrong with that?"

"Nothing, Miss." The officer closed his notepad. "We'll be in touch. We may want to set up a command center here in case this is a kidnapping. I'll let you know." The cop left us in stunned silence.

Kidnapping! The thought had never entered my mind. I looked from Thomas to Garrett. Garrett had his eyes closed.

"Garrett?" I heard my voice tremble.

He nodded. "I'm afraid, that is entirely possible. Men of Master Harley's stature are often victims of kidnapping."

My heart leaped into my throat. I swiped at the sting of salty tears in the corner of my eyes. Garrett pulled me into his arms. "There, there Miss Mari."

The pounding on the door made us jump out of our skins. Thomas hurried over and looked through the peephole before yanking the door open.

"I just heard!" Peg rushed in. "Any word?" She headed to the kitchen. "I'm going to make us a pot of cinnamon tea."

The hours ticked slowly by, punctuated by intermittent telephone calls and refills of caffeine-free tea.

"His parents! Shouldn't we notify them?" Peg asked as she stirred sugar into her fourth cup of tea.

Garrett shook his head. "No. That would only make matters worse. They'd fly in. We'd have to get a limousine to pick them up. I'd have to go there to personally attend to them. Once here they would try to order the police around. No." He shuddered.

Thomas re-entered the living room. "That was the police. They said there was some kind of battle between motorcycle gangs last Tuesday leaving twelve injured and nine dead in Bellefontaine. They're requesting information to see if Harley was one of them. They plan to set up a command center here tomorrow."

"No!" I jumped up. "Not Harley! He's not like that!" I began pacing the room.

Around ten o'clock that night we heard a loud clanking, and sputtering engine came up the drive. Collectively, we turned toward the door as it opened. Harley stood in the entrance with his helmet in his hand.

He was wearing a red and black vest with patches. It was splattered in blood. Harley raised a shaky hand to his face and rubbed his eyes. His knuckles were scraped and looked painfully raw. The hands were filthy as though he hadn't washed them in ages. Dirt streaked fingers continued to swipe his blue-gray eyes. Upon closer inspection, his eyes appeared red, glassy, and he blinked rapidly.

"Oh, Master Harley, what have you done?" Garrett carefully examined him. He gently tugged the vest off.

I gasped at the sight of his, blood-soaked, shirt and rushed to help Garrett remove it. He was wrapped in bandages that had become soaked with blood. "Harley! What happened?"

"He's on drugs," Garrett stated coldly, "again."

"Do you mean he's a dope head?" Thomas sounded shocked.

"He was once. He promised me he would never again get messed up with dope. I'd know those symptoms anywhere. He's high."

"Not by choice," Harley mumbled. He rubbed his chest gingerly. His fingers came away with blood. He stared at his digits as though he didn't recognize them.

Peg gathered our cups and left the room. We could hear her banging things in the kitchen. She was angry. "Fool! Stupid!"

"Harley doesn't break his promises. Something must have happened." I grasped his face and tilted his head, so I had a better view of his eyes. Not only were they glassy, but they had a reddish tint.

"Took a ride with Red's Motorcycle Club." Harley's words came out slurred. He swayed unsteadily. Thomas grabbed him and guided him to an armchair.

"Harlan Christian Robert Davis!" Garrett thundered, his Scottish Brough becoming pronounced. "You've put me through the pits! I've had it!" He stormed from the room.

I chased him up the stairs. "Garrett! Wait!" I grabbed his arm at the landing.

He stood before me with his hands bunched into fists and his jaw clenched. "Miss Mari, please unhand me."

"You aren't going to abandon him, are you?" I implored him. Harley would be devastated if Garrett left.

"He once told me he felt like I was more of a father to him than his own flesh and blood." Garrett continued up the stairs and down the hall to his rooms. "This is how he treats me? Getting drugged up?" He hauled out his suitcase and began packing. "I thought he learned his lesson after his stint in rehab! Oh no! Here we are years later, and he's drugged!"

"Garrett, Harley loves you. He said you and Brad were the only family he truly had. That you'd always be there for him." I choked back tears as I fought for Harley's honor. "He said he'd die for you. You can't abandon him now! Not after all the good he does. He's the kindest, most generous person I've ever met. He told me everything he does you guided him in the right direction. Harley said you helped him find Christ through the Church of Jesus Christ of Latter-Day Saints. You showed him what it means to do service for others in need."

"I've had it, Miss Mari! I always have to bail him out of trouble!" Garrett slammed the lid shut and opened another suitcase.

"So, you're just going to abandon him?" I felt my anger boiling to the surface. "How much good has he done compared to the bad? I bet you find his good deeds far outweigh the bad."

He sat on the bed and sighed. "I know it. It's just when he gets the devil in him, he does it up right and proper. No holding back with him."

"But, isn't that part of what you love about him? Doesn't his zest for life, adventure, his kindness, and generosity of spirit count for anything?"

"Yes, Miss Mari," he sighed. "I do love him like a son."

"Then, why are you packing like you're going to abandon him?"

"I won't abandon him, but he can feel like I might. Maybe then he'll..."

"He'll what? Truly feel alone? You have to admit, he has overall treated you with respect, honor, and like family. Don't do this to him! Please!"

"Garrett!" Thomas yelled. "Harley's having some kind of fit! He's thrashing around. What do we do?"

"Lay him on the floor," Garrett looked at me, sighed, and headed down the stairs.

Harley was shaking uncontrollably. Garrett rushed to him. "Let's turn him onto his side. Peg, hand us some pillows to keep him propped. Mari, please get a blanket. Thomas, call the police and let them know he has returned home."

I draped the blanket over Harley. I then went into the kitchen and got a cold, moist cloth. Bringing the dish rag with me, I returned to the living room and knelt beside him. I cradled Harley's head and tenderly wiped his face clean of blood and grime.

In under five minutes, Harley stirred. "What...what happened?" He croaked, licking his lips.

"Ssh...rest easy, my love."

Garrett gently pulled the blanket away and gazed at his injuries. He clucked like a mother hen as he studied the wounds. Garrett left and returned with a first aid kit and bandages. "Who treated your injuries?" He set the supplies out.

"A nurse named Patsy."

"She did a good job stitching you up. I imagine the blood is mainly from your ride home?"

"Yeah," Harley closed his eyes.

"This is going to sting." Garrett poured disinfectant onto cotton balls and dabbed the wound clean.

Harley hissed with each swipe across his chest. "Dang!"

"Just a few minutes more." Garrett wrapped his torso in clean bandages.

"Shouldn't he go to the hospital?" I asked.

"No," Harley muttered, "No hospital."

"Why not?"

"News would get out about a man of his stature being stabbed. Questions would be asked. The police would take him in for questioning about the stabbing. If it becomes known he was involved with a motorcycle gang, he might be facing charges even if he had nothing to do with the recent fight in Bellefontaine. It wouldn't take long for the biker gangs to find out. Then he'd become a target. And they would cause harm to him, his friends, and his business reputation." Garrett explained.

"Oh!"

"We just need to make sure his wound doesn't become infected." Garrett studied Harley. "What kind of drugs did you ingest?"

"Patsy said it was painkillers and antibiotics."

"Dope." Garrett peered into Harley's eyes. "Your pupils are dilated. How much did you ingest?"

"Dunno." Harley's response was slow and slurred. His head dropped toward his chest.

"Dear boy, what have you gotten yourself into?" Garrett clucked and fussed over him.

Peg returned, carrying a tray. She had brewed another pot of herbal tea and made some finger sandwiches. Blowing lightly, she lifted a cup to Harley's lips. "Sip."

She turned to Thomas. “We need Wanda. She’s a nursing student and can tell us what to do. Maryanne’s phone number is in my wallet. She’ll give you Wanda’s number.”

Thomas grabbed her purse and began rifling through it. “Here it is. I’ll call.” He left the room and entered the kitchen where another telephone rested on a counter.

A few minutes later, he came back. “She’ll be here as soon as she drops her kids off at her mother’s house.”

Wanda arrived thirty minutes later. She quickly assessed the situation.

“What did he take?”

“We don’t know.” Thomas lifted his hands and shook his head.

“Harley, wake up.” Wanda shook his shoulder. “Wake up.”

“What...huh?” He roused briefly before going back to dreamland.

“He has to go to the hospital. I’m guessing since you called me instead of taking him to St. Rita’s you want to keep this under the radar.”

“If possible.” Peg gathered the cups. “He was also stabbed, but he says a nurse took care of that.”

“I suggest you take him to Van Wert County Hospital. They’re good. Just make sure you have a logical answer to questions about the stabbing and the drugs.” Wanda continued to look at him with a critical eye. “With drugs in his system, he needs professional monitoring. I also think he may have lost quite a bit of blood. He may need a transfusion.”

I helped wrap the blanket around him. “Wanda, he’s cold.”

“Shock setting in. We need to get him to the hospital quickly. Keep him wrapped in the blanket.”

Garrett and Thomas carried Harley to the Bentley. They laid him in the back seat. Wanda slid in and lifted his head onto her lap. Garrett tucked another blanket around him. I sat in front. Peg and Thomas followed in Thomas’s car.

We pulled up to the emergency room entrance, and I rushed inside to get a wheelchair. Wanda pushed him into the ER, I got his insurance information and wallet from Garrett.

He was wheeled into an examination room as Peg, Thomas, and Garrett entered. "I'm afraid we can only allow family inside." A nurse explained as she prepared to take his blood pressure.

Harley opened his eyes. "That'd be Garrett and Mari," he mumbled, his voice barely audible.

Peg, Thomas, and Wanda went to the waiting room.

The nurse looked at the cuff and retook his pressure. "It's very low. His bp is seventy over forty-nine." She then took his heart rate. "It's slow. Fifty-five beats per minute. Does he take any medication?"

"No," Garrett answered. "His pulse is normally around sixty and his blood pressure around one hundred twenty over seventy-five. He was given antibiotics this week for his chest injury."

The nurse carefully removed his shirt and bandages. "Looks like a stab wound. How'd he become injured?"

"I was sharpening my knife at a friend's home and dropped it. I tried to catch it, but tripped and accidentally stabbed myself." Harley grimaced and sucked in air as the nurse prodded the wound.

That was the only time I heard Harley lie. But I understood why. He didn't want the police to be involved.

"Who stitched you up?"

"A nurse friend from near Columbus was visiting the people I was with. She sewed me up."

"She gave you antibiotics?"

"Another friend had some. He also gave me painkillers so I could come home."

"What did he give you?"

"I don't know."

"The doctor will be in shortly." The nurse drew blood and took the vials to the lab.

The doctor entered carrying a clipboard. "Stabbed yourself, eh?" He looked up and quirked an eyebrow at Harley.

"Yes, sir. I dropped my knife. When I tried to catch it, I tripped and stuck myself." His voice was barely a whisper.

Harley was given a blood transfusion and kept in the hospital for three days before he was released.

###

Harley, you recovered that day and went out of your way to prove your worthiness to everyone. I loved you before that, during and after the bad episodes. I love you still. How I long to hear your voice, smell your fresh outdoorsy, Irish Spring, and Old Spice scent, to see the twinkle in your eyes, and the smile on your lips. I miss the gentle comfort of your arms around my shoulders. It doesn't feel real that you are gone.

I will love you forever.

Last night I dreamed about you just as I have many times since you died. In my vision, I am walking through Tecumseh following the trails. I kept turning as I felt your presence. The whistling of the wind through the pines sounded like you were talking to me.

"Mari," came the soft sigh of your voice.

"Harley?" I asked as I peered into the woodland. "Is that you?"

"I'm not dead."

I whirled around trying to find you. A vague shape appeared to my left, off the trail. You turned and walked further into the woods. Your form was like a mist.

"Harley?" I took a tentative step in your direction.

"Mari," you sighed.

"Harley! Wait!" I stumbled over plants and roots as I hurried after you.

"I'll love you forever. Do not give up on me," you crooned.

"I won't. Please don't go!" I pleaded, dropping to my knees.

"Wait for me, Mari. Wait for me." Your voice echoed as you slowly disappeared.

I woke with the feeling you had been in my room. It was as though your arms had been around me, giving me comfort. I could smell the lingering scent of Irish Spring soap and Old Spice.

###

I couldn't shake the feeling that Harley wasn't really gone. So, I went to visit Garrett. He was in the midst of packing up the house when I arrived.

"Miss Mari," he paused to wipe the sweat from his brow. "What brings you here?"

I stepped inside and looked around. Gone were the games in the room to the right of the foyer. The living room was bereft of furnishings we had used to watch movies and sleep on during those wonderful weekend get-togethers. The pictures on the walls in the hall had been taken down. Gone was the music and everything that proved Harley had lived here. The house was nothing more than a shell. A building that once was home and sanctuary to the most wonderful man I had the privilege of being in love with.

My throat closed with sadness. I could only stand there and look around as I fought to hold the tears at bay.

"Miss Mari?"

"Why not live here, Garrett?" I choked. "Where is everything?"

"For the same reason tears are coursing down your cheeks. The memories overwhelm me." He rested his hand on my shoulder. "The stuff is in storage."

"But, what if he didn't really die, Garrett? How will he find you if you move away?"

"Ah, Miss Mari. It would be nice if he were alive, but he's not."

"I dream about him every night. He's standing in the moonlight, and he pleads with me not to give up on him. Not yet." I looked tearfully at Garrett. "Please, just hold on a little longer."

"If it will bring you peace, I'll wait to put the house on the market for a few months longer." He sighed and pulled me into his arms for a hug.

Chapter Eight

Harley

April

Months of torturous treatment and physical therapy went by. It was taking a long time to recover from the surgeries due to the aggressive cancer treatments making me so sick. Each day was a struggle. There were days I couldn't feel my leg and others when it felt like my limb was being roasted over a campfire. Sometimes it was as though a thousand pins were being jabbed into me like I was a giant pincushion.

The therapist tied a belt around me and made me practice getting up from my bed. I had to hold the bed rail with one hand, push up with the other and grasp the walker. I had to walk using the walker. Since my leg wasn't functioning properly, that meant I had to swing my hip out while lifting the knee as high as I could and planting my foot down carefully in front of me. The therapist had me doing strengthening exercises where you raise the knee up and kick with the leg, swing it side to side, forward and back, heel on the floor and then the ankle. It was tiring. I was told I would probably have to use a walker or cane for the rest of my life and I will always walk with a limp.

I was a fall risk, so I was not allowed to get up on my own. It was humiliating to have to urinate into a bottle. I can only imagine what girls went through.

My parents visited daily. Mother chattered about all the shops, museums and art galleries she's been to. Father droned on and on about Wall Street and the state of the economy, politics, and the cost of gasoline. Their constant chit-chat often left me not only feeling drained but with a killer headache.

The recliner was my best friend. At least I could sit and look out the window and watch people, the flowers, birds, and squirrels. My ability to walk more than a few steps was severely hampered by the numerous surgeries I had undergone. Physical therapy left my legs feeling shaky, and I had to use a walker to move around my room. I wasn't allowed to shower by myself. I had to have an orderly help me bathe. I have never felt so helpless in my entire life. Even meals were an ordeal. I couldn't convince them to not give me coffee or tea. I rarely got the juice I requested. Cutting, chewing and swallowing became draining for me as though the life was being sucked out of me.

When asked about prayers, I asked for a Mormon Priest to visit. Father must have intervened because the minister from a Lutheran church showed up and prayed for me. If Garrett had been here, he would have honored my wishes.

I spent many days trying to remember dates and numbers. I finally dredged up from the furthest recesses of my mind, the telephone number to WOSL one morning. I wondered if Mari still had a morning show. With trembling fingers, I dialed. It rang four times before being picked up.

"WOSL radio. This is Gypsy Mar. What can I play for you?" Mari's sweet voice came over the line.

I was filled with joy and could not find the words I wanted to say.

"Hello? Is there anyone there?"

I closed my eyes, savoring the sound of her voice. How I longed to see her.

"Hello?" She queried. "What kind of prank are you trying to pull? I'm going to hang up now."

"Mari," I whispered, my throat went dry, and my voice cracked. "You have any Steppenwolf? How about some 'Ride With Me'?"

"What did you just say?" Shock filled her voice. "Who are you?" I could hear a switch being flipped. She had taken us off the air.

"It's me, Harley." I could hear my voice choking up with emotion. Mari had to believe me. She just had to.

"Harley is dead." Her voice deadened. She must have switched back to on-air status because I could hear her speaking into the microphone using the station call signs. Then she was back. "Now tell me, who you really are and why you're playing this mean-spirited game."

"Harley. No game. I'm not dead, Mari. You have to believe me."

"You're some kind of sicko to play this game. Harley died in January."

"Mari," My voice cracked. Even I wouldn't have recognized it. What made me think Mari would? My spirits fell as I realized the two people I loved the most didn't believe me. "I'll prove to you I am who I say I am. Ask me anything that only you and I would know."

"Did Thomas put you up to this?" She demanded. I could hear both anger and tears in her voice.

I heard the sound of the broadcast booth door opening. "Gypsy Mar? What's going on?" Hixson thundered. "We can hear your conversation over the radio."

"Harley," she choked.

Hixson must have grabbed the telephone from her. "Who are you?" He growled.

"Harley," I whispered as my voice faded.

"Harley's dead, you pervert. Quit harassing her." He disconnected the call.

I sat back in my recliner and closed my eyes. Wetness streaked down my cheek. It was disheartening to think no one believed me or recognized my voice. I was so desperately lonely for them. Tomorrow I will try again.

I lifted the receiver once again. This time I called home.

"Hello? Davis residence. Garrett speaking."

"Garrett," I sighed in relief. "Did my father ever call you?"

"Who is this?"

"Harley."

"You again! You called back in March pretending to be Mister Harlan Davis."

"No, Garrett. It's really me, Harley Davis."

"You are a very sick young man."

"Yes, I am. I need you so much, Garrett." I sighed. It sounded like he believed me.

The phone was silent. All I could hear was the snap and crackling hiss of the electrical hum on the lines.

"Garrett? Are you there?" I felt my emotions sinking. "I can prove who I am. Ask me anything, anything that only you and I would know. Please, Garrett, please!" I pleaded.

"I'm here." He grated. "You need psychiatric help. Do not call here again."

The line went dead. My spirits plummeted. I couldn't get anyone to believe me. Depression was setting in, but I vowed to never give up. Eventually, one of them will realize who I am. They had to. They just had to.

The next day I called WOSL.

"You're listening to WOSL radio on the beautiful Ohio State University Lima campus. This is Gypsy Mar. What can I play for you?"

"Got any Steppenwolf? How about some 'Foggy Mental Breakdown'?"

Mari must have taken us off the air because I heard the snapping of switches.

"You again? What is wrong with you?"

"Mari, ask me anything only the two of us would know. Please, humor me." I pleaded.

"Oh, all right." She paused. I heard the telltale hiss and whine of a record being cued. "'Foggy Mental Breakdown' by Steppenwolf on Steppenwolf 7." She then returned to the telephone.

"No. I don't want to do this. You are some kind of sicko to keep playing this game of yours."

"Please," I begged. I was desperate. I wanted Mari to believe me so badly I could hear it in my voice.

"Give me one good reason why I should listen to you and believe what you're saying. One good reason and not because you love me."

I sat in my recliner silently. There has to be one reason I could give Mari.

"Well?" She sounded impatient. I could almost see her tapping her pencil on the playlist clipboard.

"I'm thinking."

"You don't have one." She hung up on me.

I rested my head and pulled my blanket up to my chin. I usually do not cry easily. Knowing I can call the people I love, and their disbelief got the better of me. Finally, I allowed myself to give in to self-pity. The tears ran freely. It hurt so badly to not have anyone I loved believe me.

Father walked in and saw my tears. “Quit being a sissy, Harlan. The physical therapy is necessary to get you back on your feet. The treatments are needed to beat this sickness.” He sat in the other chair and opened his newspaper. I often wondered how many newspapers he read in a day.

“Father, did you ever call my house in Lima to let Garrett know I was alive?”

“Of course not. Garrett would have flown back here and fussed over you. That is not in your best interest.”

“Father, I believe I know what is in my best interest.” I fiddled with my blanket.

“Oh, really? Look at you, sitting there and crying like a sissy.”

“I’m not a sissy. I’m not complaining about the physical therapy or the treatments. Those things are benefitting me. I’m tired of always having to fight you for everything that is important to me. It is sucking the life out of me.”

“Nonsense.” He shook out the newspaper and re-folded it.

Mother entered the room carrying a tray of bagels, lox, preserves, juice, and coffee. “I got these from the deli across the street. Much better than the horrid food served here. They said to just bring the tray back.” She set the tray on my bedside table and wheeled it over to me. “Hon,” she glanced at my father. “Have some coffee.”

“Thank you, dear.” He held his hand out for the hot beverage.

She busied herself spreading lox and preserves on a bagel and then handed it to me. “Eat, Harlan. You need to eat to keep your strength up.”

“I’ve eaten, Mother.” I smiled at her. “But, I wouldn’t mind a snack.” I took the proffered morsel. “May I have some juice?”

“Certainly. It does my heart good to see your appetite coming back.”

"Thank you, Mother. This is delicious." I nibbled on the treat. Mother had her ways but, in a pinch, she normally came through. I just wished it was consistent.

"I brought you some coffee, Harlan." She reached for the container.

"I don't drink coffee, remember?"

"Oh, yes," she said absently. "That whole Mormon thing. Why not come back to the Lutheran church?"

"Because I believe in the teachings of the Church of Jesus Christ of Latter-Day Saints."

I closed my eyes and wondered how long they would visit today. Sometimes it was a short thirty minutes, others lasted most of the day. Today they stayed past lunch and only left when I went for therapy and more testing.

The next morning, I woke up with a phone number in my head. I dialed it and was pleasantly surprised when Thomas answered.

"Thomas?" I queried. "Is it really you?"

"Yes," he drew out the word. "This is Thomas." He sounded wary. "Who are you?"

"Did I wake you? I'm so sorry! I forgot you don't get up before eight thirty."

"Who are you, man?"

I could almost see him pacing and shaking his head from impatience. It felt good to hear his voice.

"I said, who are you?" He barked.

"Harley," I rasped. Treatments made my voice come and go. At times I sounded like an old man whose voice rang rusty after years of consuming alcohol.

"Harley, huh? I wondered when you'd get around to harassing me. What you're doing to Mari is reprehensible. How dare you keep badgering her, tearing her heart apart. You're a bastard to be playing this sick game on us."

"No! Wait! It's really me!" I pleaded.

"Yeah, right." He hung up.

I settled back in my bed. How can I make them listen to me? As I pondered the question, the physical therapist hustled in.

"How are you doing today?" She went to the window and yanked open the shades.

"Just peachy," I mumbled.

"Ready for a walk and then some leg strengthening?" She pulled the walker beside the bed and then tied the belt around me.

"Sure. More torture."

"Now, now Mister Davis. We like to think of it as exercise. How will you ever get strong enough to leave here if you don't exercise?"

I looked at her at the mention of leaving the hospital. "Do you really think I'll ever get out of here?"

"I do, indeed. It's just a matter of time, treatment, and mind over matter."

She was the first person to hint I might eventually leave the hospital. My spirits rallied around the mere suggestion I might someday be going home.

Later that morning I called WOSL radio during Mari's show.

"You're listening to WOSL radio coming to you from the Ohio State University Lima campus. What can I play for you?"

"Got any Steppenwolf? How about some 'Skullduggery'?"

"Steely Dan, 'Reelin' in the Years,'" she announced and then flipped the switch to take us off the air.

"You again!"

"Mari, please..."

"You have some nerve bothering Thomas! Yes, he called me and told me about your early morning phone call to him! Leave us alone!"

"Mari, please don't hang up. I don't think I could take that again," I begged.

Something in my voice must have gotten through to her because she didn't disconnect us. "Ask me anything only you and I and maybe Garrett would know. Anything at all and I'll try to answer."

The line was deathly silent for minutes. I could hear her cuing a song and announcing it. "This is Gypsy Mar with some Joe Cocker 'With a Little Help From My Friends.'"

"When was the first time we slept together?" She asked after flipping back to off-air mode.

"Technically? After the Steppenwolf concert when I got sick. Sexually? Never. The law of chastity kept me honorable."

"When was the last time you drank coffee?"

"With my parents in 1971. I do not drink caffeinated beverages. They are bad for your health."

The silence was deafening.

"Okay, let's say, I'll agree to talk with you until I catch you lying." Mari sounded cautiously hopeful. "Let's just say you're alive. Where are you? Why does Garrett think you're dead?"

"The Cancer Institute of New York." I lay back against my pillows. My energy was dwindling rapidly. "My father told him I died."

"What?!" Her voice rose in indignation. "How could he do that? Why would he do that? Does he have no morals or compassion?"

"I don't know. Please tell Garrett, I'm alive."

"Okay, I will. How are you doing?"

"They say I'm slowly turning the corner on this cancer due to aggressive treatment. I had to have several surgeries to remove tumors from my leg. I'm slowly regaining the ability to walk." I sucked in a breath of air. My energy was gone.

"Oh, that is great news."

"I wish I could talk longer, but I'm exhausted."

"Oh! Of course! How thoughtless of me! Give me your phone number. I'll call you sometime soon."

I rattled off the numbers on the phone and my room. I wrote down her home number on a slip of paper and tucked it into the tray drawer. After we hung up, I called the nurse's station and asked them to add Mari and Garrett to the list of people who could receive updates about me.

Chapter Nine

Mari

April

"Hello?" I answered the phone in the kitchen. I had just gotten home from my shift at K-Mart.

"Hi, Mari." Harley greeted. "Did you play any Steppenwolf on your show?"

"Yes, I did. I played 'Rock Me,' and 'Screaming Night Hog' in your honor." I felt myself at war with my emotions. He sounded like Harley in some ways. In others, he didn't. His voice had taken on a raspy tone similar to how drunks often sounded.

"I dig it. How was your day?" He sounded tired.

"It was busy." I was still leery. I couldn't believe it was actually Harley on the telephone. "How are you doing?"

"I had another round of treatments, and I'm learning how to walk again." The weariness in his voice testified to his exhausting day.

"I don't understand. Why do you have to learn how to walk?" I could feel a lump in my throat as I thought about what he must be going through.

"I lost a lot of muscle in my leg from the surgeries. They had to reattach some and create replacements for others. I couldn't walk until recently. At best, my balance is precarious. At worst, my leg gives out. So, I have daily physical therapy to regain use of my leg and the ability to walk unassisted."

I was shocked at his disclosure. It must be really rough on him. He valued his independence, ability to walk, shoot hoops, and most especially, to ride his motorcycle. To be unable to walk without assistance must be torture. My heart cried for him. If he really is my Harley, the suffering he was going through had to be devastating. Harley was not a complainer. He stated the facts and whether he likes or dislikes things, but he never came across as griping about the situation.

"Tomorrow, I'll probably feel sick from the treatments, so I thought I'd call you tonight."

"What do you want to talk about?" I asked softly.

"Hmm..." The pause lasted several minutes. "You love me, correct?"

"If you're really Harley, yes. I love you very much."

"If I can convince you I am me, would you do something for me?"

"You know I would."

"Good to know, because I thought after the quarter ends, maybe you and Garrett can come out here? I'd pay all costs." The timbre of his voice took on a hopeful child-like quality. I could almost picture him cupping his chin, giving me an impish grin, and batting his blue-gray eyelashes.

"Garrett will take some convincing," I mumbled. "I don't know. You need your funds for the hospital and treatments and stuff, don't you?"

"I have plenty of funds, so no need to worry. Mari, I really want to see you both. I miss you so much." The longing in his voice was heartbreaking.

"I'll see what I can do. I'm not even sure I can get off work with the recent layoffs we've had." I tucked a strand of hair behind my ear and settled myself on the floor.

Chapter Ten

Harley

April

I hope Mari can convince Garrett to come. I was desperate to see the people I loved and know they felt the same about me. My parents probably loved me in their own way, but I often felt like a failure around them.

Their lifestyle and mine clashed horribly. They were bourgeois while I was more down to earth. They valued money and what it could bring them. I saw wealth as a means to provide service to those less fortunate. I'm not a saint, not by a long shot. There's a lot of devil in me that I constantly battle. Still, our politics, spiritual beliefs, and way of life did not match.

"Do you remember going to the race track a few weeks after my run-in with the motorcycle club?"

I lay back against my pillows and closed my eyes. I pictured Mari sitting and frowning at the mention of my fight with an outlaw gang.

"Yes," she spoke slowly. Distaste was evident.

"Do you recall what we did?" I propped myself back up and stretched. I love hearing her voice on the other end of the telephone.

"Tested your new motorcycle," she answered softly.

"Do you remember what happened?" I leaned forward and reached for the table tray. I poured some water into a glass and sipped.

"Do I remember what happened? You have got to be crazy! How could I forget?" From the sound of her voice, I could picture her shivering at the memories of that day. "You scared me half to death, Harlan Davis!"

"I'm sorry. I didn't mean to do that," I spoke softly. "had actually planned an exceptional day and night. Unfortunately, things didn't go quite like I hoped."

"What had you planned?" She asked, curious.

“A picnic lunch, some sightseeing and then a romantic dinner in New Weston. I was going to renew my promise to you to never hurt you like I did a short time before that. I wanted to promise you a lifetime of love.”

“Oh, Harley,” she sighed, “instead it ended in disaster.”

“That’s putting it mildly.” I chuckled and then gasped as a bolt of pain shot through my leg.

“What? What’s wrong?” Mari instantly picked up on my distress.

Fortunately, the pain ended as quickly as it started. “It’s nothing. Just a little cramp in my leg.”

“That didn’t sound like a little cramp,” she fretted.

“Really, I’m okay.”

“Okay,” she whispered.

“So, tell me. What do you remember about that day?”

###

Mari

That day was bright with sunshine befitting my mood. The ugliness of the recent weeks with Harley and the motorcycle club were behind us. He was my generous, loving, kind, service oriented, honest, prankster Harley again. His face crinkled with joy. His smile lifted my spirits. He was mine again.

“Here’s your helmet, jacket, and boots. Just bring them with you.” He handed them to me and headed out the door.

“Did you get a new bike?” I fumbled with the helmet.

“Yeah. I had my pit crew customize a Hog for me. My Sportster Ironhead XLCH is toast.” He tucked my arm in his and smiled at me.

“My new ride is a Harley-Davidson XLCH Ironhead. It came with an 883cc engine. I had them modify it for more power. It has a larger engine. Other changes include a big gas tank, passenger seat, and hard case saddle bags. It’s black and chrome, and huge compared to my old Hog.” He guided me into his Bentley. “We’re meeting my pit crew at the race track. We are going to put it through its maiden paces." He smiled his lopsided grin and said, "Hopefully, it'll pass muster, and we can ride it to dinner while one of my guys brings the car home."

"Are you going to be doing the testing or one of your crew?" I asked, awaiting his response. I just knew what he was going to say and I didn't like it. Knowing him, there was no way I was going to change his mind.

"Me." He had a gleeful look on his face much like a kid at Christmas with a new train set.

"Ok," I wasn't sure I liked the idea. "Do you think you should?"

Harley was going to ride an unproven bike. It scared me. I know he's raced cars and motorcycles in the past, but the thought of watching him out there on the tracks, possibly getting hurt, unnerved me.

"Harley, are you sure you've recovered enough? Shouldn't you let one of your crew," I used air quotes around the word "crew" for extra emphasis, "do that the first time out?" I tightened the seatbelt.

He looked quizzically at me. "Mari, you know I'd never ask my staff to do anything I wouldn't do first."

"I know," I said glumly. I was scared he'd get injured again so soon after his recent disaster.

"What's wrong, love?" He turned to look at me. His hand rested lightly on the steering wheel, and the other held the key.

"I'm worried you'll aggravate your injuries."

"You worry too much, love."

"Really?" I could feel tears threatening to gush forward.

"I'm healed, Mari. They even took the stitches out last week."

He turned onto Interstate 75 toward Dayton and a little over twelve miles later merged onto US 33 West toward St. Mary's, and Grand Lake. We then turned north at New Weston.

New Weston is a village boasting 174 residents. The racetrack is between the New Weston and Burkettsville. We had to pass through New Weston. The main street started with clapboard style houses, then the central part had businesses and a church. It was all very Americana.

What must have been the entire village came out to gawk at the Bentley. I felt like I was in a one-vehicle parade as we drove through.

We arrived outside Burkettsville about an hour and ten minutes after leaving his place. Burkettsville is a tiny village of about 279 people and similar to New Weston.

The racetrack is between the two villages. It was a simple affair of about a half mile asphalt and dirt track. To me, however, it looked ominous as though it was laying in waiting to swallow some unsuspecting biker.

Chapter Eleven

Harley

April

There is a half-mile dirt and asphalt race track between New Weston and Burkettsville. I occasionally use it to performance test my modified motorcycles. The owner, Merle, and I had an arrangement allowing me access to the track during non-racing hours. The track is banked twenty-four degrees in the corners and eight degrees on the straightaway.

My pit crew was already present when we arrived. They had brought my new bike on a flatbed truck. Ken was using our pace bike to check the condition of the track while Edward and team rolled my sled down the ramp. Once on the ground, they inspected it, preparing it for performance testing.

"How's it looking?" I asked as we approached. I draped my arm over Mari's shoulder. She reached up, took my hand and lightly kissed my palm.

"Mighty fine, Mister Davis." Edward paused when he responded. "Mighty fine." His tone of voice did not sound quite right.

I looked at him for several long minutes. He ducked his head and began studying his clipboard.

"Safe enough to take Mari for a spin?" I unbuttoned my shirt and put on a white undershirt.

"Better put her through her paces first." Edward continued to look down at his notes.

"Gotcha," I nodded. His responses meant they were concerned about how it handled.

"Miss Mari?" Adams took her arm and guided her to the grandstand seating area. "Best you sit over here so you can watch all the activity. Okay?"

"Uhm, sure." Mari glanced between Edward and me. "Is something wrong?" She asked as Adams steered her away from the pit.

"Nah, Miss Mari. Just bike talk is all it is."

As Adams guided Mari away, I quickly removed my jeans and donned a pair of leather race pants. The leggings had pads along the calves and knees. They were designed to protect my calves and knees from the track and any accidents that might occur.

"Okay, Edward. Give it to me straight."

I slipped on my leather jacket and connected it to my racing pants. The jacket had built in padding at the elbows and forearms. Both the top and bottom of my outfit were vented to allow cool air in and keep me from overheating.

"What's got you concerned?" I stepped back and looked at the black monster. The Harley looked lovely and wickedly beautiful.

"Excessive vibration." Edward scratched the back of his head. "Don't know what's causing it to rock."

"The cam?" I frowned. We were testing the bike with the original but had engineered our own version to replace it if the cam proved to be defective like many of that year's model.

I stepped out of my shoes, and into my racing footwear. These are heavy duty leather boots with aluminum or alloy buckles, a reinforced shin plate, and medial guard.

"Maybe, but passed all the tests we've run."

Edward handed me a hard spine protector. "Better wear this. I know it kind of restricts your movement, but they'll pad your back."

"Worried the engine might blow? Is that why you put Mari in the grandstand? To keep her safe?"

I rubbed my face in contemplation of what I was being told. I had expected minor problems but not something as dangerous as the engine possibly blowing out. I looked back at the grandstand and suddenly found myself wishing I hadn't brought Mari out here. Why couldn't I have scheduled another day to test the monster?

"What's your best guess?" I asked as I looked at the spine protector then back at the stands.

Mari waved and blew a kiss. I pretended to snatch it out of the air and place the kiss against my heart. I returned her gesture with my own.

"How likely is it? The engine blowing, that is."

"Fifty-fifty." Edward looked me in the eye. "I'd be lying if I said I wasn't worried."

"That bad, huh?"

"Yeah. Mister Davis, I really wish you'd let me put it through its paces."

"Nothing doing. I can take the chance as well as anyone." I put on the spine protector. With a minor adjustment, I still had a full range of motion while protecting my back. I pulled on my gloves. They are very thick at the knuckles and have rivets on the palm to protect my hands.

Finally, I donned my brain bucket, also known as a full-face helmet. Properly decked out, I walked around the motorcycle, checking the brakes, making sure the turn signals, and headlights worked. The taillights had painters tape covering them, and the mirrors had been removed.

It was a beauty. The tires were designed for road racing with grooved threads so they could grip both pavement and dirt. The exhaust pipes allowed for more kick and quicker throttle response. The suspension had been lowered, so it had a hunkered down traction enhancement. The bike frame was sixty-one inches instead of fifty-five, and the engine was 1200cc for power, 317cc over the current model available. I then mounted the sled and looked over the instrument panel. Everything seemed good.

Still, Edward doesn't get worried over nothing. I turned again and looked over at Mari. When she noticed me looking at her, she waved and blew me a kiss.

I pretended to catch it and hold it close to my heart before sending a kiss back to her.

Ken returned. "Track's good as usual."

"Thanks." I waited patiently for Edward to give me the green flag. The wait felt like an eternity.

Edward consulted with Adams and Ken. He then called Doctor Wilson over. I guess he was going over contingency plans with them. Doctor Wilson took a folding chair halfway down the track and settled himself to watch the test.

Edward nodded to Ken, who started the pace bike and headed out ahead of me. Adams climbed into the bed of the truck.

Edward held the green flag loosely. After glancing at each crew member, he raised his arm. I waited patiently for him to bring the flag down. When he did, I kickstarted the engine and slowly rode down the track. I wanted to make sure the engine was good and warm before actually putting it through its paces.

Chapter Twelve

Mari

April

I sat in the stands and watched as Harley got dressed in a racing outfit. It was hilarious how modest he was, probably because I was there. I had already seen most of his body when Harley got sick after the Steppenwolf concert, and I helped him dress for bed. Not to mention, when he donned the t-shirt I had given him earlier that day, and he put it on in the street.

Harley once explained that modesty involved the law of chastity. This fundamental teaching of the Church of Jesus Christ of Latter-Day Saints included maintaining the purity of the body as well as the mind. Sexual activity outside of marriage is not permitted. I had never experienced a relationship where the guy didn't try to pressure me into having sex. I never gave in. I wanted to be a virgin for the man I married. Still, it was refreshing not to have to deal with the octopus arms, so many guys seemed to sprout.

With Harley, I was free to be me, and I knew he loved and respected me. Even when the devil got in him, and he did things to break my heart, I never doubted his feelings for me. Somehow, I knew he'd come back around. He kept his promises.

He wheeled his Hog onto the track. He sat there looking at Edward for several long minutes. I wished I could hear what they were discussing.

Harley kept looking in my direction. My heart swelled with love. I placed my fingers to my lips and blew a kiss. He reached out, grabbed it and held it over his heart before returning the gesture. Such a simple thing made me grin like a love-struck fool. What was I thinking? I am so in love with him, it's not funny. This complicated man worked his way into my heart. He taught me what it's like to truly love someone through all the joys and heartaches life tosses at you.

Edward raised his hand. It held a green flag. When he swished it downward, Harley started the motorcycle and headed down the track. He rode at a snail's pace. I wondered why. Harley continued riding slowly through two complete circuits of the track. The third time around he picked up a little speed.

One of Harley's men sat near me and made marks on a clipboard.

"Brian?"

"Yes, Miss Mari?" He glanced at the bike and made another notation. He adjusted the binoculars and made another note.

"Why is he going so slowly?"

"It's nothing to concern yourself with, Miss Mari. He's just testing the limits."

"Of the bike or himself?" I gasped as the cycle wobbled slightly. Could something be wrong with the machine? Is that why he rode so slowly?

"Both. An expert rider always knows his own limits and what his Hog can handle." Brian pointed to the corner.

"He's downshifting. Next, he'll start braking. This will set up the suspension. Then he'll give it gas all the way through the corner and launch back onto the straightaway. He's not leaning off. That means the weight is distributed evenly. As he progresses to higher speeds, he might need to redistribute weight, and he'll lean off."

"What is leaning off?"

"It's the positioning of the body to get the greatest possible influence of a bike's lean. Picture an imaginary line running right through the center of the front tire." Brian drew a sketch to illustrate what he was saying.

"On an inside corner, you want as much of your body between that line and the ground. The more you go in that direction, the less your bike needs to lean."

Brian jumped up, made a quick notation. "Ah... damn!" He hurried toward the pit.

I looked at Edward and saw him waving a black flag. A glance down the track caused my heart to stop. Smoke was billowing out the back end of Harley's motorcycle.

The pit crew jumped into the flatbed truck and raced toward him. The doctor leaped from his seat and jogged toward Harley, carrying a black medical bag.

I ran out into the middle of the track and saw Harley yank his headgear off. He slapped his leg with one hand while swinging the helmet.

I started to jog toward them when Brian grabbed my arm.

"Best you stay right here. Harley doesn't look hurt."

I watched as the pit crew hoisted the bike onto the truck and headed back.

"Harley?" I shouted. "What happened?"

"Overheated. It's most likely a water leak from the coolant reservoir." He wiped the sweat from his face and greedily gulped the water Ken handed him. "Good thing it only held water and not a mix of coolant."

The entire crew gathered around Brian as he read his notes. That's when I noticed a vapor trail.

"What's that?" I asked pointing.

Harley looked in the direction I was pointing. "That's a vapor trail created by the water leaking from the coolant reservoir."

I sighed with relief. "It's not the engine smoking?"

"Nah. Just water." He started to put his arm around me but paused.

I reached out and pulled his arm around my shoulder.

"Mari! I stink!" He protested and pulled his arm back.

"Who cares?" I grabbed his hand and held it in place on my shoulder.

"We brought a replacement reservoir. Shouldn't take longer than a couple of hours." Adams chimed in.

"Mister Davis, why don't you take Miss Mari to an early lunch?" Edward said as he continued looking at the motorcycle.

Harley looked at me. "I'd rather stay and help. Okay with you, Mari?"

I shrugged, "Sure. I'll watch."

I was given a folding metal chair to sit on. The crew clustered around the bike. They took great pains to remove it from the truck without causing additional damage.

A deep sense of foreboding settled over me as I watched the activity. It was as though the day had darkened, and some evil presence was trying to gain a foothold over us. All color seemed to fade into gray as though I was watching a black and white horror movie. I shivered at the sudden cold feeling I had.

Chapter Thirteen

Harley

April

I watched her turn back toward the grandstand. I felt bad she had to sit around and watch us guys work on a motorcycle. Most girls would prefer doing anything other than watching men tear apart a motor vehicle. Then again, Mari wasn't a typical beauty. She had brains and looks.

Quickly, I shrugged off my racing gear and donned overalls. We became a beehive of activity as the guys clustered around the bike, removing the various parts to the water pump and reservoir.

Occasionally, I glanced in Mari's direction. I felt terrible leaving her sitting on the chair with nothing to do. Grabbing a bottle of water, I jogged over to her.

"I thought you might like a drink." I removed the cap and handed it to her.

"Thanks." She took it and sipped. "How much longer?"

"Just a few more minutes and it'll be ready to test again." I leaned over and kissed her cheek. "Thanks for being such a sport."

"Sure."

"We're ready for you, Harley!" Edward called.

"Be right there!" Turning to Mari, I said, "Got to go, love." I planted a quick peck and sauntered back to the pit.

"Brian, would you make sure Mari's attention is occupied while I change?"

"Sure thing, Mister Davis." He grabbed his clipboard and headed toward her. As he walked away, I heard him snickering.

"I can hear you!" I called out and laughed.

"Mister Davis, I really wish..." Edward ran his hand through his hair, and then rubbed his chin. He left a grease mark on his face.

"No, Edward. You men did all the hard work. I'll do the testing." I shook my head to emphasize my point.

"The risky stuff, you mean." Edward frowned at me.

"Yes," I said as I did leg stretches. After that, I bent down and then straightened my back.

"Just don't go out in a blaze in front of your girl," Edward mumbled. He tapped his clipboard and scribbled notes.

"I don't intend to crash," I mumbled as I got mentally prepared for round two. I shrugged my shoulders, shook my arms, and turned my head from side to side to loosen the muscles.

Once again, I dressed in my racing outfit. I straddled the Hog and put on my full-face helmet. The raceway seemed daunting this time around. At least the time it took to replace the cooling system allowed the track to dry.

I sat studying the dirt stretch. It's only a quarter mile. Then there's an asphalt stretch of the same length. Just a half-mile track. Not a long distance. So, why was I nervous?

Edward raised his hand, holding the green flag. When Ken came back from checking the roadway and gave the thumbs up, Edward brought the flag down. I started the Harley and waited a few minutes before slowly driving down the track.

The first lap was nerve-wracking. I was extremely aware of every bump, each shimmy, vibration, and noise the bike made. The bike, for the most part, sounded normal.

For the second time that day I made two slow circuits before easing into a faster speed. The first lap was relatively easy. The cycle handled superbly. No signs of water leaking, no shaking. On the second lap, I noticed a slight shimmy, but it was nothing to be worried over.

There was a slight vibration on the third lap. It became a little more noticeable as I rounded the corner. Still, it was within normal operating constraints. I began performance testing in earnest.

Each time I completed a lap, I ramped up the speed by ten miles per hour. Everything was handling almost perfectly until the eighth lap when I hit eighty miles per hour. The vibration became a noticeable shake as I entered the corner, making the bike hard to control.

I eased back on the throttle and started to apply the brakes when the engine began whining. Soon, stuttering accompanied the increasingly loud whine. Generally, as I come out of a turn, I apply gas. Instead, I continued to brake as I pulled out of the corner and glanced at Edward. He waved a black flag.

Trouble.

Big trouble.

As I angled toward the pit, I felt a shift in the engine vibration and noise. The bike was shaking and rattling so hard it slid sideways. Smoke began billowing from the engine. It could only mean one thing; the engine was going to blow. The Hog skid out of control. I ditched the bike as best as I could and immediately went into a roll away from the monster.

I looked over at it as soon as I was clear. The engine exploded in a deafening roar. Flames shot upward licking the engine. The black flag was replaced with a red one being waved. In no time my crew was all over it, dousing the flames.

The doctor we had on standby rushed to my side. He rapidly removed my suit and began prodding me.

"I'm fine. What in the heck happened?" I sounded shaky.

I watched as my crew began the process of determining what went wrong. Ken measured the distance from where I entered the turn to where the engine failed. He then took measurements from where the black flag was issued to when it changed to red.

I heard Mari screaming and turned to face the stands. She was running down the track. I grabbed my outfit and pulled it back on.

"Mister Davis, I need to finish examining you," Doc Wilson said as he tugged the top back down.

"I can't let Mari see me almost naked," I complained. "Make it snappy. I'm telling you, I'm not hurt. Just a few scrapes, scratches, and bruises. I'm fine."

"When did you injure your chest?" He studied the slash marks from my run-in with Satan's Hounds.

"Weeks ago. It's not bleeding," I said as I looked down.

"I'm your personal physician, why wasn't I informed?" He looked at the wounded area.

"I was in a hospital out of town. When I got out, I couldn't get an appointment until next week. You are one busy dude. How'd you fit today in?"

"Today is Saturday." He started looking over the rest of my torso.

"Oh, yeah. I forgot."

"I need to see your legs. I'll get a blanket for your concerns about modesty."

Chapter Fourteen

Mari

April

I was never so terrified and wanting to clobber that man in my entire life! Seeing him enter that turn and losing control of his bike was terrible enough.

Brian leaped to his feet and ran to the pit. The entire crew, including Doctor Wilson, was jumping onto the flatbed truck. They carried an assortment of equipment with them.

An obscenely loud screech emanated from the far end of the track. Harley was sliding sideways close to the ground. He launched himself outward and tucked into a roll. Seconds later there was an earth-shattering explosion as the engine blew apart.

All I could envision was Harley laying on the ground, bloodied and maybe dying. Horror and terror completely engulfed me. Dimly, I became aware of someone screaming. The shrieking continued and was joined with the loud hammering of my heart.

Watching the engine explode was cause for a heart attack. I jumped from my seat and ran down the track screaming his name. I just couldn't lose him now! Not so soon after becoming engaged, and all the bad stuff we had just gone through.

"HARLEY!" I raced toward the accident. My legs pumped rapidly like pistons, propelling me toward him. That old saying about fear making a person able to do unbelievable feats is true. I never ran so fast in my life. Sweat streamed from every pore. My breathing became shallow, and I began to feel light headed. As I neared the wreck, I slowed to a walk. My heart was a huge lump in my throat. I was so scared.

Harley looked up from what the doctor was doing and slowly rose. He pushed past everyone and limped toward me.

"I'm okay, Mari." He pulled me into his arms, and gently brushed the hair from my face. His thumb lifted my chin, so I looked up into his eyes. "I'm okay," he repeated, and tenderly kissed my lips. “You’re shaking.” Harley kissed the tears running down my cheeks. “Hush, hush, sweet Mari,” he murmured.

“Then, why are you limping?” The practical side of me took over even though I remained frightened. I hiccupped, gasping for air. “You scared me to death, Harlan Christian Robert Davis! Don’t ever do that again!” I feebly pounded my fists against his finely muscled chest.

“Hush, my love. I’m okay.”

Chapter Fifteen

Harley

April

I was so intent on reaching Mari, I didn't notice the limp. I glanced down and saw my boot had a bulge. I draped an arm over her shoulder, and she slipped her arm around my waist. She guided me to the pit. The doctor came back over.

"I told you, I needed to check you over." He chastised me. "Now, let's take a look at that ankle, shall we?"

"I think it's sprained." I removed the boot, wincing at the pain radiating from my ankle.

"I'd say you may be incorrect in that assessment." The doctor gathered his supplies. He wrapped ice in a cloth and pressed it against my ankle. "You might have a fracture or a serious break."

"Dang! That hurts!" The cold was shocking.

My ankle swelled rapidly. It flushed red and felt hot, almost like a fever.

"Does this hurt?" He gently manipulated my foot.

"Yes," I hissed. I couldn't suppress the groans. Movement without the boot was sheer agony.

"Is it broken?" Mari asked. She peered over my shoulder at my foot.

"He appears to have a fracture." Turning to me, he said, I'm going make a splint. Then you are going to be driven to the hospital for x-rays and a cast. Until you get there, you will keep your leg elevated. I will follow you."

"Hey, doc, why not take him in your car? I can have one of the guys bring his car to his house, and Garrett can pick them up." Edward stood with his hands on his hips and shook his head.

"Don't say it, Edward," I warned, "I am so not in the mood for a lecture."

"Even better." Doctor Wilson said and motioned for the guys to help me up.

Edward and Adams carried me to the doctor's car. They slid me into the back seat so I could sit with my leg stretched out on the seat.

Chapter Sixteen

Mari

April

"We were supposed to go to dinner that night. Your trip to the hospital nixed those plans."

###

Harley

"Boy, did it. Ruined my plans for the night."

###

Mari

I got the impression you had something special in mind. I figured it had to be special from the way you kept it so secret." I smiled at the memory.

###

Harley

"I did. I had planned to propose to you again. Kind of to make up for the way I acted, getting involved with Red's Motorcycle Club. I felt horrible for the way I treated you. I know I broke your heart during that fiasco. I'd give my left nut to turn back time and make it so that stupidity never happened. I hurt so many people that week. You, Garrett, Thomas, and even Peg."

###

Mari

“We all forgave you.” I choked up hearing his heartfelt confession.

###

Harley

“I know you all did.” I yawned. “I’m getting tired, Mari. I should let you go. We’ve been talking for over an hour.”

###

Mari

“Oh, dear! How thoughtless of me!”

###

Harley

“I enjoyed talking with you.” I smiled and lay back, feeling content.

“Good night, my love.” She sounded wistful.

“Sweet dreams until we talk again,” I said.

Chapter Seventeen

Mari

May

Harley called me at WOSL. He sounded panicked. His voice cracked as he talked.

"Mari, please. I need you and Garrett to come here. I don't understand what they are planning to do with me. Please come!" He pleaded.

"I can't promise, but I'll see what I can do." Something in his tone finally made me get off the fence. During our telephone conversations, he had shared details of our relationship only Garrett might have known. The desperation he expressed made me think I should believe he is my Harley.

###

I raced from the station to a pay phone. I dialed the number he had given me in April. Still, I had to make sure before I went begging to Garrett.

"The Cancer Institute of New York. How may I direct your call?" The operator asked.

"Admissions, please." In a matter of minutes, someone from Admissions answered.

"Could you tell me if Harlan Christian Robert Davis is a patient there?"

"One moment, please."

I heard the rustling of papers over the static in the phone lines.

"Yes, he is. Shall I ring his room?"

"Please." I figured if he answered, then I had my answer.

"Hello?"

It was him! The same voice I had talked with during my show. "Harley!" It was time to accept the voice on the other end of the telephone was indeed my Harley.

"Mari? Are you okay?"

“I am now. I just wanted to make sure.” I was so excited I could barely talk.

“Okay,” he chuckled. Even through his laughter, he sounded worried.

“I won’t keep you. You need to rest. I’ll call you soon.”

“Go through the operator and have them reverse the charges. I’ll pay for it.”

“That’s not necessary. I’ll talk to you soon.”

I raced from Galvin Hall to the parking lot and hopped into my car. In some ways I was still so conflicted, I decided to skip class and go see Garrett. Could it really be true, or was I in some kind of dream state and hallucinated the call to the hospital? He had to know! He’d be thrilled to learn Harley was alive. Alive! My Harley was alive! Joy filled my heart to bursting. From what he said, he was beating back that hateful cancer.

I had to keep reminding myself that the caller could be a prankster. Maybe he had some science fiction way of redirecting the call to the number back to a place in Lima, Ohio. Science fiction movies show that kind of stuff all the time. Maybe I was being ridiculous in those thoughts. The man I talked with knew stuff that Harley would not have talked about to anyone other than Garrett or me. I was at war with myself. A huge part of me wanted so badly to believe it was Harley calling the radio station. An almost equally big was the side of me saying this was a sicko who likes playing on people’s emotions.

I slid to a stop at the gate, unlocked it and swung it open slowly. The gate was heavier than I remembered. I then pushed the call button.

“Yes?” Garrett answered.

“It’s Mari. I forgot to buzz first.”

“It’s always a pleasure to see you, Miss Mari. Leave the gate open. I’ll close it after you leave.

I hurried to the door and waited with unbridled energy for Garrett to answer. He pulled it open and beckoned me inside. I stared at the barren walls and rooms. Coming here and seeing it so devoid of furniture, art, and games made me sad. It was as though Harley never existed, or at the very least, never lived here.

"Garrett!" I rushed into his arms for a much-needed hug. "It's so good to see you still here."

"Only for a month or so, Miss Mari. Then I'm off to California and a new family."

"Garrett, what if I could prove Harley is still alive? Would you still go to California?"

"Oh, Miss Mari!" He groaned. "Is that pervert finally getting to you?"

"Garrett, he told me things only we would know."

"Such as?"

"What happened after the Steppenwolf concert in December of 1975. The last time he drank coffee. Harley even told why he doesn't consume hot caffeinated beverages."

"Miss Mari, you do realize anyone can get the information about Mormons not drinking caffeine, right?" He spoke gently, as though I was a misguided child.

"Yes, of course. But, Garrett, he gave me a phone number, the name of the hospital and his room. I called the Cancer Institute of New York, and they had him listed. They put me through to his room. Garrett, it was him!"

"Oh, Miss Mari," he moaned.

"No, Garrett! I've been talking with him almost every night since April. We talked about stuff only the two of us, and possibly you would know."

Garrett studied me for many long minutes before sighing. "Give me the phone number."

I dug the slip of paper, with the telephone number on it, out of my purse and handed it to him. He studied it before reaching for the phone. I leaned close to him so I could hear what was said.

"Hello?" Harley's voice sounded raspy.

"Master Harley?"

"Oh, thank Heavenly Father, Mari, got through to you!"

"When you were five years old, what did you call me?"

The line was silent for an excruciating time. Finally, Harley responded.

"Bobo an. I couldn't say Boban to save my life."

"And what is Boban?"

"It's Scottish Gaelic for dada."

"Oh, Master Harley! It is so good to hear your voice," Garrett choked back a sob. His whole face suffused with joy and tenderness. "What can I do for you?"

"Can you come to see me? I'm scared. They're planning something, but no one will tell me what. Please!"

"Absolutely, Master Harley. It will take me a few days, but I will come."

"And Mari?"

"If possible, I will bring her too."

Chapter Eighteen

Harley

May

I couldn't wait until Mari's shift at K-Mart was over before I called her. Just hearing her voice for even a few minutes lifted my mood and made me smile.

"Hello?" She sounded breathless. I must have called just as she got home.

"Hi, love. What Steppenwolf song did you play for me today?"

"'Drift Away.'" She paused, "'Desperation,' 'Disappointment Number,' 'Lost and Found by Trial and Error,' 'Hodge, Podge, Strained Through a Leslie,' and 'Resurrection.'"

"Wow! Those would have taken a third of an hour," It made me happy she played so many songs for me.

"Do you remember going to see the castles?" Mari asked.

"I remember the castles. Piatt if I'm not mistaken. They were the Mac-A-Cheek and Mac-O-Chee. Lovely old homes."

"How did we get there?"

"In my Touring car." I grinned. She was still testing me.

"Did we stop anywhere along the way?"

"At a diner in Bellefontaine."

I closed my eyes and pictured that day. It was simply wonderful. I settled back in the recliner and closed my eyes as memories washed over me. One of my favorite sweet memories was the time we visited Mac-A-Cheek and Mac-O-Chee castles also known as the Piatt Castles in West Liberty, Ohio.

###

"Where are we going that we have to head out so early?"

"Early?" I laughed. "It's almost nine."

"Oh. I thought it was earlier." Mari reached for her helmet.

"Not this time," I shook my head and took the helmet from her. "We're going in my Touring Car." I smiled at her shocked expression.

"Your Model T?"

"Yep. It's befitting where we're going. As for where we're going, the ride will be about an hour there and back. That leaves us with six hours to sight-see." I was dressed in pressed tan slacks, a pinstripe shirt, a string tie, and a tweed jacket.

"Can you drive it with your ankle in a cast?"

"I can." I wiggled the ankle with the cast and was promptly rewarded with twinges of severe pain. I pursed my lips trying to keep the groans in.

Mari looked me up and down. "I just bet you can, Mister Groan."

"Honest! I can drive it." I ran my hand through my hair.

"Okay, if you say so," she shrugged. "I better change into one of the dresses you bought me." She rushed upstairs.

Mari returned about fifteen minutes later attired in a forest green dress I had purchased for her when my parents visited the previous year. It was accompanied by an emerald necklace.

We stopped at Don's Hamburger in Bellefontaine for a quick meal around ten thirty. The place opened at eleven, but it took us almost thirty minutes to park and wade through the people surrounding my Touring car. I guess a lot of them had never seen a 1920's vintage vehicle.

"What are you going to have?" Mari leaned across the table and pulled the menu away.

"I'm thinking about a hamburger and a bowl of chili. How about you?"

"A cheeseburger and fries." She sat back against the booth seat and gazed at me. "Where are we going?"

"West Liberty."

"What's in West Liberty?"

"Something I'm sure you'll enjoy since you love antiques." I couldn't help myself. I grinned wickedly at her. How I love teasing Mari. The way her face turns red makes me giddy with playfulness.

"Harley," she said as she sipped her water.

"Mums the word." I pretended to zip my lips shut.

"Oh, you wicked little boy!" She exclaimed and burst into laughter.

"That's me, devil Harley." I winked ominously at her which made her giggle even harder. "You so get me, Mari."

"So, what's the plan for today?"

"We are going sightseeing. After that, I have a special surprise."

Mari was amused by the people gawking at the car. I had to gently encourage people to move so we could exit the parking lot.

"Excuse us, please." I reached around a man who was peering inside the vehicle.

"Is that one of those kit cars? You know, you buy the kit and build it?"

"Nope. It's the real deal. 1920's vintage Touring car."

"Cool!"

I got the car started, and we drove away leaving a growing crowd behind.

The Piatt Castles are an interesting bit of architecture. They are two gothic style structures built to resemble castles but on a much smaller scale. They are situated near the Shawnee village, Mackachack. The two homes are only three-quarter miles apart. Mac-A-Cheek is slightly smaller than Mac-O-Chee. These 19th-century homes were built by Brigadier General Abram Sanders Piatt, and his brother, Colonel Donn Piatt.

Both homes were constructed using limestone, have multiple floors, painted ceilings, frescoes, and intricate woodwork. Looking at them from the outside you get a gothic feel like they belonged on the Moors of Scotland. Inside, you get a sense of stately, baronial, glamour. Rooms are filled with Native American and military artifacts, and fabulous furnishings spanning two centuries.

Arriving in my Touring Car enhanced the impression of old wealth and royalty. I really wanted this date to go well after the fiasco of the last one. During that date, I wound up with a fractured ankle. Thank Heavenly Father I had a walking cast.

I grasped her hand and tucked it close to me as we walked to the entrance of Mac-O-Chee. To call these homes castles is a bit of a misnomer. They are châteaux with gothic architecture.

The floors are inlaid. Richwood covers many of the halls and rooms. The painted ceilings are breathtaking. Looking at Mari's face lighted up in wonder told me I'd made the right choice in selecting the castles for what I hoped would be a very special date.

###

Mari

Garrett ushered me inside when I arrived at Harley's home. Harley was leaning against the stair rail post. His injured ankle crossed his other foot. I didn't notice his outfit as I reached for my helmet. I wondered how he could ride a motorcycle with his foot in a cast. He had borrowed a vintage Harley-Davidson 1952 K model from his company. Edward delivered it personally on Wednesday.

"We're going in my Touring car," he said.

I looked sharply at him and whistled. He looked absolutely fabulous in tan slacks, matching pinstripe shirt, tie, and an old-fashioned tweed jacket like you would picture Ernest Hemingway wearing. On Harley, the outfit made him so sexy. The colors accentuated his beautiful blue-gray eyes, and I found myself fighting a losing battle not to stare at him. He looked hunky. No male model in a suit and tie could hold a candle to him. My heart fluttered in a staccato rhythm as I ogled him.

"I...um...I better change into one of the dresses you bought me." I made a mad dash up the stairs and into a guest room where he kept the dresses for me. I didn't dare bring them home.

Mom would grill me to death about where I got them, and from whom. How I shouldn't hang around a man, who bought women clothing. Then she'd alternate with how he must have wealth and did he expect me to sleep with him. Finally, she'd claim we were middle class, and he was upper class so of course, he'd expect sex. There'd be no convincing her otherwise.

I stood in front of the armoire looking at a lovely assortment. I finally pulled out my favorite, a forest green dress that went midway down my calf, an emerald necklace, and black shoes.

Harley was standing next to the door when I came down the stairs. He grinned, grasped my hand and bent to kiss it.

"You look ravishing, my love," he murmured.

"And you look divine." I felt my face redden.

Harley was the epitome of a gentleman, and he is so dashing. I wondered again for the millionth time how I managed to attract him.

We ate an early lunch at Don's Hamburger in Bellefontaine. A crowd of people surrounded Harley's car.

The men were running their hands over it and whistling.

"It's a 1920's Touring Car," Harley said as he gently pushed his way forward. "Excuse us, but we need to get into the car and leave. I hope you enjoyed seeing my vehicle."

He ushered me into the passenger seat and then entered the driver's side. We slowly pulled away.

The Piatt Castles were simply divine. Technically, they weren't castles, but they did remind me of fairy tale palaces with their chimneys, high ceilings, and ornate woodwork. Breathtakingly gorgeous. We spent considerable time touring both homes. By mid-afternoon, both of us were hungry. I don't know what it is about walking outdoors that whets the appetite, but ours had kicked into high gear.

We went back to the car. Harley hefted a picnic basket and cloth from the boot of the vehicle.

Grabbing my hand, we strolled back across the grounds to a shaded area. Harley spread the cloth on the ground and set the food-laden basket on it.

Garrett had spared no expense in preparing this meal. We feasted on finger sandwiches made with cucumber, cream cheese, pimento cheese, fruit, ham, and chicken. Accompanying them was a selection of coleslaw, potato salad, bean and mushroom salad, assorted fruit and cheeses, and chocolate cake. All to be washed down with Vernors.

After gorging ourselves, Harley reclined back, propped up by his elbows and smiled at me.

"I am so lucky to have you in my life, Mari." He sat up, steepled his fingers and looked at me as though he was contemplating a serious matter.

"What is it, Harley? Is something wrong?"

"No," he grinned shyly. "everything is right. Mari, I am so sorry for how I treated you recently. I solemnly promise I will never hurt you like that again."

"Thank you," a blob lodged in my throat. "I…I appreciate that. All is forgiven." I swiped my eyes with a napkin.

Harley nervously reached into his jacket pocket and pulled out two items. "This first gift is a bottle of the Jontue perfume you liked so much."

"Thank you," I accepted the gift-wrapped box. It was the second bottle of my favorite perfume Harley had given me.

The next item was a jewelry case. Harley inched onto his knees and held it out to me. "Mari, with this gift, I reaffirm my love and devotion to you."

He opened the box. Inside was a gold butterfly necklace. The wings encased opals. "This necklace is to accompany your engagement ring and is a token of my love for you." He looked so intense and nervous. "Mari, I ask again if you will consent to be my love, my wife. Will, you be mine forever and share this journey of life with me?"

"I will. Harley, you are the love of my life." Once again tears threatened to overwhelm me. "It is an honor to marry you and travel down the road of life, sharing your adventures, creating memories, and loving each other."

He whooped with joy and leaned forward to kiss me with tenderness.

Thus, ended a very special date. I had my Harley back.

Chapter Nineteen

Harley

May

Garrett was able to arrange a flight for the 26th, three weeks away, close to the Memorial Day weekend. Mari would not be joining him. She had to help her family move. I was very disappointed. Seeing her would have put me at ease.

I was right. My parents had been in conversation with my multitude of doctors. It seems there was no longer any sign of cancer in my body. I was being sent home to recuperate with plans to return in three months for a checkup and follow up treatment and examination. Physical therapy would continue three times a week at my parents' home. The other four days I was supposed to work with a trainer in the swimming pool.

I wished I was going home to Lima. Unfortunately, the day Garrett was scheduled to arrive was the day I was released from the hospital. There was no way to contact him. It seemed karma was working in overdrive to keep me from those I loved the most. I guess Heavenly Father had a lesson for me.

Mother was all atwitter about my coming home to Sagaponack. The day I arrived at the family estate, the place was buzzing with activity. The entire entrance was decorated with a banner proclaiming my homecoming gala that night. The foyer was festooned with all manner of flowers, garland, and strategically placed art. The chandelier was being decorated with colored lights.

"Mother," I said, looking up at her from my wheelchair. "I don't think I'm ready for a gala."

"Nonsense. We're celebrating your beating that horrid cancer."

"I'm in remission, not cured." My energy was flagging.

"Really, Harlan, it's not as though you are expected to dance all night. Just one with me, one with your sister, Elizabeth, and a few debutantes. That's not too much."

"The trip from the hospital has exhausted me. May I go to my rooms?"

"Of course. Rest until dinner. We will eat at eight. Our closest friends will be in attendance." She motioned for a manservant to push me to the lift.

My suite had been redecorated. It now resembled a boudoir for some man in the Victorian era. The outer reception room contained mahogany tables, ottomans, chairs, and a wine cabinet. The seating was dark green, and the lanterns matched. Spittoons sat next to each chair. Disgusting.

The master bedroom had drapes made of heavy burgundy damask with gold trim. My bed was perched up with sliding boxes underneath. Drapes and canopies surrounded the brass frame. A thick blue and gold comforter and matching pillows adorned the top. Cabinets and shelves made from walnut burl separated the marble top table from drawers.

Both rooms had color coordinated oriental rugs and oil paintings.

The bathroom held a claw foot pink marble tub and a standalone matching sink. There was both a toilet and a bidet.

I found the suite ugly. It was not my type at all. How I missed Garrett. He'd have made sure my rooms were untouched. I watched dispassionately as the manservant turned down the bedding.

He turned and began to lift me. "I can stand and get to the bed."

"Very well, Sir. Mister Harlan Davis, I shall remain to offer assistance getting into the bed." He bowed and stood to watch me.

I rose from the chair, stepped onto the sliding platform, and climbed into the bed.

###

The manservant returned at precisely seven o'clock with a gray tuxedo, matching pants, white shirt, tie, and black shoes. There was also a silver-gray cummerbund to go with the outfit. He insisted on helping me dress and then taking me in the wheelchair to the formal dining room. Once there, he handed me a cane and escorted me to my place at the table. It was seven thirty, and all the dinner guests had already been seated.

Father stood with a wine glass in his hand and lightly tapped it with a spoon. He cleared his throat as everyone turned to face him.

"I'm sure you have heard about my son's battle with cancer. It's been a long, hard fight for all of us. Tonight, I'm happy to announce he has won that war. The cancer is gone. Harlan, would you like to say a few words?"

I slowly rose, placing my hands on the table to steady my balance. I had no idea Father expected me to talk and was at a loss for words. "Thank you for coming. It's always a pleasure to see good friends and family. I am currently in remission and other than tiring easily, I feel pretty good." I sat back down and glanced at my mother. She was beaming with happiness. I nodded to her.

The first course consisted of Caesar salad with herb crusted croutons and raspberry vinaigrette dressing and ceviche of shrimp with avocado and orange.

Ashley sat next to Elizabeth who was on my right. She whispered to my sister and then looked at me. "Welcome home, Harlan. I'm glad you bested that awful cancer. Tell me, is it true you'll never walk without a cane or walker again?"

"What? No! I will eventually not need either of those. I will, however, most probably, walk with a limp."

Mother noticed I had eaten very little of the first course. "Harlan, do you not like the dishes?" She reached over and gently caressed my face.

"They're delicious, Mother. My appetite hasn't recovered from all the treatments. I'm pacing myself so I can enjoy the rest of the meal."

"Are you certain? I can have Cook make you something else."

"I'm sure."

The second course included Almond crusted salmon with baby peas, carrots and asparagus spears in a Chardonnay butter reduction. Served along with it was a delightful lump crab cake with Tabasco butter.

As I nibbled these two wonderful dishes, I noticed Elizabeth whispering to Ashley. Ashley, in turn, glanced surreptitiously in my direction and giggled.

“I heard he can’t make love anymore. I bet that Mari girl wouldn’t want him now.” Facing me, Ashley asked, “Isn’t that right, Harlan? She abandoned you. Otherwise, she’d have come to see you in the hospital.”

“She thought I was dead, Ashley,” I said quietly, trying to hold back my temper.

By the time the third course was presented I was weary of Ashley and Elizabeth’s snide remarks. The wait staff placed dishes of Oysters Casino in front of us.

The main course was baked lobster, which I thoroughly enjoyed. It was followed by desserts of chocolate cakes with pockets of chocolate sauce and black cherry topping, Jack Daniels chocolate chip pecan pie with Chantilly cream, and Pavlova with rhubarb. Being the glutton that I am, I would have normally eaten every dish served and polished dinner off with the Pavlova. Since being diagnosed with cancer and the brutal treatments, my appetite dwindled dramatically. I chose the Pavlova but only ate a bite.

After dinner, Father ushered us into the ballroom. The other guests began arriving, and I was expected to greet them. My energy was seriously fading before the dancing started.

Chapter Twenty

Garrett

May

The 26th started out rough. I had packed the night before but forgot to include my toiletries and sleepwear. They had been set out ready to be placed in my bag. Now, I could not find them. I wasted precious time looking everywhere before I checked the bathroom. The entire kit and pajamas were on the counter.

Heavy traffic, due to an accident on Interstate 75, almost made me miss my flight. Upon arriving at the airport, I was dismayed to find the parking area virtually full. I circled around for a half hour before finding a space.

"Mac an donais! Damn!" I pounded the steering wheel. "Forgive me, Heavenly Father. I must make this flight."

Grabbing my travel bag, I rushed from the car. My thoughts were on Master Harley. He needs me more now than ever before. I have to get to him. It was bad enough I couldn't book a flight for three weeks. It seemed as though the Devil was trying to keep me from him.

I ran into the airport and up to the ticket counter. "Here is my ticket."

The airline attendant looked at the flight number. "I'm sorry, sir. That plane just left. I can book you on an afternoon flight."

"Mac an donais! Damn!" I cursed for the second time. Swearing is very unusual for me. Frustration was getting the best of me. I wanted to punch someone. Instead, my time was spent sitting in a lounge, reading the Book of Mormon.

The flight to New York was not uneventful. A two-hour trip lasted the better part of the afternoon. A mechanical malfunction had us changing planes in Cleveland. I believe I set my own personal best in swearing that day.

I arrived at five o'clock. The airport had a rental car company. I had arranged for a vehicle based on getting there in the morning. Naturally, the car was no longer available. I had to make new arrangements. Fortunately, they had a full-sized vehicle. The rental agency was kind enough to give me directions to the hospital. I have never liked driving in New York City. The traffic and crazy drivers are enough to scare the life out of an older person.

I finally reached the hospital around seven o'clock. I strode up to the reception area.

"May I help you?" Asked the receptionist.

"I'm here to visit Mister Harlan Christian Robert Davis. If you would be so kind as to direct me to his room."

She spent several minutes looking up the requested information. "I'm sorry, sir. Mister Davis was discharged earlier today."

"I see," I frowned. "Thank you." I stared at her for a long time.

From the expression on her face, I must have been a sight to behold. She may have thought I was psychotic. She reached for the telephone.

I turned and headed back out to the car. He had to be in the care of his parents. Once again, I found myself fighting city congestion. I arrived at the Davis estate at around ten o'clock. There was a banner proclaiming a welcome home gala that night. Surely, they couldn't be so cruel as to force Master Harley to attend a gala when he just got out of the hospital? We'd see about that. I squared my shoulders and marched to the door.

I impatiently pressed the bell until the butler opened it. It took all my willpower to keep from rushing past him.

"May I help you, sir?" The butler asked. He was a different one from the previous year. Seems the Davis family was always hiring new staff.

"I'm here to see Mister Harlan Davis," I drew myself up to my full height of five foot ten inches.

"May I see your invitation?" The butler held out his hand.

"I am here at the request of Mister Harlan Davis. If you'll step aside."

"I'm afraid, I can't let you enter." The butler placed his hand on my shoulder and tried to bar my entry.

My patience with this young fool was gone. "Enough! Unhand me immediately!"

His hand dropped. "Sir, you must have an invitation."

"We'll see about that requirement." I gently shoved past him and went inside.

He followed me, protesting my entry, as I strode down the hall to the ballroom. "But, sir!"

At the doorway to the ballroom, I heard Harley speaking. He sounded like he was whining, something he never does.

"But Mother, I'm not up to dancing anymore. I'm tired." His voice was raspy.

Entering the room, I was aghast at how pale and weary Master Harley looked. I pushed past dancing couples and hurried to his side.

Turning, I spoke briefly to Mistress Davis. "There'll be no more dancing for him."

"This is a gala celebrating his homecoming." Mistress Davis glared at me. "You were not invited."

"Are you trying to kill him? He was just discharged from the hospital!" Anger suffused me at how callously they were treating him.

Master Harley looked at me and tears streamed down his cheeks. "Garrett, is it really you?"

He sounded so weak, it burst my heart to see and hear him in this condition. I could not believe he was expected to dance at a gala.

"Aye, it is," I said as I lifted him into my arms and carried him from the room.

The wheelchair was parked outside the formal dining room. I gently settled him in the seat and lifted his legs onto the rest. A blanket had been draped over the back. I tucked it around him.

"Now, Master Harley, do you wish to spend the night here, or are you up to traveling to New York where I have booked the penthouse at a hotel."

"No! I don't want to stay here. I want to go with you. My medication is in my rooms."

"We'll go up and get it and some clothing too, eh?"

"And my violin. I don't want to leave it here even though I have one in Lima. But, I don't know where they put it."

I went back into the ballroom and stepped over to Mistress Davis.

"Mistress Davis? Harlan would like to know where his violin is."

"Hmm...? Oh, that. It's in the music room."

"Very good. Thank you." I exited and quickly made my way there. I grabbed his violin and some of his favorite sheet music. I took the instrument and music to the car before returning for Master Harley.

"Are you ready, Master Harley?" I pushed him to the elevator.

"I am. I can't wait to get out of here."

We went to his rooms to get his personal effects and clothes.

His rooms had been redecorated in a manner not at all befitting my beloved employer. They were downright ghastly. In his suite, I selected several comfortable outfits, underwear, and two sets of pajamas. Tucking his medicine into a pocket, I grabbed his prescriptions. I will have them filled when we get back to New York City.

"Garrett? Do you think you can bring my walker and cane? I can't believe I was expected to dance when I have trouble walking."

"I'll find a way."

I grabbed both items. Master Harley could carry his medicine bag and the cane. His personal effects and clothing were in a duffle bag, which I slung over my shoulder. I balanced the folded walker on the handles of the wheelchair. It was a bit awkward but manageable. We went back to the ground floor.

Waiting by the elevator was his father. "Excuse us, Mister Davis," I said and attempted to go around him.

He quickly blocked our path. "You are not taking him anywhere, you mongrel!" His face turned a dark red and veins stood out at his temples.

"He is my son. If I had followed his wishes, he would be dead. Instead, he is alive and well. Cured."

"I'm in complete remission, Father, not cured," Harley whispered and licked his lips.

"His current condition is due to our efforts, not yours. You are nothing but a servant. Of course, you'd do whatever he wanted. Do you know he is bankrupt?"

"I. Am. Not. Bankrupt!" Master Harley's face flushed with anger. "I have plenty of funds. How do you think you never got any bills? Insurance? Even fully covered there would have been some charges. I paid for them. I even had long distance phone service installed so I could talk with Mari."

"You are delusional," Mister Davis spat. "You, servant, are not taking him anywhere. He belongs here! Away from your influence, we'll finally get him to behave like a member of high society and not like some free spirit biker rebel hippie!"

"Tsk, tsk, such animosity," I responded as Harley looked on. He seemed a little paler and more than fatigued.

"Harlan was released to our care! He will remain here!"

"Mister Harley is an adult. He can choose where he stays."

"I want to go with Garrett, Father," Master Harley spoke up.

"You will not!" Mister Davis grabbed the wheelchair and attempted to wrestle control from me.

"Unhand the chair, Mister Davis. Do not make me get physical with you," I growled.

To my surprise, Mister Davis punched me. Without thinking I connected my fist to his face. He flew backward and hit the wall. I quickly rolled Master Harley out of the house to the car. Once he was settled on the passenger side, I closed the door. I had just finished putting the wheelchair into the trunk and slid into the driver seat when Mister Davis ran out. I started the car and sped away, leaving him chasing us.

I glanced at Master Harley. He had a pallor I didn't like. "Are you okay, Master Harley? Shall I take you to the hospital?"

"I'll be fine. I'm just exhausted. I don't understand how my parents could expect me to participate in a formal dinner and then dance with the debutantes! Ten! I just got out of the hospital! My energy is low."

Master Harley glanced at me. He lifted a hand to his eyes. I reached into my shirt pocket and handed him a handkerchief.

"Thank you." He dabbed at his eyes. "I am so glad you got here." He slid across the bench seat. I draped my arm over the back. He nestled into the crook of my shoulder.

"The pleasure is mine, Master Harley. We'll rest at the hotel for a few days. I'll change my flight back to Ohio. We'll make short flights with a day or two rest period in between."

"Sounds good to me." He yawned. "I missed you." Master Harley snuggled like he did as a young child. "I love you, Garrett."

"And, I missed you." It was so miorbhaileach, meaning wonderful. "I love you too, Master Harley." I could not begin to describe the emotions flying through my heart. "Aye, it is good to have you back."

Love swelled in my chest for this young man who had come to mean the world to me.

Chapter Twenty-One

Mari

June

Right after the Memorial Day Weekend, my parents told me we were leaving for Texas in a couple of days. I knew my family was moving. I just didn't think it was so soon. A few days prior, I met with the DJ's and my other friends. I took photos of everyone. Judy, Thomas, and Peg were seated outside Galvin Hall under a tree. Mike and John were in the hall outside WOSL. The rest were inside the radio station. It was a sad day.

As luck would have it, my car decided to have a mechanical issue three days before the move. Ken came out and looked at it.

"Well, Miss Mari, this is a double-edged sword. On the one hand, it's the water pump. The problem is this is a custom manufactured part. We'd have to order the parts to rebuild it. That could take up to six weeks."

"Ken! I don't have six weeks! We leave in three days!" I paced and glanced at him. "Let me think about it. I'll call you tomorrow."

"Ok, Miss Mari."

I watched him leave. Dad came over to me and put his hand on my shoulder.

"I put an advertisement in the paper. It's not like we can take three vehicles to Pasadena."

"What if I don't want to move?"

"That's up to you. Do you really want to stay here with your young man gone?"

"I... yes I do. Dad, he's not gone."

"Oh, Mari," Dad sounded sad and pulled me into his arms. "Come with us. You can always go back once we're settled in. Besides, your Mom needs your help, and I need you to help Dee drive the Dodge."

"Okay." I sniffled as tears threatened to come.

The next day I called Ken, and he came over.

"The guys and I talked. We came up with a plan. How about Davis Motors buys the car for six hundred dollars. We'll hold it for a year. That way you'll have the money to fly back. If you don't, after a year one of us will buy it from the company. I have the cash in my pocket and a bill of sale showing you sold it to us."

"You guys would do that for me?"

"Of course. It's what Mister Davis would have wanted." He pulled out the money and handed it to me along with the bill of sale.

I hugged him hard. "I will be back!"

Ken motioned for the tow truck. In no time my beloved Satellite was hitched up and towed away.

It felt like a huge part of my heart died. There were so many memories of Harley and me sitting in the car after classes talking until late at night. When I sat in the car these past few months, I could almost feel his arm draped over the seat with his hand resting on my shoulder. From the corner of my eye, it felt like I saw his silhouette facing me. A whiff of his scent, a tinkle of his laugh drifted in wraith-like, unseen, barely heard, but comforting at the same time.

Now that I knew he was alive; those sensations were bittersweet as I wondered when and if he'd return to Lima. I had spent the past week helping Garrett restore the furnishings so the house would be ready if Harley returned. I moved my clothing, books, photo albums, drawings, journals, records, tapes, and stereo into Harley's home at Garrett's urging. My belongings were put into a guest room. It felt good to have the house put back in order. I felt the home was patiently waiting for Harley's homecoming.

The day of the move arrived way too soon. I had closed my checking and savings accounts the previous afternoon. I was carrying twenty-one hundred dollars in my purse.

We were up at the crack of dawn with last minute packing. I had saved some tapes for the trip. Naturally, they included Steppenwolf, Creedence Clearwater Revival, and Gordon Lightfoot. Dee brought tapes of the Rolling Stones, the Beatles, and Deep Purple.

The Dodge Colt was loaded with personal effects. It was a white car with a blue denim top. As vehicles went, it was a sorry specimen. It was slow to accelerate and brake. Heaven help you if you had to go up a hill. It would only do so if you drove up the incline backward. If you weren't doing fifty by the time you hit the freeway, you were risking your life.

The day was sunny, unlike my mood. I didn't want to drive in the afternoon. Dee and I fought over it. I was, shamefully, less than pleasant to my sister. In fact, I was downright mean, and I had no excuse for it. She's the best sister a girl could have. You could count on Dee to cover your back.

Dee applied an astringent to her face multiple times a day. The scent was arid at best.

"Why do you use that stuff?" I asked as I popped in a tape of 'Cosmo's Factory' by Creedence Clearwater Revival.

"To keep my pores clean and remove excess oil. Don't you?"

I didn't think her skin was oily, but she did. Dee has always been beautiful where I considered myself average in appearance.

"Nope. Never needed to."

That night we stopped in Nashville, Tennessee around five. We had traveled four hundred miles.

The next day I asked Dad for a map outlining our route.

"You don't need one. Just follow us."

"But, Dad, the Dodge is accelerating very slowly. What if we get separated?"

"Get on Interstate 10 to Houston. You know our address."

Dee insisted on driving in the morning. I wanted to because I wanted to face the rising sun. Somehow driving with the sun setting at my back made me feel like death was coming. After all, the sun had set on my dreams of what might have been with Harley. Driving during sunrise made me think of what might be when Harley returned to Lima. Perhaps we could have a wonderful future.

So, we fought like siblings do.

"Dee, I really prefer driving in the morning when the sun is rising."

"So, do I," Dee stated.

"I drove yesterday afternoon."

"I said no. I'm driving."

It went on for hours. I called Dee selfish.

She told Dad at lunch about our fight. Dad gave me a stern lecture, which only served to make me angrier. I was so mad, I ignored Dee for the rest of the day. It was very childish of me, but I couldn't seem to stop myself. I was so going to return to Lima.

We stopped in Jackson, Mississippi after having gone four hundred fifteen miles. The motel had a swimming pool. It was a welcome relief to play in the water.

On the final leg of our journey, outside Baton Rouge, Louisiana, our car had difficulty getting onto the interstate, and we got far behind. Mom and Dad exited the freeway without warning in Baton Rouge. As we drove westward on the Interstate, we saw them on the feeder road, too late for us to take the exit.

"What are we going to do?" Dee asked as she looked out the window.

"They'll either get back on, or we'll drive to Pasadena, Texas on our own." I saw another exit just before an entrance ramp. "Hold on! I'm going to try to make this exit and then drive like a snail. Hopefully, they will spot us."

When Dad caught up with us, he motioned for us to pull off the road. I pulled into the parking lot of a gas station. Dad proceeded to yell at me for not keeping up with them.

"I would have, if I hadn't been saddled with this slowpoke car," I snapped back at him. "We have to be going forty or fifty miles per hour before we get on the freeway, and you just took off leaving us behind."

"Humph!" Dad muttered. "We're stopping for lunch on the other side of Beaumont." He marched to his car with his back ramrod straight like the Marine he had been.

We left Baton Rouge and headed for Lafayette. We hit Interstate 10 West. Between Lafayette, Louisiana, and Beaumont, Texas there is a long expanse of water. It is called the Atchafalaya basin; a huge swamp. Driving down the freeway, we saw cypress stumps poking up through the murk.

On the Louisiana side, there were exhibits advertising alligators. The only time I'd seen an alligator I was seven and we were going through Florida. Those creatures were kept in captivity. These gators were wild. The exhibit boasted a swamp boat ride guaranteed to show you gators. We didn't stop.

On the Texas side, there was Lost River. Beyond that was Beaumont. West of Beaumont was a shack claiming to have the best fried alligator and crawfish around. They were right. The deep-fried alligator, mudbugs, and frog legs were simply divine.

A few hours later, after stopping for lunch, we were in Houston, Texas. Houston was huge! The only other cities I'd been in that equaled or surpassed Houston in size were Los Angeles, Chicago, Washington D.C., and New York.

We arrived in Pasadena. Pasadena was definitely an oil and gas company town. Off Highway 225 there were a lot of refineries. They gave that side of the city a peculiar odor.

Dad did not like where our mobile home was located, so he booked extra days at the motel. The place he finally selected was next to a well-known honky-tonk called Gilley's.

Country and Western music with live performances from some of the greatest country musicians around. Mickey Gilley was often there along with Loretta Lynn, Roseanne Cash, and Emmy Lou Harris to name a few.

There was a weekly radio broadcast called 'Live from Gilley's.' I didn't listen to the radio show. The music on Friday and Saturday nights was loud enough to hear from our home a field away.

With our home settled, I began the onerous task of helping unpack. Some items that we couldn't lay flat due to lack of space were shipped. The moving van arrived three days later after Dad called the company and informed them of the location change. In only an hour most of our stuff was in the mobile home.

Once everything was unpacked, I started calling the airlines for flights to Dayton, Ohio. For some reason, I could not book a direct flight from Houston to Dayton. The cheapest and only one I could get had me flying into Atlanta, Georgia and then to Dayton, Ohio. The same thing happened when I tried to get a flight to Cincinnati.

To make matters worse, the next available flight was July first. I wanted to call and either speak to Garrett or leave a message about my return date. Dad refused to let me make a long-distance phone call. The only public phone booth I knew of was out of order. Just my luck.

At least I would be in Houston for my sister's wedding. Dee had been dating Frank while we were in Lima. He was flying in so they could get married. There was a white wedding chapel along the freeway. They were fairly inexpensive and looked lovely. Dee selected it and picked June 15th for the ceremony.

Dee wore a simple white wedding gown that made her look even more beautiful than she already was. She had baby's breath woven into her hair, accentuating her eyes. Her lacy veil and train came down her back and trailed behind her.

Frank was decked out in a dark blue tuxedo with a white boutonniere.

Mom had on a black dress. Dad wore a matching suit. I was dressed in a purple and blue striped dress with the pearl necklace Harley had given me. It was the only jewelry I could wear around Mom without getting the Japanese version of the third degree. I wore my engagement ring on a chain and tucked into my neckline.

The backdrop had gold interwoven with yellow and white. It was deliciously elegant.

I took snapshots of the ceremony with my Polaroid camera. Mom dabbed at her eyes with a handkerchief while reaching up to tuck a stray strand of hair behind Dee's ear. Dee moved away and stood next to me. She leaned in close and whispered, "Looks like I beat you in getting married. Just teasing." She giggled.

Her words made me sad. If Harley hadn't gotten sick, we'd be getting married next month. July 19th was our selected date after I decided I didn't want to be a June bride.

"I know. I'm really happy for you." I smiled. Back in Lima, when I first learned Dee was getting married, Garrett recommended a jeweler. I had purchased a piano jewelry box for her rings.

Chapter Twenty-Two

Garrett

June

During the few days we stayed in New York, I purchased the penthouse we were staying at. The short flight from New York to Harrisburg was brutal on Master Harley. I worried about him. He looked so frail and had lost quite a bit of weight since I last saw him back in January. While in New York, I had booked us into a bed and breakfast suite in Smoketown, about fifty minutes from Harrisburg. We would rest here for two days before venturing on to Cleveland, Ohio.

I made special arrangements to have dinner provided. We would venture out for lunch. The hotel recommended a nearby restaurant called the Good' N Plenty. It was opened in 1969 and served Pennsylvania Dutch meals. It had a comfortable, relaxed atmosphere.

I had the Pork and Sauerkraut with a side salad and filling also known as potato and bread with butter, parsley, onions, eggs, milk, salt, and pepper. It is prepared like a casserole.

Master Harley ordered their PA sampler of white chicken and meatloaf with pepper cabbage and Chow Chow. The latter is comprised of fresh vegetable renderings from canning including carrots, onions, cauliflower, peppers, beans, a lot of vinegar and a little sugar. For dessert, he had Shoofly pie, also known as either Molasses pie or cake. From the way Master Harley scarfed his meal, it seemed as though he hadn't eaten in days.

I was glad to see him eating so heartily. Master Harley loved good food, and I hoped his consumption of large meals would help him regain the weight he had lost.

After lunch I had him walk around the gift shop and the grounds using his walker. I followed close behind him with his wheelchair in the event he needed to sit.

We then returned to our suite. I insisted Master Harley rest until dinner was served. Room service brought us a meal starting with clam chowder, a side salad, T-bone steak, green beans, baked beans, and Creme Brule. We sat on the balcony to eat. Then once again, I was pleased to see Master Harley eating with gusto.

Afterward, I suggested we walk up and down the hall. Then I took his wheelchair and walker to the ground floor. I took the elevator back up to where Master Harley awaited.

"Shall we descend the stairs and sit in the lobby?" I hooked my fingers onto the back of his belt. This way, if Master Harley should stumble or fall I could keep him upright and then carry him to a chair.

"Okay. I know I need to keep exercising my leg muscles." He looked down with a frown. "It's just hard, but I will persevere."

"That's the Master Harley I know. Ready?"

He nodded, grasped the banister with both hands, so he was standing sideways. Tentatively, he took one step down, made sure his leg was stable before bringing his other down. It almost looked like he was crab walking. Slowly, in this manner, we made our way to the lobby.

"Master Harley, keep hold of the banister. Let me get past you and carry the walker down to the ground floor so you can use it to walk to the wheelchair."

He nodded with lips pursed and a grimace on his face. I hurried past him and stationed the walker so he could grab it with one hand and then the other. I pushed the wheelchair close so he could sit.

"Don't sit until you feel the edge of the chair against your legs. Wouldn't do to have you miss the seat and fall."

"Yeah, that'd be a disaster."

I pushed him into the lobby seating area. Next, I put the wheelchair at a ninety-degree angle to a plush armchair. Master Harley heaved himself up and turned so he could sit. Once seated I went to the reception desk.

"May I order from room service and have it delivered over there?" I nodded toward Master Harley.

"Certainly sir. I'll place the order for you. Your room number is?"

"Ten."

"What do you desire?"

"Hibiscus tea if you have it. If not, any herbal tea would be fine, and apple pie for two."

She nodded and lifted the phone receiver.

I returned to the sitting area and sat next to Master Harley. "How are you feeling?"

"A bit tired, otherwise, I'm doing fine." He glanced around the room. "I like this room. It's elegant and comfortably homey at the same time. Reminds me of our home in Lima."

"It is indeed, lovely here, Master Harley." I generously tipped the young man who brought our order.

"Master Harley, I took the liberty of ordering us a light snack." I placed a dish with a slice of pie on the end table next to him. "Tisane? It's hibiscus with ginger."

"Yes, please. It sounds delicious." Master Harley balanced his plate on his lap, picked up his fork, and took a bite of his pastry." He closed his eyes and grinned as he savored the morsel. "Cinnamon topped apple pie. Yum!"

I smiled like an indulgent father. It made me feel so fabulous to see him enjoying the simplest pleasures. "Master Harley, I thought we would rest tomorrow and then leave for Cleveland the day after. We'll exercise your legs on the grounds and then do some strength training."

"Okay," he said and sipped the Tisane.

###

Once again, the short airplane trip was hard on Master Harley. The ride from Smoketown to Harrisburg and the airplane trip exhausted him.

In Cleveland, I also booked us into a two-room suite at The Tudor Arms. With the city looking more and more likely to default on its debts later this year, prices were inexpensive as some hotels tried to lure tourists in.

I arranged for us to visit the Lakeview Cemetery. It would be a nice place for Master Harley to take a leisurely stroll around the grounds and to see the amazing architecture.

I ordered a hearty breakfast of omelets, sausage, cantaloupe balls, muffins, biscuits with milk gravy, and orange juice. Room service brought our meal up within fifteen minutes.

"Master Harley, do you feel up to a stroll after breakfast?"

"Here in the hotel, or someplace interesting?" Master Harley buttered a biscuit and scooped gravy onto it. He tucked into his food ravenously.

"I thought we could visit the Lakeview Cemetery or the botanical gardens. I think you'd like Lakeview it has all kinds of trees, botanicals, and historical monuments such as James Garfield's resting place. Plus, they have a lot of places to sit and relax."

"I'd like that." He gulped his orange juice and dug into his omelet. "I am so hungry."

"I took the liberty of ordering us a lunch to take with us."

We finished eating. While Master Harley was in the bathroom getting dressed, I placed our trays in the hall. I placed the wheelchair by the door facing the restroom.

"I think I'd like to walk."

"That's fine, Master Harley. I'll follow behind with the wheelchair. We'll do it like we did in Smoketown."

"Okay. I'm ready, are you?"

He pushed his walker to the entrance. We went down the hall to the stairs. Once in the lobby, he sat in his wheelchair while I drove the car to the unloading area. In no time, we were on our way to a day of leisurely strolls.

Lakeview Cemetery is simply amazing. The grounds boasted a multitude of horticulture plants including Moses Cleveland Trees, Gingko Biloba, Chestnut Oak, Sweet Bay Magnolia, Japanese Maple, and Weeping Canadian Hemlock to name just a few. There were benches strategically placed throughout the grounds for visitors to rest and take in the beautiful scenery. We sat often and enjoyed the view. Master Harley alternated between walking and riding in his chair.

We sat near the James A. Garfield Memorial to eat our picnic lunch.

The Memorial had Master Harley in awe. He allowed me to push him as we toured it.

"Garrett, it has three different types of architecture. Am I correct in saying they are Romanesque, Gothic, and Byzantine?" He spoke excitedly.

"Yes, I believe so."

"Is that sandstone I see? And look at all the exterior sculptures! The outer balcony has terra cotta panels and life-sized figures! Let's go inside!"

"Okay, Master Harley!" I chuckled at his exuberance. It reminded me of our cross-country trip back in 1970.

I wheeled him inside. "It's simply marvelous."

Master Harley gawked at the interior. There were stained glass windows and panes. "Look, Garrett, the original thirteen colonies, a map of Ohio, and panels showing events from 'War and Peace.' There's an awful lot of mosaics."

I had to smile at his excitement. He was totally absorbed. "They are divine."

There were deep red granite columns and a twelve-foot white Carrara statue of the President. I was so immersed in viewing everything, I failed to notice the silence for quite a while.

I turned to ask him if he wanted to go into the viewing area. Master Harley was sitting with his head bowed. He gripped the wheelchair so hard his knuckles turned white. The pallor had returned.

"Master Harley, are you feeling ill? I was alarmed. How could I be so callous not to watch out for him?

"Hmm?" He glanced up at me. "I'm exhausted, Garrett, but I didn't want to interrupt your enjoyment here. I know how much you like gardens and architecture. Almost as much as you love antiques. I'm sorry."

"Oh, Master Harley!" I moaned. "It is I who should be sorry. You just got out of the hospital a few days ago. Let us go back to the hotel and rest."

It was after three when we entered our suite. By then Master Harley was so tired and weak I had to turn down the covers and lift him onto his bed. I tucked him in like I did when he was a toddler.

I was so ashamed of myself for not paying more attention to his health. Master Harley was asleep before I finished smoothing the blanket. I sat in the armchair and watched him. He looked haggard. How could I not notice his fatigue?

We would dine in our room. Around seven, I ordered dinner from room service. I ordered a salad, soup, steaks, baked potato, chocolate cream pie, rolls, and root beer.

The next day, I insisted we only venture out for lunch and dinner. I wanted him well rested for the flight to Dayton.

###

The trip to Dayton was smooth. After picking up our car at the airport, we checked in to the hotel. Tomorrow we would leave for Lima. I drew a hot bath for Master Harley and insisted he take a long soak.

With Master Harley in the bathroom, I telephoned Thomas. I felt it would be important if he and Peg could be at the house when we arrived. At least that way Master Harley would have other people who cared about him there.

I know hc's hoping to see Mari. He knew she was helping her family move. I didn't have the heart to tell him she went to Texas. She was supposed to leave a message on our home telephone telling me when she'd be back. I checked every day. There were no calls from Mari.

Chapter Twenty-Three

Harley

June

My excitement kept building when we left Dayton. In ninety-minutes I would be home. I would wait for Mari to return home from her job.

Garrett told me she had moved her stuff into a guest room in my house. I don't know why since she only helped her family move to another town. Maybe, it was more convenient for her to stay at my place to go to work or school. Her family might have moved an hour or two away from Lima. It didn't matter. What was important, was she'd be waiting for me or would come home once her shift ended.

"I am so looking forward to being home, Garrett." I snuggled under my blanket and watched him drive.

"So am I, Master Harley, so am I."

"Tell me, have things changed much? I've been gone for thirteen months. I imagine there are differences."

"Some, but not much." Garrett glanced at me. "I rearranged a few pieces of furniture. That is about all. We can put it back to how you want it."

"No need. You have excellent taste. I'm sure it's fine." I stretched. The ride was tiring me out. I wanted to nap, but my mouth wanted to talk about Mari.

Garrett stopped the car when we pulled into the driveway. I sat gazing at my house. Home.

We arrived home. How sweet it felt to be home. My sanctuary where I was free to be me, to relax, and enjoy life surrounded by those I loved and good friends. It felt wonderful. Thomas's and Peg's vehicles were in the circle in front, but not Mari's.

"Garrett, where's Mari? Is she working today?"

He turned to me with a sad expression. He reached out and gently lay his hand on my leg. "Oh, Master Harley, I don't know how to tell you this." He turned back and stared out the windshield.

"Tell it to me straight. Has something happened to Mari?"

He sighed, "I don't know. The last time I heard from Miss Mari, she was going to help her family move to Texas. She planned to help them move and then return to Lima. She was supposed to call and leave a message about her plans. There haven't been any messages."

"Texas! You mean she went to Texas?" My heart thundered hard in my chest. "And you haven't received any messages? What does that mean? Did she move to Texas? Has she given up on me?"

Despair took up residence. I had fought so hard to survive so I could return to Mari.

"No, Master Harley, I don't believe that for a second. Mari fought for us to believe you were alive. She wouldn't give up on you. Her belongings are here. Maybe she couldn't get a flight for weeks, or the move is taking longer than anticipated."

He drove the car into the circle and parked in front of the entrance. "Shall we go in? Do you want to walk, or should I push you?"

"I'll walk," I sighed.

Garrett exited and got my walker out. I slowly rose and grabbed the device with first one hand and then the other. Garrett slipped his fingers under my belt to make sure I didn't fall. Once I was stable, I stepped up onto the entrance way and moved toward the door.

He opened the door and ushered me inside. Thomas stepped forward and grasped my arm. "Welcome home!"

"Thomas, let's get him seated. He looks tired." Peg hurried to my side.

Garrett pulled me against his chest and slipped his arms under me. He carried me to my recliner and gently deposited me in it.

"Welcome home, Harley!" Peg leaned forward and wrapped her arms around me. "Flash, Mike, and Hixson will drop by in a bit. Judy is out of the country, and Lori is working at the station until sign off."

"Do you guys mind helping Garrett with our bags?"

Thomas jumped up, "On it!"

"Are you hungry? We got some of your favorite Chinese dishes. For dinner, Flash is going to cook up something special."

"I'm famished." I started to rise. I wasn't, but I didn't want to disappoint my friends. Knowing Mari was in Texas made me lose any appetite I had.

"Stay put. We're going to eat right here." Peg busied herself setting out the food while Thomas took our bags to our rooms.

"Are you cured?" Peg asked.

"Not yet. I'm in total remission," I replied as Peg handed me Vernor's ginger ale.

"See? I remembered." She placed a tv dinner tray in front of me.

"Thank you." I forked a bite and chewed it slowly. "This is delicious," I complimented them. They had picked out my favorite dishes.

Thomas ambled over to the stereo and put on Steppenwolf's 'Slow Flux' album. Soon hard driving rock and blues wafted into the room. I leaned back in my armchair, closed my eyes and let memories of our weekend get-togethers wash over me.

The music, the camaraderie, and the food made for great times. I opened my eyes when I sensed movement near me. Peg was removing my dish.

"I can do that, Peg."

"Nonsense," Peg stated in that matter of fact manner of hers. "You just got out of the hospital and flew home. The least we can do is pamper you. Harley, you must rest. Someday, Mari will return, and you want to be in the best health possible."

"Are you sure she's coming back?" I asked.

"She said she was but didn't know exactly when."

Thomas brought me a lap blanket and tucked it around me. Peg handed me a cup of my favorite herbal tisane. It felt strange being pampered by my friends, but I appreciated their efforts.

Flash and Hixson arrived shortly after four. They came in carrying bags of food and baking supplies.

"We are going to feast tonight!" Flash grinned wickedly. "How does Lobster chowder, steak tartare, baked potatoes, salad greens, biscuits, and banana cream pie sound?"

"Sounds delicious, Flash."

"Shall I assist you in the kitchen?" Garrett asked.

"Nothing doing. You just had a grueling week rescuing Harley and bringing him home. I got this covered."

"If you guys don't mind, I'm going to take a nap." I reached for my walker, but Garrett placed my wheelchair in front of me."

"You'd best use this, Master Harley. It will be easier to use the elevator at the back than to try to climb the stairs."

I dutifully sat in the chair, vowing to myself, someday I wouldn't need it. My rooms looked almost exactly like I'd left it. It was a relief to be home. I remained sitting, gazing at it for many minutes.

"I moved some things to make it easier for you to maneuver in here. I hope you don't mind, Master Harley."

"Not at all, Garrett. It feels like home; my sanctuary."

Garrett hovered near me as I got onto my bed. "Ah!" I moaned in pleasure. "It's great to be here, even if only for three months before I have to go back."

"It's wonderful to have you home. Rest now. I'll come to get you when it's time for dinner."

"Thank you, Garrett." Emotion threatened to overwhelm me.

"For what, Master Harley?"

"For being you, and everything you've done for me. I'm grateful and lucky to have you in my life."

"Thank you, Master Harley. The feeling is mutual." He tucked a light blanket around me.

"I love you, Garrett," I murmured as I closed my eyes.

"And I you, Master Harley." Garrett's words brought comfort and contentment to me as I drifted into slumber land.

All too soon I was awakened by a gentle shake of my arm. "Master Harley, it's time to get up."

I stretched, yawned, and sat up. "I was tired," I said and grinned at Garrett. It felt so good to be home.

"You've only been out of the hospital less than a week. Your stamina isn't back to normal. It will be in time. Right now, we need to focus on physical therapy and rest."

I stood and did a couple of stretches. "The scent of Flash's cooking is making me hungry." I settled into my wheelchair.

"It's a pleasure to have you back." Garrett deftly maneuvered the chair into the elevator.

"When did you add the elevator?"

"When I learned you might be coming home. We had those two unused closets directly above each other."

"How are the guys doing at the shop?"

"They found a larger facility that could hold the motorcycle business. It's in Delphos. The automobile repair and vintage car business remain at the location in Lima."

"I guess more staff were needed?"

"Aye, indeed. You now employ three hundred people between the facilities. All are veterans." Garrett paused outside the dining room. "And with the three companies in New York, Davis Enterprises now consists of over five hundred. Most of them are also veterans. While you were napping, I took the liberty of transferring everything back into your name."

"You didn't need to do that, Garrett. I have plenty of funds in my Swiss account."

"I know you do. It just felt right. I did maintain my name and Mari on your accounts."

"Very well."

Garrett pushed me into the dining room. We were greeted by all the employees. The sliding glass doors to the patio had been opened to accommodate everyone.

"Mister Davis," a blond man grasped my hand and pumped it vigorously. He was using crutches and had a prosthetic leg. "Name's Allen Winters. I am so grateful for your company. I had been unemployed since I was discharged. Now, here I am gainfully employed with benefits and profit sharing."

"You're welcome," I smiled, "but I think thanks should go to Edward and the guys who ran the operations while I was gone."

I noticed all the guests had lined up to introduce themselves. It was heartwarming. Flash, Peg, Hixson, Thomas, Mike, and Lori scurried between the kitchen and dining room bringing platters of food which were placed on the sideboard.

Peg decided it was her duty to make sure I had plenty to eat. Thomas took charge of pampering Garrett to his amusement. The food was scrumptious as usual. I never realized how much I enjoyed Flash's cooking and vowed to help him finance his dream restaurant.

The employees all left after dinner. Lori gave them take home bags for their families. The WOSL gang, Garrett, and I retired to my game room. I was content to watch them play.

Mari was uppermost in my mind. I wish she'd call. I wanted so badly to hear her voice and know she was okay whether or not she planned to return to Lima. As long as I knew she was safe, I could deal with the possibility of her not coming back. At least I hoped I could.

It was shortly after nine o'clock when the telephone rang. Garrett answered and then came to me. "It's Mari."

I stood and using my walker went to the phone in the entrance hall. I sat on the chair beside the table and took a deep breath. "Hello?"

"Harley! You're home? I wish I could have been there. I'm calling from a pay phone, so I have to keep this short. I'm flying into the Dayton airport from Atlanta at eleven o'clock in the evening on July first. That was the earliest I could get. I'll send you written information on the airline and flight number."

"I can't wait to see you," Joy filled my heart. "I love you and miss you."

"I can't wait either. I miss you so much. I love you. I have to go now. Bye." She disconnected.

"Bye," I said to the telephone receiver.

Chapter Twenty-Four

Mari

July

July first finally arrived. Mom and Dad accompanied me to Houston Intercontinental Airport. The drive from Pasadena was an hour long, and traffic was intense at noon. They called it the lunch hour rush.

"Mari, are you sure you want to go back to Lima?" Dad asked. He was a retired Marine and still held his body straight and looked like ex-military.

"Yes, Dad," I fidgeted. I felt a desperate need to tell them why I wanted to go back. I glanced out the window.

"There's nothing there for you. Your young man died." He glanced in the mirror at me.

"What young man?" Mom sat up and asked. "Why I do not know about him?" Her Japanese accent was becoming heavy.

"It's okay, hon." Dad steered onto Highway 225.

I looked out the window and noticed the Shell refinery sign was still missing the 'S,' so it read 'Hell Refinery.' The entire area sure smelled like it could have been the Devil's home.

"Mom, Dad, he's not dead. We thought he died, but then he called us from a hospital in New York. He's home now. His name is Harlan Davis. He's Mormon, and I plan to convert to his religion. We're going to be married." I said in a rush. I dreaded this moment since my first date with Harley; the trip to Wolf Park.

Dad gripped the steering wheel so hard his knuckles turned white. "How long have you been engaged?"

"Well over a year." I found myself nervously twirling my hair around my finger. I hadn't done that in years.

"What kind of man is he?" Mom asked. She turned in her seat to look back at me. Her high cheeks looked even more pronounced, giving her a chipmunk appearance.

Here goes, I thought to myself. "Harley's a good, kind, and generous man. We met at college." They would never believe all the times our paths crossed from Portland, Oregon, Chehalis, Washington, Seattle, Washington and Lima, Ohio before officially meeting at the Ohio State University-Lima campus. There are days when I still don't believe it myself.

"Does he have a job? How will he support a family?" Mom asked.

"Hon…" Dad started to speak.

"What? We need to know that Maru will be well cared for."

I took a deep breath before answering her question, "He's a businessman, Mom."

"What kind of business can a college student have? He sells dope?" Mom sounded agitated.

"No, he doesn't sell dope," I gulped. Better not let Mom know he did dope in his teens. I'd never hear the end of what a bad man he was if she found out that little tidbit.

"Well? What does he do?" Mom's voice rose another octave.

"He's a mogul," I whispered.

"What? Speak up," Mom was getting more demanding in her questions. That was never a good sign.

"I said, he's a mogul."

"A mongrel? Low class," Mom harrumphed.

"No, mother, a mogul not a mongrel. He's actually very high class. He owns Davis Enterprises which includes three businesses. They customize motorcycles for police departments throughout the country and Canada as well as for individuals. They also maintain and repair automobiles, and restore vintage cars."

"He's a grease monkey. Oh, Maru, you can do much better than a garage mechanic."

"He's also part owner of a resort Lodge at Lake George in New York, a restaurant, and another vintage car company."

"What is his worth, Mari?" Dad asked.

I hesitated a long time, prompting Dad to ask again. "Well, Mari, what's his worth?"

"Is that really important?" I tugged on a lock of hair. At this rate, I was going to be bald before we reached the airport.

"Yes, it is. A Father always wants to know his daughter will be financially stable."

"Did you ask the same questions of Frank before he and Dee got married?"

"I knew he was working at K-Mart, so no."

"But, you're asking me because Harley owns several businesses. I don't see how that is fair."

"Just answer the question, Mari." Dad switched to his military tone of voice.

"The last I knew, he was worth over a billion in his own right, plus had inheritance money from his father's side of the family, which he never touches. The resort, he inherited from his maternal grandparents. He opened his first business when he was sixteen."

"How old is he?" Dad asked.

"He'll be twenty-seven in September." Boy, I never wished I could get out and hitchhike to the airport so badly as I did at that moment.

"And still in college? Is he a graduate student?"

"No, he's either a junior or senior undergrad. He can't attend college full time and still run his businesses."

By this time, we had entered Interstate 45 headed north. I was sweating from being interrogated.

"You mentioned motorcycles," Dad said.

I cringed, knowing where he was headed.

"Does he ride?"

"Yes, he does."

Dad hesitated and glanced at Mom before asking, "Does he belong to a biker gang?"

"He's in Hell's Angels?" Mom gasped.

"No, mother, he isn't. He doesn't belong to any. Yes, he considers himself to be a biker. A hobbyist biker because he likes to ride. He has also raced."

"You said he's a billionaire?" Dad asked.

"Yes," I replied nervously.

"Too high class for us," Mom said.

There it was, the elephant in the car. Why did class have to matter so much to Mom? Her own family before World War Two was rich.

"No, he's not."

"You said he was kind and generous?" Dad changed the subject away from wealth. "How so?"

"Well, he donates to charities. He provides holiday meals to the soup kitchens. These meals include turkey, ham, chicken, veggies, soups, salads, dressing, potatoes, gravy, rolls and assorted desserts. I'm not talking about just Thanksgiving and Christmas either. He does New Year's Eve and day, Valentine's day, Ides of March, April Fool's, Memorial Day, Picnic June, 4th of July, Picnic August, and Back to school in September. In September, he also provides school supplies and clothing for the needy, including winter garments. Halloween, Thanksgiving, and Christmas with presents for the children." I paused.

"His company is made up of almost all veterans. I think there's three or four he brought over from Sagaponack. Everywhere he's taken me, people come up to him and want to tell him their progress."

"He races? Cars or motorcycles? Mom asked.

"Both."

"Too dangerous. You going to be a widow."

I ran my hand through my hair and stared out the window. This hour-long drive has got to be the longest in history.

"You not go." Mom said. "Too dangerous you marry this man. He reckless."

"He's very safety conscious," I said.

"You ride a motorcycle with him?"

There was the other elephant. I didn't know that many elephants could fit in a small car.

"Well, Maru? You answer me."

"On the back of his."

"You sleep with him? You know…have sex?"

"Technically, no," I sighed. My face was turning a brilliant shade of red.

"No?" Dad asked, "What about those overnight trips?"

"What overnight trips? How come I not know about them?"

I sighed again. Would we ever get to the airport before I burned in the lake of fire? "Wolf Park at Battleground, Indiana, The

Steppenwolf concert in Provincetown, Rhode Island, and The FCC Licensing in Pontiac, Michigan which you knew about."

"Not the first two. Did you sleep with him?" Mom said.

Another sigh escaped my lips. "Technically, no." This was rapidly becoming the longest car ride of my life and in history.

"What that mean?" Mom's voice was rising in pitch and volume.

"It means after the Steppenwolf concert, he felt sick, so I lay down and held him until he fell asleep. That's all."

Finally, I saw the signs for the airport turn off. The longest car ride of my life was coming to an end. Hurray!

"You not go. You no marry this man. He not good enough for you. He buys you clothes? Jewelry?"

"He bought a few outfits to wear when I met his family. He bought some jewelry as gifts."

"You his mistress," she harrumphed.

"No, I'm not."

"He high class, we middle-class. You marry middle-class, not his type. He tire of you and dump you for someone in his society."

"Harley isn't like that, Mother. Give him a chance, and you'll find out he really is very caring, kind, respectful, generous, and loyal. Dad, his three businesses in Lima are almost all staffed with veterans. One of them is his secretary. She's an older lady. There are only three or four who aren't."

"Nice to know he respects our military. How well are they paid?"

"Much higher than average with yearly bonuses, health insurance, sick and vacation, profit sharing, and others. Harley's very loyal to his staff. If one of them gets fired, they really brought it upon themselves. He also has three other businesses under his umbrella company."

"Your sister moved back to Ohio," Mom sounded sad. "And now, you too."

"Don't worry Mom, you'll see us again. When Harley and I get married we're going to have two weddings; one in the temple, and one at the church. Non-Mormon family and friends will be able to go to that one."

Dad found a parking space, and we entered the airport. I hugged and kissed both parents before boarding. An hour later I was in the air headed toward Atlanta, Georgia, and a three-hour layover before getting on the flight that would take me to Dayton, Ohio. Thomas and Peg would pick me up and take me to Harley's home. I could hardly wait to see the love of my life again.

Chapter Twenty-Five

Harley

July

I was so excited I could hardly rest. I found myself pacing with my cane much to the dismay of my physical therapist.

My physical therapist wanted me to use the walker for a few more weeks. That afternoon he gave me a thirty-minute lecture about taking things slowly.

Peg and Thomas convinced Garrett that we should stay home and they would pick Mari up at the airport.

"Don't worry, we're quite capable of picking Mari up at the airport. We aren't new to it, you know." Peg said.

Thomas nodded in agreement. "Piece of cake. Or is it pie? I always get it mixed up."

"It's cake, you goofball," Peg chided.

I don't think time ever passed so slowly as it did today. I must have looked at my watch a million times before it was nine o'clock that night.

"Please call me when she lands," I begged them before they headed out.

"Relax, dude," Thomas chuckled. "We'll let you know. Now, we'd better hit the road before we miss her flight and she decides to rent a car."

"Go! Go! Be careful!" I ushered them out the door.

"Master Harley, you look tired. Sit in your armchair and rest. You don't want to be worn out when Mari arrives."

Garrett fussed over me like a mother caring for her infant. I loved him for his devotion. I was so lucky to have him in my life.

"You're right, as usual, Garrett. All the excitement has me wired. I feel like I have, as the veterans would say, ants in my pants."

"Oh, my!" Garrett chuckled. "They do have a colorful way of phrasing things, do they not?"

"Aye, they do," I laughed.

“How about a light snack? It’s been hours since you ate dinner. I’ll make a cheese and fruit plate, and hibiscus with ginger tisane.”

“Sounds lovely.” I stretched and yawned.

The tension was increasing the nearer the time came for Mari’s plane to land. Only three or four more hours and she’d be here in her new home.

“I’ll make something more substantial for when Mari arrives.” He said as he went toward the kitchen.

“Hmm…” I closed my eyes and relaxed for the first time today. In a little over three hours, Mari would be here.

I could hear Garrett around in the kitchen at the back of the house.

He hummed ‘Loch Lomond’ a Scottish folk song in Gaelic. He has a great singing voice. I never tire of hearing him sing.

“Here you go, Master Harley. May I join you?” Garrett set a plate and a steaming cup of tisane before me.

His question startled me. “Of course, you may. You don’t need to ask.” I was puzzled by his sudden change in demeanor. “What is it? Why did you ask?”

Garrett paused for a long time before responding, “With you and Miss Mari getting married soon, I return to being your manservant.” Garrett perched on the edge of a chair and sipped his beverage.

“Nonsense, Garrett.”

“It is proper protocol for me to step back and become a servant again, not a companion.”

“Excuse me?” I sat up straight. “One, you are not a companion or a servant even though I pay you. Two, you are family…part of my family.”

“Master Harley…” he began.

“I know Mari will agree with me, Garrett. You are family. I don’t want to ever hear you refer to yourself as a companion or servant again. You are my equal, my confidant, and a member of my family. Have I ever done anything to make you feel otherwise?”

“Thank you, Master Harley. I’m honored to be a member of your family. No, you never made me feel like a servant.”

"You don't need to ask permission. This is as much your home as it is mine and now Mari's." I sat back. "My family, Garrett. You're part of my family. Forever. You're stuck with me."

"Thank you, Master Harley," he dabbed his eyes with a handkerchief.

"I know I depend on you a lot, but I want you to understand how much I love you. You've always been here for me. I intend to do the same for you. And you know, if anything happens to me, you will be well cared for."

"Thank you, Master Harley. The feeling is mutual."

"Don't you know by now, I consider you to be more my dad than my father can ever be."

"That's quite an honor."

"The honor is mine. I am fortunate to have you."

The hours ticked by slowly. We sat in companionable silence nibbling on snacks. The quiet was occasionally punctured with small talk.

"I'd like to do a 4th of July picnic with the WOSL gang and my employees. Do you think that's possible?"

"Probably not this close. Why not just have your radio friends over? We can do a company-wide picnic in a couple weeks."

"Okay."

One o'clock in the morning came and went. Thirty minutes later, Thomas called.

"Harley," he sounded worried. "Mari wasn't on the plane. Peg is checking to see if she got on another flight from Atlanta."

"No! What do you mean she wasn't on the plane?" Panic set in. "Do you think she's okay?" I asked, wringing my hands.

"She probably missed her connection. I'll call you when we know more." He hung up.

"Problem, Master Harley?" Garrett asked with concern.

"Mari wasn't on the flight," I said miserably.

My heart sank. This rollercoaster I've been on all day sapped my energy. I hated feeling weak and helpless.

"Don't worry, Master Harley. I'm sure she's fine. She may have missed a connecting flight."

"I hope you're right, Garrett," I said glumly.

###

Mari

Wouldn't you know it? My flight out of Houston got diverted to Dallas due to weather. I had to make a plane change in Dallas that would take me to New Orleans where I had another change and finally on to Atlanta. It didn't make sense to me because the path was virtually the same, only Dallas was further north.

Naturally, I missed the flight from Atlanta to Dayton. I'd have to wait until three. That meant I'd arrive in Dayton around four-thirty. The one saving perk was my seat was upgraded from economy to business at no additional charge, and I was given food vouchers.

The lines at the pay phone booths were long. It was an hour before I could get one. By then, it was two in the morning.

"Davis residence," Garrett's voice came over the line. He sounded tense.

"Garrett? It's me, Mari."

"Miss Mari! Is everything okay?"

"Just fine, Garrett. Changes in my flight made me miss the connection in Atlanta. Is Harley awake?"

"One moment, Miss Mari, I'll put him on."

"Hello? Mari? Are you okay?" Harley asked. From his tone, I could tell he was worried.

"I'm fine. My plane got diverted to Dallas and then New Orleans where I had to make a connecting flight to Atlanta. I missed the plane to Dayton. The next one leaves at three. So, I should be in Lima at around six. Please let Thomas and Peg know if you hear from them."

"I will." Relief flooded his voice.

"And, Harley?" A deep yearning filled my heart. Oh, how I wanted to see him, hold and kiss this fabulous man. I missed him so much.

"Yes, love?"

"Try to get some sleep. You and Garrett both, okay?"
"I'll try."
I hung up the telephone and found a lounge to settle in for the long wait for my next flight. I ordered a Coke and a sandwich. I pulled out my journal and began writing about the events of today.

###

Harley

Thomas called within five minutes of my conversation with Mari.

"Harley? We can't find out anything. All they could tell us was that she didn't get on the plane in Atlanta."

"Mari just called," I said. "She had to fly into New Orleans and make a connecting flight to Atlanta. Of course, she missed the plane to Dayton but will be on the three o'clock flight from Atlanta arriving in Dayton around four or four-thirty."

"That's good. Peg and I will camp out until she gets here. See you in a few." He hung up.

Garrett brought me a cup of cocoa with marshmallows. I sipped the sinfully delicious beverage. Garrett makes cocoa using chocolate shavings instead of the store stuff.

At some point, I must have fallen asleep. I woke up laying on the sofa with a blanket tucked around me.

"Good morning, sleepy head," Mari's voice drifted into my sleep addled brain.

"Mari!" I bolted upright and rubbed my eyes. "When'd you get in?"

"About an hour ago. Peg and Thomas are upstairs sleeping in your guest rooms."

"Why didn't you get some rest too?" Happiness filled my heart to bursting.

"I wanted you to see me first thing when you woke up." Mari smiled. "The flight here was excruciatingly long. I wish I could have been here when you got home."

"You're here now. That's all that matters." I held out my arms. "Come and sit beside me."

Mari stood gracefully and settled on the sofa next to me. I turned to face her. She tilted her head slightly. I cupped her chin and pulled her close for a long, sweet kiss. "I've missed you so much," she sighed.

"I've missed you too, my love." I murmured into her ear.

We continued kissing for several minutes. I felt like I was a starving man who had just been thrown a feast. I couldn't get enough of the taste of her luscious lips, and I was drunk on her presence.

"Lay your head on my chest. Get some rest." I pulled my blanket around both of us. I gazed at her beloved face. She looked so tired. Dark smudges circled her eyes, and there was a weary cast to her forehead and cheeks as though she hadn't slept in weeks.

"Hmm…" Mari sighed as she lay her head on my chest and melted into my welcoming embrace. She was home.

Chapter Twenty-Six

Harley

July

"Wake up sleepy heads," Peg gently nudged my shoulder. "It's almost noon."

"Noon?" I sat up and rubbed the sleep from my eyes. Stretching, I yawned and ran my fingers through my tousled hair.

Mari stirred and arched her back. "Good morning," she grinned at me. "How did you sleep?"

"Very well," I mumbled. I was beginning to realize the challenges I was going to have with Mari living in my home. My traitorous body was already reacting.

"Me too." She stood up. "If you don't mind, I need to take a shower."

"Um…I don't mind," I gulped. "Go right ahead," I mumbled as inappropriate visions of Mari in the shower flitted through my mind. Just great! Now my brain was joining my body in the rebellion. I just couldn't win. Thankfully, I was Mormon and practiced the law of chastity. Otherwise, Mari would be in trouble. Big trouble.

Deciding I needed a cold shower, I slowly made my way upstairs to my rooms. I spent a good half hour under the cold spray before my treasonous body quit reacting inappropriately. By the time I got back downstairs, everyone had assembled in the kitchen.

Garrett was in his element, whipping up a lunch feast. Baked chicken with marinated vegetables, fruit, salad greens, rolls, and apple spiced pie.

"Come sit beside me," Mari beckoned. She sliced open a roll and spread a pat of butter on it.

"Smells wonderful." I took my seat and filled my plate. "I'm hungry," I said as my stomach let out an earth-shattering rumble to the amusement of everyone in the room. "I couldn't ask for a more perfect day. I'm back home and surrounded by the people I care about and love." I looked at each person and smiled.

"Awe…shucks," Thomas grinned back. "We love you too, man."

"So, what's the plan for today?" I savored a bite of chicken.

"We thought we'd leave after lunch. Give you and Mari some time together. Garrett asked us to run some errands for him. We'll be back here around dinner time." Peg scooped more fruit onto her plate.

"You both are going to relax," Garrett said.

"And what about you?" I asked. "Last night had to be rough on you too."

"I'll rest. I promise." Garrett chuckled.

"Someone has to look out for you, too, you know."

"Harley, can you get in the pool or the jacuzzi? A nice long soak sounds fabulous to me." Mari asked as she polished off her fruit.

"I can," I nodded. "My physical therapist has me working out in the pool. I could go for a soak in the jacuzzi."

"Let's go, Thomas," Peg said, "They need some catch-up time."

Both stood. "We'll be back," Thomas and Peg said in unison. I'd noticed when I arrived home they often said the exact same thing together. It was humorous, almost like they were an old married couple instead of just dating.

Mari rose, "I'm going to change. A nice long session in the jacuzzi with my fiancée is just what I need."

There went my traitorous body again as I pictured Mari in a swimsuit. "I'll join you," I said. "I mean, I'll go change too," I hastened to explain. I didn't mean to sound like I was going to change with her. "I'll meet you back down here." My face flushed red.

"Oh, Harley, she got you tied in knots?" Thomas chided as he walked toward the door."

"Yes," I gulped, "I mean no. Oh, I don't know what I mean!" I hurried as fast as my walker let me toward the elevator. Peals of laughter followed me down the hall.

Mari was waiting for me by the time I got back downstairs. She was wearing a blue speckled one piece that accentuated her curves. A blue towel was draped casually over her shoulder.

"Wow! You look ravishing," I looked her up and down. "Is it new?"

"Yes, I bought it during my layover in Atlanta."

I let out a low wolf whistle. "I could almost forget my vow of chastity with you dressed like that," the devil in me spoke up.

"Should I go change into shorts and a t-shirt?"

"No, no. C'mon let's go."

"I'll bring cold beverages," Garrett said.

"Why not join us, Garrett?" I asked.

"I'm going to sit in the gazebo and read." He ushered us out the door.

Mari walked slowly beside me. She carefully removed anything in our path that might trip me. Occasionally, she grasped my elbow and steered me around an obstacle.

"Mari, I can do this," I laughed. "It's so endearing how protective you are."

"You kept me safe. Now, it's my turn, love."

I loved hearing her call me her love. It filled my heart with joy. I thank Heavenly Father for bringing her into my life, albeit in a most unorthodox manner.

Once we got to the jacuzzi, she insisted on helping me sit on the lip. Once I was securely seated, Mari entered the water, turned and held her arms out to me. "Take it slow. I got you."

I slipped into the water, and Mari grasped me. She then slid me backward to the bench. I reached over and turned the jets onto gentle. The hot water and bubbles felt soothing.

"How was your trip home?" Mari asked.

"Here you go, ice cold herbal tea." Garrett handed each of us a glass.

"Thank you," Mari sipped. "This is so good."

"Thank you, Miss Mari. I'll check back with you in a bit."

"Garrett rescued me." I swallowed the cool beverage.

"Rescued you?"

"I was released from the hospital the same day he arrived. When they got me to my parents' home, there was a big banner proclaiming a gala in my honor was being held that night."

"The same day you got out of the hospital?" Mari gasped. "What were they doing? Trying to kill you?"

"It sure felt like it. I was in no shape for dinner and dancing. I took a nap, but it wasn't long enough. Dinner had about fifty people, and the dancing had a hundred. I was expected to dance with ten debutants. I could barely walk with a cane, let alone dance unassisted. I'm ashamed to say, I leaned heavily on the girl's arms."

"Your parents are something else."

"Garrett came bursting in just as I thought I was going to collapse. He lifted me into his arms, placed me in my wheelchair, took me to my rooms where he packed a bag, got my favorite books, and my violin. When we got to the ground floor, he got my cane and walker. My father accosted him. Garrett clocked him, and he was out cold."

"He did what?" Mari gasped. "Garrett knocked your father out?"

"Yes, he did," It was the first time I'd ever seen Garrett hit someone."

"Did you fly straight here?"

"Heavens no! Garrett arranged for short flights of an hour or two. We stayed several days in New York at a penthouse suite. We had room service, walked the grounds, and ate at several restaurants featuring cuisine from Saigon, Cuba, and New York local food. We flew into Harrisburg and stayed in Smoketown for a couple days. There we practiced walking from our rooms to the lobby and around the grounds. From there we flew to Cleveland. During our stay, we visited the Lakeview Cemetery. The grounds are beautiful, and the Presidential tomb is something to see. We then flew to Dayton and stayed overnight before coming home. Garrett took great care of me and made sure I was well fed every step of the way."

"Sounds like you had a wonderful return trip." Mari sounded wistful. "I wish I could have been here when you arrived."

"I did," I said. "What matters is you're here now." I leaned toward her. "I want to adopt him."

"That'd be fantastic! But, what about your family?"

"That's the problem. I need to have my attorneys sort out the legal quagmire especially where inheritances are concerned."

"Do you have to go back to New York?"

"I return to the Cancer Institute of New York in September. They'll do testing and another round of treatment. Mari, I know university classes start in mid-September. If I can schedule it for early September, do you think you can accompany Garrett and me?"

"Absolutely. I'm going to try to get my job back at K-Mart. I'm sure Peg and March will cover my shows at WOSL."

Garrett knelt down and placed a fruit and cheese tray beside us on the lip of the jacuzzi. "Something to snack on. I'll return to refresh your beverages."

"Thank you very much, Garrett," Mari said.

"Yes, thank you, Garrett." Facing Mari, I continued, "You don't need to work, you know. I can support both of us."

"I know, but it doesn't seem right. I don't want you to support me financially until after we're married." She twirled a lock of hair around her finger. "I mean, by me living here, you are kind of supporting me because I don't have to pay rent, utilities, or groceries. I don't want you to feel like I'm here for what you can give me."

"Ah…Mari, no! I'd never feel that way about you. I know you'd never be here for the money. You're the kind that gives…generosity of spirit, and money."

"At least let me pay rent and for my share of the groceries."

"Nonsense. Get a job for university tuition, books, gas, clothing, spending money if you want. I'll not have you paying me to rent a room here or for food. I want you to live here."

"If you insist."

"I do insist. You don't know how much I want this." I took a sip of my drink.

"Okay," she paused, and a mischievous grin spread across her face. "It's not like we're sleeping together or anything."

"What?" I sputtered, and my beverage came spurting out my nose, much to her merriment. "Heavens! The law..."

"I know. The law or vow of chastity prevents that," she giggled.

"We're soulmates. In you, I have found my better half as they say." I said, trying to regain some semblance of dignity and failing.

"So, have I." Mari fidgeted, "I have to admit something."

"What?" I sat straight.

"When I thought you were dead... well, it was like my world ended." She hiccupped. Tears glistened in her hazel eyes. "I...I wanted to die."

I reached out and pulled her into my arms. "I'm glad you didn't."

"I came close. I had a knife out and everything. Then I thought about everything you taught me, what your church says about suicide. But, it was feeling your presence and hearing your voice telling me you had not gone away and not to do it, that convinced me."

"I'm glad. We're both here now." I kissed her head. "I'm very glad you listened to my spiritual self."

"Me too."

Chapter Twenty-Seven

Mari

July

Despite what Harley said, I felt more comfortable getting a job. "I want to try to get my job back at K-Mart."

"I'll take you," Harley grabbed his leather jacket and the keys to the Bentley.

Surprisingly, Polly Workman was more than willing to hire me back. I was assigned to the lingerie department, the biggest in the department store. Unsurprisingly, she had not changed one bit.

"Mister Davis, we all heard you were deceased,' Polly hummed her tuneless song.

"The rumor was greatly exaggerated as you can see' he responded dryly.

After securing a position there, Harley drove me to Davis Motors. True to their word, my beloved Satellite was waiting for me. They had manufactured the water pump, tweaked and shined it. I gave them five hundred dollars and allowed Harley to chip in the rest after making him promise to let me pay him back.

"Here's the keys, Mari." Ken handed them to me. "We had fun fixing this gal up. Enjoy. Be safe."

"Thanks, Ken." I waved at the guys. "Thanks a bunch."

"You're welcome, Miss," he replied.

Harley looked at me. Edward had given him papers showing the financial state of the businesses. "You took very good care of the company Edward. I'm impressed," he said and walked toward me.

After returning home, we set about planning a company-wide picnic. I still couldn't believe I was living in Harley's home. My rooms, which consisted of a bedroom, dressing area, and bathroom, was down the hall from his, and Garrett's rooms. Harley bought a desk and placed it in my room. He also had a telephone added so I could call my parents anytime I wanted.

We sat at the counter in the kitchen. "So, it's settled, the picnic will be July 22," I wrote in my notebook.

"I'm going to close shop for all three businesses for that day. Give them a full weekend. And I'm going to give out the bonuses I missed last year and a little extra. Their families will be welcome. I need to hire a lifeguard for the pool and rent some play equipment for the kids."

I scribbled furiously as Harley rattled off his list. "What about tables and chairs?"

"Yeah, need to get those too, and hire some cooks. I'm going to let Flash be in charge of the food. If it turns out wonderfully like I think it will, I'm going to finance him setting up a restaurant. He did graduate this past Spring, right?"

"Yes, but he hasn't found a position yet." I kept writing. The way he read off what he wanted to be done, it was a wonder his secretary could keep up.

"Good. If it works out, it'll be a nice surprise for Flash. Food-wise, we'll need chicken, ribs, hamburger patties, hot dogs, rolls, buns, potato salad, coleslaw, bean salad, fruit salad, watermelon, melon, corn on the cob, relish, cakes, pies, cookies, candy, assorted chips, and beverages. No alcohol. Everyone knows my position on that; if not, they're going to learn. Probably throw in some steaks too."

"Slow down!" I laughed, "I can't write that fast."

"Oh, sorry. Garrett, did I forget anything?"

"Graham crackers, marshmallows, and chocolate."

Harley snapped his fingers, "S'mores! Fireworks. Tablecloths, paper plates, and plastic utensils."

I groaned at the thought of fireworks. Harley knew they scared me.

"A volleyball set."

"I think that'll be enough, Master Harley." Garrett leaned forward. "Everyone will have a good time. You can set up your sound system. We'll need tents in case of rain."

Harley snapped his fingers again. "Good point, Garrett."

I was glad I wasn't in his boardroom, although he wants me to learn his business. Just planning the picnic gave me a good view of him as a mogul. It was a far cry from when we were planning our wedding over a year ago.

"Garrett, I could use some snacks. Do you mind?" Harley stretched.

"As you wish, Master Harley. Then I'll start making dinner."

"No need. We're going out for dinner."

"Shall I make reservations for you and Miss Mari?"

"Already done and you're included."

"Me? You don't need…"

"Ah…ah…ah, yes I do." Harley winked at me.

Garrett shook his head as he stepped over to the refrigerator and began putting together a snack tray for us.

"What do you have up your sleeve, Harley?" I whispered.

Harley leaned forward and beckoned me closer. "I found a way to adopt him," he whispered. "It's an honorary adoption. As such, I had my lawyers build into the adoption all the rights a father would have. My attorney assures me there is no way my parents can remove him or take my inheritances away."

"That's wonderful, Harley!" I clapped my hands and bounced in my seat with joy.

"Now, about our wedding," he placed his fingers in the classic steeple position. "I think, we should resume planning it. What do you think?"

"We've already planned most of it. We just need to get the places and dates arranged, and send out invitations."

"Mari, you do understand, you'll have to join my church, right?" he stared intently at me.

"Yes," I swallowed hard. Joining another religion felt overwhelming, but I was willing to do it.

"Good. I'll contact the missionaries and see if they can do three basic doctrine training a week starting next week. You'll have to go to church with Garrett and me on Sundays. You will be baptized. If we start right away, we'll be able to get married August 19. After that, we can work toward your temple recommend and hopefully be married in the temple sometime next year." He paused. "Don't worry. Friends and family can participate in the wedding, just not the temple service. We can go on a month-long honeymoon with a break in the middle for my checkup and treatment."

My head swam with all the information he was spewing. "Uh…okay," I managed to croak.

"Is that okay with you?" He looked quizzically at me.

"Sure," I hesitated.

Harley leaned back against the counter. "What is it?" He asked.

"Nothing," I muttered.

"Don't give me that," he snapped. "I can tell something is bothering you."

The mogul was still in full force, and I didn't care for it. "It just seems everything is moving so fast. I just got here a few days ago."

"I see," he studied me quietly for several uncomfortable minutes. "Is it joining my church? The last time we talked about marriage, you were okay with that. This won't work otherwise. My religion is extremely important to me."

"It's not that," I protested. Harley's words stung. It was clear he would pick religion over me and that hurt.

"Then what is it, Mari?" His voice took on a steely undertone he had never used on me.

"Harley, I don't like the way you're talking to me. I'm your fiancée, not someone off the streets."

"Would you rather not get married, Mari? I've been looking forward to seeing you, being with you, and marrying you for a long time. This cancer business made me decide not to wait. But, if you'd rather…" He held out his hands and shrugged.

"It's not that, Harley. I do want to marry you!"

"Then what is it?" he grated. The muscle in his jaw clenched and relaxed repeatedly.

"It's all moving so fast. Even if we can get everything arranged in time, I don't know if my parents can fly in so soon after Dad started working at Pierce Chemicals. I'm not sure they can afford the flight. I just got my job back. I don't think I can get the time off."

"I can take care of Polly Workman. I did it before. I can do it again. August 19th is a Saturday. I'll pay for flight tickets. They can fly in Friday night and leave Sunday."

"What about classes? And WOSL?"

"Skip the fall quarter. I'm sure Peg or Thomas or someone can take your show for a month. I've already asked. Peg, Thomas, and March all said they'd pitch in and cover for you."

"You already asked? Do you have the entire wedding and honeymoon planned?" I was getting angry.

"Well, yes, based on what we'd already planned. I just moved it to fit a new schedule."

"Without involving me?" I was furious. He only thought he'd seen me angry in the past. "It's my wedding too, Harley!" I screamed at him. "I don't like this side of you!"

He looked questioningly at me. "What do you mean?"

"This…this supreme boss man mogul, that's what!" I shoved away from the counter. "I'm your fiancée, not some business conquest!" I stomped out of the kitchen and ran upstairs. I dragged out my suitcase and began flinging clothes into it.

###

Harley

"What did I do?" I watched her storm out of the kitchen.

Garrett clucked like a mother hen. "You made the final plans for your wedding without involving her."

"All I did was arrange the dates, booked the church, and arranged to have the Bishop preside over the services."

"All without asking her opinion. Master Harley, I do believe you have some serious, as they say, kissing up to do."

"Really? That's ridiculous!" I huffed.

"Yes, Master Harley," Garrett chuckled. "Don't you know, girls like to plan their wedding.'

"But, don't guys get involved too?"

"Not so much. Boys mainly help with seating arrangements and plan the honeymoon. They always clear it with the bride. Basically, a wedding is a bride's special day."

"What about the groom? Isn't it his special day too?"

"Yes, but it's more a bride's day." This is the day the bride gives herself to one man. She takes great pains to make sure she looks perfect. A white wedding gown represents purity."

"Kind of like the law of chastity? Remaining pure and free from sexual activity until marriage."

"Yes. A wedding is sacred. It is the day you pledge yourselves to each other for eternity in front of God, the congregation, family, and friends."

"I guess. I better start with the kissing up." I rose and slowly made my way from the kitchen using only my cane. "How do I always manage to get myself into trouble?"

As I made my way down the hall to the stairs, a thought occurred to me and I turned back. "Garrett?" I called out.

"Yes, Master Harley?" He appeared in the doorway wiping his hands on a dish towel.

"Suppose Mari doesn't want to join our church? Can a Mormon marry a non-member?"

"Yes, they can, Master Harley. It would be a civil marriage until death but not an eternal one. Only a temple marriage can be eternal as the couple is sealed to each other."

"I see," I said and headed back down the hall.

I stood outside her door and listened to the sounds coming from inside. She sounded very angry. I swallowed hard and rapped twice.

"Mari?"

"What?" She flung the door open. "What do you want now?" she stood with her hands on her hips.

I peered around her. There was an open suitcase. "Are you going somewhere?" Dread filled my heart. I could feel it hammering in my chest.

"I'm going to Texas," she snapped.

"But…what about us?" I stepped inside.

"You mean, what about you, don't' you," Mari shouted. She picked up the 'Steppenwolf,' the Hermann Hesse novel I had given her during our first Christmas. She held it as though weighing it. "Get out of my room!" She threw it at me.

I ducked, but not fast enough. The book glanced off my shoulder hard enough to send me reeling. I barely grabbed the bedpost and kept myself from falling.

"We're through! I'm moving to Texas," she yelled again. Mari grabbed my arm and helped steady me.

"No. Please, Mari, don't leave. I don't know what I did, but, I'm sorry." My heart was breaking. I had struggled so hard to be able to come home and have a life with her. If she left, I just knew a large part of me would die. There was no way I could envision living my life without her in it.

"You don't know what you did?" Exasperation filled her voice. "I'll tell you." She went back to throwing stuff into her suitcase. "You only planned out every detail of our wedding and honeymoon. I bet you've even planned how many kids we'll have, their names, and our entire future."

"Six," I said sheepishly.

"Six what?"

"Kids?" I winced.

"Kids?" She sounded disbelieving. "You want six children?"

"I always wanted a large family," I grinned boyishly at her.

"Two," she said.

"Five," I countered.

"Three." Mari sat on the edge of her bed.

"Four."

"Deal," she held out her hand.

I grasped it, pumped it and lifted her hand to my lips. "So, what are we going to do about the wedding?"

"I guess the dates and places are okay." She began taking her clothes out of the suitcase. "What about joining the church? I'm not sure I can meet the requirements in time."

"We'll get what we can and then take it from there. The temple wedding could be a year after you get your temple recommend. I have to get mine renewed so we can do that together."

"And my parents? Are you really willing to fly them here?"

"Absolutely, my love."

"And our honeymoon?"

"An even mixture of places you wanted to visit and mine. Such as the Grand Canyon, Glacier, Yosemite, Angkor Wat, Japan, Polynesia, and others."

"That will take some time."

"Which is why I asked the DJs if they'd cover your show and I didn't want you to go back to work. I figured it will take the fall months to do everything."

"Could we do Glacier, Yosemite, and an east coast fall colors trip first?"

"Of course. Then we could go to Angkor Wat, Japan, and finish with Polynesia."

"Can we add Australia, England, and France?"

"Whatever you want. Or we could do some in the fall and some next year… say late spring."

"That'd be great, and we could finish with a temple wedding."

"Sounds like a plan." I pulled her close and kissed her. "Now, let's get you unpacked, eh?"

She smiled and nodded.

Relief swept through me. I may have put my foot in my mouth, but I got her back. Disaster diverted.

###

Mari

What a relief! The mogul had gone back in his cave. My sweet Harley was back. Everything was right and good with the world again.

Chapter Twenty-Eight

Harley

July

With the disaster averted, I changed into a suit and went out to the Bentley to wait for Garrett and Mari. Garrett came out a few minutes later wearing his standard tweed jacket, white shirt, and dark green pants.

He leaned into the window.

"Master Harley, shouldn't I drive?"

"No. Tonight, you are being pampered. You can sit up front if you wish. I'm sure Mari wouldn't mind."

"I'll sit in the back if that's okay." Garrett climbed into the back seat.

"Fine by me."

Mari appeared wearing a floral dress and got in on the passenger side. "Where are we going?"

"There's a new restaurant in town called the Western Steakhouse. I thought we'd try it." I said as I pulled out of the driveway.

The place reminded me of a newer version of the Ponderosa Steak House. It had a western theme and an image of a cowboy riding a stallion on the exterior. A beautifully appointed salad bar adorned one section of the restaurant. Our waitress was pleasant and took our drink orders while we perused the menu.

"Mari, what are you having?" I asked as I sipped my water. I never tired of looking at her sweet face. There are still days when I pinch myself because I can't believe she's still with me after all I put her through.

"I'd like a six-ounce ribeye medium-well, more on the well-done side, a baked potato, and a trip to the salad bar."

"Very well," the waitress scribbled on her order pad.

"Garrett?" I asked.

"The shrimp and ribeye, medium, baked potato, and salad bar."

"And you, sir?" she turned to me.

"A twelve-ounce T-bone medium-rare, baked potato, and salad bar."

"Very good choices. Please help yourselves to the salad."

We loaded our plates and returned to find our drinks had been replenished and a cup of sliced lemons and limes was on the table.

"This is delicious, Master Harley," Garrett set his fork down while chewing his food. "To what do I owe this pleasure?"

I grinned and winked at Mari.

"I believe this is going to be a most memorable night, Garrett," Mari said as I reached inside my suit jacket and pulled out an envelope.

I slid it toward Garrett. "Go on, open it."

"For me?" Garrett looked puzzled as he slipped the papers out.

Garrett's expression turned from puzzlement to apprehension as he repeatedly glanced at the legal brief. "Have I…Am I…" he cleared his throat. "Am I being…"

"Relax," Mari lightly placed her hand on his arm. "You have nothing to be concerned about. It's all good."

I rose and dropped to one knee much like I did when I proposed to Mari. "Garrett, those papers are just a small token of my esteem and love for you. You have been an integral part of my life since I was born."

Garrett sat holding the papers and watching me. Tears glistened in his eyes. "Master Harley," he began.

"Hear me out," I placed my hand on his. "You have raised me, and loved me when I thought I had no one. You stood beside me when I got into trouble. You gently steered me along the right path, sometimes having to employ tough love. I can depend on you." I felt wetness running down my cheeks. Grabbing my napkin, I dried my tears.

"What that document decrees is an adoption by me, making you my honorary father. The papers grant you all the rights of a legal parent including inheritances. If I could have divorced my father without possibly entangling my inheritances, I would have. Unfortunately, I couldn't do that, so this is the next best thing. Will you, Garrett Geadasach, Geddes, consent to being my honorary father?"

"Oh, Master Harley. You honor me to the ends of this earth." He grabbed his napkin and dabbed his eyes.

What a sight we must have made. Two adult men crying like babies.

The entire restaurant had gone silent as though they were waiting with baited breath for his response. I heard someone comment, "Is he proposing to the older man? I didn't think that was legal."

Someone responded, "It's not."

I dug into my other pocket and pulled out a jewelry box.

"My answer is, yes." He sniffled.

"In this box is a ring and cufflinks with the family crest." I pushed it toward him. Once again, I felt tears streaming down my face. My voice turned raspy as I spoke. "It would be a great honor to me if you will wear these.

He opened the box with trembling fingers, put the ring on and then the cufflinks. "I am proud to wear them, Master Harley, son."

Unexpectedly, he jumped up and pulled me to my feet where he engulfed me in a giant bear hug. The people in the restaurant applauded wildly.

An older lady, coming from the restroom, paused and asked Mari, "What's the occasion?"

"My fiancé just adopted the older gentleman as his father." Mari was smiling.

"That is wonderful." The lady turned toward us. "Congratulations on the adoption."

"Thank you," Garrett wiped his tears away.

We returned to our seats.

"I've never seen two grown men cry before," Mari giggled. "Congratulations to the both of you."

"Thank you, Miss Mari."

Right about then our meals were served. We ate, talked, and laughed. When we finished our dinners, the wait staff came out bearing cakes and ice cream for everyone in the facility. I stood up and said, "In honor of my adopted father, dessert is on me." I then motioned to the waitress. "Please let the cashier know, I'm paying the tab for everyone currently here."

The rest of our evening was spent in pleasant conversation. When we got home, Garrett made us his favorite herbal tea. "Garrett, at the risk of sounding tacky, in addition to adopting you, I'm keeping you on my payroll."

"As you wish, Master Harley. Never again can your parents bar me from attending to you. My heart is full."

"As is mine."

Chapter Twenty-Nine

Mari

July

The following week the missionaries came to begin my training. We agreed on three times a week so I could be baptized before the wedding. I learned about the plan of salvation, and atonement. The missionaries joked about the church having the most rules of any Christian religion.

Between preparing to join the church, my job, and help with getting ready for the picnic, I had very little time. Yet, Harley insisted on two things; I begin learning the business end of his companies, and date night Tuesdays and Thursdays.

'So, are you and Mister Davis going out tonight?" Polly Workman stood behind me as I refilled the lingerie bins. She casually waved her hand in my face. Her wrist was sporting a new ruby bracelet that matched her short dress. Harley was at it again.

"Yes," I replied.

For a second time, Polly flashed the bracelet at me.

"That's a lovely piece of jewelry. Is it new?" I asked.

"Yes, it is. It's quite lovely and expensive, isn't it?" Polly gloated.

"I guess."

"Did I hear correctly? You two are getting married next month, hmm?" She began humming tunelessly.

"August 19th," I replied.

"You make sure you do everything womanly possible to hang onto him. He's a keeper."

I stopped folding bras and stared at her. I couldn't tell if this was her version of giving out motherly advice, or encouragement to become a red-light district, madam. "I'll do my best," I managed to sputter.

"I'm serious, Mari. Many women would give their right boob for a man like him."

"Excuse me?" I choked and turned to stare at her. "I…I don't intend to let him get away."

"I'm sure we'll be getting an invitation?" Polly asked.

"Of course," mentally, I groaned. Add another ten people to the growing guest list.

I told Harley about the conversation when he picked me up.

"So, we need to invite your co-workers?"

"Yes."

"Does she know we're Mormon?"

"No," I said glumly.

"I guess we're going to have to tell her. She needs to know she can't go around pinching or groping the guys."

"I know. I'll tell Polly next week."

"I'll go with you," Harley sighed.

"What about your guest list?" I asked, curious. He hadn't mentioned anyone.

"Naturally, it includes Garrett and Thomas. I decided to depart a little from the standard Best Man and added a Father of the Groom. That way both can be in the wedding party."

"I have Peg as the Maid of Honor."

"That ought to be a hoot," Harley snorted.

"I assume your company employees will be invited. What about your family?"

"Yeah, my employees are invited including George, Evangeline, Keisha, Jamal, Shauntelle and her brood."

"Your family?" I gently prodded.

"I'll ask, but I doubt they'll come."

"Where are we going tonight?' I asked as we arrived home.

"Someplace special." He winked.

"How special? I need to know what to wear. Are we going on your Hog?"

"Yep. So, jeans, shirt, jacket, and boots will do nicely."

"Got it. Be back in a jiffy." I raced upstairs. I leaned over the rail and called down, "What happened to your walker?"

"The therapist said I don't need it anymore. I have a foldup cane and in two weeks, might not need it except occasionally when my leg gets tired."

"That's wonderful!" I hurried into my room and changed into black jeans, a black shirt, and my boots. I grabbed my helmet on the way out.

Harley looked at me and whistled. "You are so beautiful."

He grasped my hand, and we headed out the door. Garrett was just topping up the gas tank when we came out.

"All gassed up and ready. I'll see you soon."

"Garrett's joining us?" I asked as I straddled the motorcycle and wrapped my arms around Harley's waist.

"Sort of," he mumbled.

"Where are we going for dinner?"

"Church. They're having a meet and greet potluck dinner for investigators."

"Oh," I resettled my feet.

"Watch the pipes, Mari. Don't want you to get burned."

"Got it."

The meeting house was rather simplistic in design but connotated reverence and elegance. Directly across from the entrance is the Chapel. Turning left at the entrance, you have the Women's Relief Society room on the left and the Cultural Hall on the right. Further down is the serving area or kitchen on the left.

The dinner was being held in the Cultural room. The room was getting crowded as the congregation drifted in. Harley introduced me to so many people. I felt like I was cocooned in a wealth of acceptance and love. Never have I felt that way in any other church.

Garrett walked in and strode over to us. "How are they treating you, Mari?"

"Wonderfully, Garrett." I smiled at him.

"I brought your favorite chicken and dumpling casserole, Master Harley."

"Thank you, Garrett!" He clapped his hands in joy and bounced on his feet like a toddler. "Mari, you are going to love it. He makes the best!"

Garrett smiled indulgently.

The Bishop stood at the front of the room. “Brothers and Sisters, let us welcome our investigators to our Church. When your name is called, please rise.” He then called each of our names. After the last one, the congregation applauded. The Bishop then called upon a member to give thanks.

Looking around, I noticed everyone folded their arms and bowed their heads. I did the same.

“Heavenly Father, we give thanks for the blessings you have bestowed upon us. We thank thee for allowing us to share the gospel with our investigators. Heavenly Father, we ask thee to bless the food we are about to consume and all the souls who partake of it. Amen.”

We then lined up at the buffet and filled our plates. Everything looked and smelled so good, I was tempted to make a pig of myself. With great restraint, I managed to put just a tiny scoop from each platter on my plate and still left some room. I made certain to put a fairly generous helping of Garrett’s contribution on my dish.

“Do you want a root beer, ginger ale, water with lemon, lime, or orange?” Harley asked.

“Water with orange, please.”

“You go ahead and sit down. I’ll bring it,” Harley smiled.

When Harley smiles his entire face lights up, and his blue-gray eyes become a solid blue. It makes him look even more handsome.

I sat at our table. Harley brought his plate and put it down. “I’ll be right back with our beverages.”

“Don’t rush, okay?” I didn’t want him wearing out his leg.

“Hello, I’m Sheila,” a tall, willowy woman greeted me.”

“Hi, I’m Mari.”

She slid into the seat next to me.” So, you’re the young lady Harley speaks so highly of.” Her smile was warm and kind.

“Yes, Madam, I am.” I blushed.

“He says you two are going to marry.” She said it more like a question than a statement.

“Yes, we are.” I grinned.

“Be still my heart. So many young ladies are going to be heartbroken. He’s quite a man, your Harley is.”

"I know."

Harley set our drinks down and sat beside me. "I chased after her all over the country and then had to pester her to go out with me."

"You did not," I playfully punched at his arm. "You said, 'what are you doing Friday?' and I said I was working. You said you could get someone to switch places with me. I said if you do that I'll go out with you Friday. You said Thursday. I said I had class until nine o'clock that night. You said you'd pick me up after class."

"See? I pestered you."

"Yeah, you did," I blushed.

"Oh my!" Sheila laughed. "Harley, did you really chase her across the country?"

"Unintentionally, but yes. I ran across Mari twice in Portland, Oregon, once in Chehalis, Washington once in Seattle, Washington, and at Rink's department store here in Lima where she almost got me arrested."

"Hey!" I protested. "In my defense, you looked like a bad boy biker."

"You two have quite a history!" Sheila laughed as she stood up. "I'd love to hear more about it sometime."

"Someday, she's going to write a book about us." Harley laughed.

Garrett joined us at the table. "Did I miss something?" he asked, looking between us.

"Just the history of Harley and Me," I said.

"Oh, I was there for most of it." He placed his napkin on his lap.

"Harley and Me," Harley mused. "I like it. That's what you should call the book."

"You really want me to spill your dark secrets?" I laughed.

"Hmm…" he placed his fist under his chin and thought. "My redemption." He snapped his fingers. "You can call that one Harley's Redemption. Yeah, that's the ticket." He grinned wickedly. "I double dog dare you to write them."

"Oh, you!" I laughed. "Maybe someday when we're old and gray."

"You mean silver-haired. Silver looks much better than gray."

"Boy, do you have an ego." I snickered.

"That's me, big-headed, egotistical maniac." He leaned toward me and growled.

"Don't you even think of biting me!" I laughed.

People stopped by our table throughout our meal. When we finished eating, Harley led me around the room, introducing me to the congregation. It was surprising to me how relaxed and comfortable I felt.

The following Sunday I attended my first church service. I have been apprehensive about joining the church but would do it for Harley. I think he picked up on my fear and took it as reluctance. During the week, we'd had numerous conversations about it. Each time I assured him I was fine with joining the church. The truth was, I was uncomfortable.

The church service was completely different from what I had experienced at other churches. The was no pomp and circumstance. The sacrament meeting was simple and reverent. It opened with congregational announcements and was followed by a hymn. We sang, 'I Need Thee Every Hour.' This was followed by an opening prayer. There was no formal sermon. Another hymn, 'Lead Me into Life Eternal' followed the prayer.

Various members came to the podium and gave their testament. Each viewpoint was interesting as some shared how they came to join the church. Others talked about things they learned while performing service.

This was followed by the blessing of the bread by the priesthood. It was passed through the congregation. "Do I participate?" I whispered.

"If you want," Harley murmured. "It'd have a different meaning than for members. For Mormons, the sacrament is a renewal of our covenants with Heavenly Father."

I declined the bread. It didn't feel right to participate until I was a member. I sat in quiet contemplation with my eyes closed.

I saw a vision. In my vision, I saw a dark room with a man in white robes in the center. A light shined down upon him. It was Jesus Christ. He held his arms out to me and beckoned me to come forward. I felt rather than heard him say, "Come unto me. This is the house of my Father. You are home." Behind, him the church came into view. Peace washed over me such as I never knew could exist. I had indeed come home. Gone were my fears and doubts. The Church of Jesus Christ of Latter-Day Saints was where I belonged.

After the sacrament, a young lady missionary talked about her experience in Bolivia. This was followed by a family performing a musical piece. Then another missionary shared how his mission touched him. Then there was a closing hymn and prayer.

After the sacrament, the missionaries came to lead me to the Gospel Principals class. "Give me just a moment, please. I need to speak to Harley."

They stepped respectfully away. Harley was grinning. You had an epiphany, didn't you?"

"Yes!" I hugged him. "I can be baptized whenever they say I'm ready."

He called the missionaries over and shared with them the good news. "We'll see if it can be arranged next weekend," Sister Cass Anderson said.

"Make that the week after. We have plans with people from out of town next weekend."

"How about the Wednesday before that weekend?" Sister Megan Renae asked.

"Perfect."

Both Harley and I went to the Gospel class. It was similar to Sunday school in the Baptist Church. Then I was directed to the Relief Society. "Where are you going?" I asked.

"Priesthood meeting."

"Wait! Are you a priest?"

"Almost all worthy men are priests. There's the Aaronic priesthood with four offices including deacon, teacher, priest, and bishop. Deacons are young men aged twelve to fourteen, teachers are fourteen to sixteen and priest aged sixteen to eighteen. The Melchizedek priesthood is conferred upon faithful males aged eighteen and up. They are elder, high priest, patriarch, Seventy, and Apostle. The bishop is also a member of the Melchizedek priesthood."

"Wow! So, I'm marrying a priest."

"I'm just a man, Mari," Harley chuckled as he headed to his meeting and I rejoined the missionaries.

The Relief Society meeting is for women. The teachings focus on increasing our faith in Heavenly Father and Jesus Christ. How his atonement is our saving grace. The importance of the Doctrines and Covenants, and the impact we have in performing service to those in need.

By the end of church services, my head was swimming with thoughts about what I had learned. Whoever said Mormons were not Christian had absolutely no knowledge of the Church of Jesus Christ of Latter-Day Saints.

Chapter Thirty

Mari

July

The week leading up to the company picnic was hectic. I felt like I was a chicken running around without a head. I frantically met with the missionaries, worked at K-Mart, and looked at items for our wedding. With all that going on, I still assisted with the plans for the picnic.

"Keisha, Jamal, and Shauntelle with her kids are coming," I hollered to Garrett as I hung up the phone.

"I think that's everyone," Harley said. "And our WOSL friends will be joining us."

'Where are we going to put everyone?" I scribbled furiously in my notebook. "Keisha and Jamal, Shauntelle, four children, Thomas, Peg, March, Maryanne, Lori, Judy, Mike, Flash, and Hixson. That's sixteen."

Garrett placed a plate of fruit, cheese, crackers, and cookies on the kitchen counter within easy reach of us.

"Eighteen, George and Evangeline are coming too," Harley grinned.

"Eighteen! We only have a five-bedroom house, and three of them are taken. Keisha and Jamal will share a room as will Evangeline and George. That takes up our two guest rooms."

"March, Thomas, you and me will sleep in the living room like we used to do during those weekends with the WOSL gang," Harley added.

"No, Master Harley. You are still in recovery despite how well you feel. You will bunk in with me," Garrett said. "Mari and Maryanne can share your room."

"Flash can have his room," I suggested.

"No, Miss Mari, that honor is now yours as his fiancée."

"Peg and Maryanne can bunk with me," I said. "Harley has a king-sized bed. It'll hold the three of us."

Harley nodded his agreement. “Should work.”

“That leaves Hixson, Flash, Mike, Lori, Judy, and Shauntelle’s children,” Garrett commented.

“Do we still have those inflatable mattresses?” Harley asked.

“Yes, we do. We have four.”

“We can set the mattresses up in the game room, living room, and dining room. We can blow them up ahead of time and stack them in the laundry room. When it’s time for bed, bring them out. I think the kids would love sleeping in the game room, don’t you?”

“Aye, I do, Master Harley.” Garrett lovingly placed a hand on Harley’s shoulder. “I’ll check them and make sure they are still in good shape. If not, I’ll replace them. I’ll pick up an extra one just in case we need it.”

“Flash is going to arrive Thursday to begin prepping for the barbecue. I’ll go with him to help select and I’ll pay for the food,” I said. “I know, you will give me cash.” I sighed. “Can’t I contribute?”

“You are, by being my fiancée. Soon, my funds will also be yours.” Harley said.

“Aren’t you going to have a prenuptial agreement?” I asked as butterflies flitted in my stomach.

“No need,” Harley said. “I trust you with all my being.”

“Thanks. I think.” I mumbled as I twined a lock of hair around my finger.

“Don’t you have to work Thursday?” Harley cocked his head and grinned.

“At five. We should be finished way before then,” I paused, thinking how best to ask my question. “That reminds me. Would it be okay to invite my sister, Dee, and her husband, Frank?”

“Sure, why wouldn’t it be?” Harley shrugged.

“Great. Thanks.” I rose and went to the telephone to call her. Boy, was she shocked to find out I was in Lima.

“When did you return?” Dee asked.

“July first,” I replied.

“Why?” She sounded incredulous.

“I’d rather tell you in person. So, can you guys come?”

“I’ll have to ask Frank, but I think so. Where is it being held?”

"You know where the Country Club is? The Harlan Davis home is near there." I proceeded to give her the address and directions.

"How are you involved in this?"

"I'll tell you when I see you. Bye, Sis." I returned to the kitchen where Garrett was busy preparing dinner.

"Are you sure, you're working Thursday night?" Harley asked.

I reached for some cheese. "Yeah. Why?"

"What happened to date night?"

I stared at him. "Oh, no! I traded with Karen so I could have Saturday off." I wrung my hands. "I have tonight off."

"Today is Tuesday," Harley commented. "Okay, we'll just have one date night this week. We'll go to a movie after dinner."

"That'd be great!" Relief washed over me. "Want to see 'Foul Play'?"

"I think 'Convoy' and 'Heaven Can Wait' is still in the theaters," Harley suggested.

"You choose. Any of those movies are fine with me."

"'Convoy,'" he rubbed his hands gleefully.

"'Convoy' it is." I hugged him. Oh, how I loved this man-child of mine.

"We'll need to leave a little early to drop by K-Mart and talk to Polly Workman." Harley winked at me.

I groaned. I really didn't want to have that conversation. By the time we finished dinner, I was a nervous wreck.

We pulled into the parking lot. Amazingly, we got a first-row spot. Harley hurried around to the passenger door and opened it for me. From the number of people gawking through the window, you would think they had never seen a vintage Bentley.

Harley grasped my hand, and we walked into the store.

"My God, Mari!" Karen gushed. "He drives a fancy car! Girl, have you got it made. Look at that rock on your finger!" She fawned over my engagement ring.

The band was silver karat and held a black opal with pink, blue and large green patches. The stone was shaped like a diamond. "What kind of stone is it?"

"Black Opal. From what I've been told it's the rarest of this type of stone. He had the band designed."

"Oh, wow! It must cost a fortune." She peered at him.

"I wouldn't know. Harley never said how much." I squirmed under her scrutiny.

"How come you never wear it here?"

"It wouldn't be safe," Harley piped up. "Expensive piece of jewelry, she'd be a target."

"Karen, uh…is Polly in?"

"Yeah." She nodded in the direction of the back room. "In her office."

"Thanks." I led Harley toward the back corner. Polly's office was through the storage room and up a flight of stairs. At the door to her office, I hesitated before knocking. "Miss Workman?"

"Hmm...?" she hummed. "Oh, Mari," she peeked around me, and her voice became a purr, "and Mister Davis. To what do I owe this unexpected pleasure? Hmm?"

"We wanted to talk privately with you about my upcoming wedding." I struggled to get the words out.

"Do you need more time off?"

"No!" I hastened to add, "We wanted to tell you about the ceremony."

"We're members of the Church of Jesus Christ of Latter-Day Saints, commonly called Mormon," Harley spoke with such self-assurance. I was so proud of him.

"Mormon?"

"Yes, Ma'am. As Mormons, we live by a lot of rules most people do not pay any attention to. Since our wedding will be taking place in our chapel, there are certain expectations we have of members and non-members."

"You are trying to tell me what to do?" She applied another coat of red nail polish.

"Not so much that, but rules of conduct to save everyone embarrassment."

She sat back. "Okay. Spill it."

"A man should be dressed in suit and tie. No cut-offs or ragged t-shirts. He must wear underwear, and his manhood should be…shall we say restrained? A woman is expected to wear a knee length or longer demure dress. No showing off cleavage or body parts that might be deemed sexual in nature."

"How archaic," she commented.

"That may be, but we practice the law of chastity which not only means sexual conduct is reserved for marriage, but also we remain modest."

"But, I've seen you in here looking like a biker."

"There's nothing immodest about wearing a shirt, jeans, boots and leather jacket. I'm asking that everyone who plans to attend must be dressed modestly."

"I'll need to buy a new dress," she hinted.

"If you'll tell Mari your size, I'll make sure to get you something appropriate, including shoes. If anyone wants to attend but can't afford an appropriate outfit, I'll do the same for them. Just give Mari the information."

"What about jewelry?"

"I'm sure you have some nice pieces in your collection to choose from."

"Well, okay, then. I'll inform everyone."

"Thank you."

"What about gifts?"

"That's not necessary, but if someone wants to get us a little gift, a donation to a soup kitchen would be appreciated." Harley took my arm. "Now, if you'll excuse us, we have a date."

"Have a good evening."

We walked down the stairs. I turned to Harley, "I'd like a brief word with Karen and Susan. I know some of the ladies at church volunteered to be the bride's maids, but I'd like to ask them too."

"Go ahead. I'll hang out near the dresses." He laughed.

I walked over to them. "Karen, Susan, can I speak with you?"

They came over. "Susan, I know you're married, but I'd like it if you were my Matron of Honor. My sister is going to be my Matron of the Bride. I know, it's different from most weddings."

"It would be an honor. Congratulations, Mari." Susan said.

"Thanks. Karen, will you be a bride's maid?"

"I'd love too!" she squealed.

"Okay, we'll need to find some time to do fittings. I've picked out the dresses. I think you'll both like them."

I motioned to Harley. He came and stood beside me. "This is my fiancé, Harlan Davis of Davis Enterprises. Harley, this is Susan and Karen."

Harley took the hand of each in turn and planted a chaste kiss on the back. "Pleased to meet you lovely ladies."

"Oh my!" They fanned their faces with their hands.

From the way they swooned, I thought I was going to have two fainting women on my hands.

As we walked to the car, Harley snickered. "Have much drama around here?"

"You don't know the half of it," I said.

The movie was less entertaining than my co-workers, but we still had a good time.

Chapter Thirty-One

Harley

July

With all the excitement of the upcoming baptism tonight, I came across an advertisement for a lodge in Arizona. The advertisement specified condors could be seen from the property which abutted canyons. I want to see these majestic birds fly.

"Hey, Mari?" I called when she entered the living room.

"I'll be ready in fifteen minutes," she said, heading toward the stairs.

"I want to ask you something."

"What is it?" She came over to me.

"See this lodge?" I pointed to it in the magazine spread.

"It's lovely."

"How about after the wedding reception, we fly there and spend a couple of days?"

"That'd be nice. I'd like that."

"I'll make reservations." I stood and walked to the foyer.

Mari ran upstairs. After a few minutes, she came back down carrying a small bag. "Towel, change of clothes, and stuff," she said. "I'm ready." She sounded nervous.

"Garrett?" I called out.

"Yes, Master Harley?" He entered the room wiping his hands on a kitchen towel.

'We're ready to go." Turning to Mari, I said, "You'll do fine. A piece of cake." I took her bag and slung it over my shoulder.

"Very good. Let me put the towel up, and I'll bring the Mercedes around." Garrett said and walked back down the hall.

"I am nervous." She smoothed her dress. "Who am I kidding. I'm scared I'll do something wrong and shame or embarrass you."

"That won't happen, love." I held the door open for her.

We stood side by side waiting for Garrett to bring the car around. When he did, he hopped out and held the back-seat door open for us.

###

Mari

When we arrived, the missionaries and my sister were waiting. I hugged each.

"I'm so glad you could join us," I said to Dee. "Where's Frank?"

"He had to work."

Harley ushered us into the Baptism room. There was a table for refreshments. Chairs had been set up in rows. At the front of the room, a podium had been placed to the left of the baptism font. Members were already mingling.

Soft music was playing. The song was 'All Creatures of our God and King.' A member of the priesthood stepped to the podium and said a prayer. He then talked about how baptism is the symbolic death of sinful life. The person being baptized is reborn to spiritual life and the service of God and his children. By being baptized, it is the symbol of death and resurrection.

The congregation then sang hymns while I was led to the changing room. I removed all my clothing except my white undergarments and put on a white jumpsuit. Once I was attired properly, I was led from the changing room to a set of narrow stairs leading to the baptismal font. Members of the priesthood stood ready to assist me into the water.

"Mari, having been commissioned of Jesus Christ, I baptize you in the name of the Father, and of the son, and of the Holy Ghost. Amen."

I was then lowered into the water. Every part of my body had to be immersed. If any part remained above water, the process would have to be done again.

"It's cold!" I sputtered upon being raised back up. The witnesses affirmed the immersion was complete and I was helped out of the font and up the steps. I returned to the changing room. After drying off and changing into dry underwear and my clothing,

I went back to the baptism room. Once again, music was playing softly.

"Congratulations!" The missionaries clustered around me, hugging me.

"How does it feel?" Sheila asked. "Do you feel cleansed?"

I paused. I did feel clean, not externally, but from within. "Why, yes. Yes, I do!" My voice was full of wonder.

Dee smiled. "I'm happy for you, Sis." She hugged me. "You'll have to tell me what it's like to be Mormon."

"Thanks, Dee."

Harley brought over two plates filled with finger sandwiches, fruit, and cookies. He handed one to each of us before returning to the table for his own.

"Congratulations, Miss Mari," Garrett said.

"Thank you. Dee, this is Garrett, Harley's father."

"Pleased to meet you, lass." Garrett nibbled a sandwich. "I'm his honorary adopted father."

"Piffle. You're more Harley's father to him than his biological one."

"Mari's right, Garrett. Adopted or not, honorary or not, I consider you to be my father." Harley said from behind him.

"Dee, the young man is Harlan Davis."

"I know who he is. Any relation to the Harlan Davis of Davis Motors?"

"I own the company," Harley replied. "Pleased to make your acquaintance again. I believe we met at WOSL," he leaned forward and whispered, "beer blast in '75."

"How does Mari know you?"

"We met at the Ohio State University-Lima campus. I'm her fiancé."

"Fiancé?"

"Yes," I quickly chimed in. "I want to ask you to be one of my Matrons of Honor, my Matron of the Bride if you will."

"I'd love to." She hooked her arm through mine. "Boy, Mari, when you pull a shocker, you sure go all out. Will Mom and Dad be able to come? I mean, they did just move to Texas."

"Harley is flying them in on Friday."

"Where's your engagement ring?"

Harley suddenly patted his pockets. "Right here." He pulled it out and put it on my finger.

I held my hand out to Dee. "It's black Opal with a custom designed band."

"It is gorgeous." She looked at me. "Hey, it matches your butterfly necklace."

"Harley gave me that too." I gazed adoringly at him.

"Don't eat too much. We're all going to dinner." Harley said as he nodded to Garrett.

Harley announced dinner invitations to his favorite Chinese restaurant. The crowd was thinning, so we said goodbye. By the time we got to the entrance, Garrett had the car waiting for us. He seated Dee in front.

Dinner was great. A number of the congregation joined us. We had fun talking about our baptismal experiences and getting to know each other.

"If I were ten years younger, I'd have made a play for your Harley," Sheila whispered. "I now see I wouldn't have made the cut. You have him all sewn up," she laughed.

"Yeah, I chased after her so hard until she caught me," Harley chuckled.

After dinner, we dropped Dee by her car and followed her home. Harley wanted to make sure she got there safely. That's my fiancé, always looking out for others.

Chapter Thirty-Two

Mari

July

"Is Frank the guy that used to work in the storeroom in the lady's department at K-Mart?" Harley tapped his finger on the end table.

"Yes. Why?" I asked as I accepted a cup of ginger tisane from Garrett.

"I never cared much for him."

"Why? I used to have a crush on him." I sipped the tea. "This is perfect, Garrett. Thank you."

"You're welcome, Miss Mari." Garrett perched on the sofa.

"I don't know." Harley reached for a scone. "There's just something about him I don't trust. I think he's going to break your sister's heart someday." He stretched and yawned. "Almost time for me to go to bed."

I suddenly felt very tired. I guess it was all the nervousness and excitement of the day that wore me out. "I think…" I stopped in mid-sentence as I saw Harley rubbing his calf. "What's wrong?" Fear gripped me like an iron fist.

"Hmm…? Oh, nothing. I just had an itch."

"Are you sure?" Try as I might, I could not keep the fear out of my voice. Chills ran down my spine.

"Relax, Mari. It was just itchy." Harley stopped scratching and stretched again.

I looked over at Garrett. He was scrutinizing Harley. "I believe he's okay, Miss Mari."

Relief flooded me." Thank Heavenly Father."

"You worry too much," Harley grumbled. "It's off to bed for me."

"Good night, my love," I kissed him.

I wrapped him in a hug and didn't want to let go of him; ever. I wished we could stay entwined in each other's arms for eternity.

According to our church's teachings, if we marry in the temple, we will be sealed forever.

###

Harley

July

Mari had to work this evening. Normally, tonight would have been date night. She and Flash met up and went shopping for the picnic. I was a little jealous. I wanted to go with them, but I had a physical therapy session this afternoon.

"Master Harley? Your therapist is here." Garrett announced.

"That's fine, Garrett. Please show him in."

"Hello, Mister Davis." Steve, my physical therapist, was a large muscular man. He looked like a jug-head with his blond crew cut.

"Hello, Steve. Are we going to the exercise room or the pool?"

"We're going to do both. Let's start in the exercise room with leg lifts." He pulled out a device and checked my blood pressure and pulse. "Very good." He put it back into his bag and stood up.

He followed me down the hall and around the corner to the end where my exercise room waited.

"Leg lifts," I sighed.

Leg lifts were followed by leg crunches and then the exercise bicycle.

"Doing good, Mister Davis. How about trying the treadmill? We'll go at the slowest pace." Steve complimented me.

"Okay." I climbed off the bike and went to the treadmill. Steve was true to his word. He set it to the lowest setting and flat with no incline. After ten minutes I was drenched in sweat.

"Time for a few laps in the pool. How are you feeling?"

"Like I've had a workout. I used to be able to do these with ease." I draped a towel around my shoulders and headed to my locker room.

'You will again. You're really regaining ground rapidly." Steve followed me and changed into his swim trunks.

Together, we headed outside to the pool. The water was refreshingly cool to my hot body. I began swimming laps with Steve sitting on the edge in case I got into trouble. I dove a few times. My body sluiced through the water easily. I love swimming.

We spent an hour in the pool and then got out. Garrett brought snacks and beverages to us.

"Thank you, Garrett."

"Protein packed. Good choices. Mister Davis needs to eat high protein to help rebuild his muscles," said Steve.

We consumed the treats and then went inside to shower and change.

"Keep this up, and you won't need me by the time your wedding day arrives."

"You are coming to the wedding, right?"

"I wouldn't miss it. See you next time, Mister Davis."

"Be safe, Steve."

Fifteen minutes later, Mari and Flash rushed in carrying bags of groceries. Both Garrett and I hurried to help them.

"I've got to get to work!" Mari grabbed her smock.

"I'll take you." I grabbed both jackets and helmets. "Flash, put your things in a guest room tonight. Tomorrow, we'll move you. Unfortunately, with the number of people staying this weekend, I can't give you a private room."

"I understand. We'll sort it out later."

###

Mari

July

The next couple of days were crazy. Flash spent all his time in the kitchen preparing dish after dish of mouthwatering food. Thankfully Harley had restaurant sized freezers and refrigerators to store not only the food for the picnic but also our meals leading up to the gathering.

The WOSL gang arrived Friday and were pressed into picking up people at the Dayton airport. I think they were in heaven driving Harley's vehicles. Garrett drove the limousine to ferry Keisha, Jamal, George, and Evangeline home. Thomas drove the Bentley with Jimmie and Tyrone, while Peg had the Mercedes with Chantal and Laila.

Hixson and Mike were in charge of pumping up the air mattresses, checking them for leaks and going to get two more. Harley gave them cash and the use of the minibus.

Lori and Judy assisted Flash in the kitchen. Harley was told to sit back and relax. I ferried snacks out to him and kept him company. We talked a lot about our upcoming nuptials and honeymoon. Professor Schmidt arrived carrying potted plants.

"I thought these would make nice table decorations." He placed them on the patio.

"Thank you," Harley said.

"They're beautiful," I exclaimed. The blooms were a riot of colors, blue, pink, red, yellow, purple, and white.

"Congratulations on your upcoming nuptials. I am planning to attend." Turning to Harley, "I would never have guessed you are Mormon. Maybe, I should think about joining."

"You'd have to keep it in your pants," I blurted much to my horror and embarrassment.

"Chastity, huh? Maybe not, then," he laughed.

"I am so sorry." My face must have been bright red because it certainly felt like it was on fire.

"No harm, Mari. I'll see you tomorrow. Good to see you back among the living, Harley."

"Good to be back, Professor." Harley walked with him to the door.

A few minutes later Hixson and Mike came in with two additional air mattresses. They took them to the laundry room and began the process of pumping air into the six of them.

A half hour went by before the airport vehicles arrived. Shauntelle's kids tumbled from the cars. Jimmy, Chantal, Tyrone, and Laila stared at the house.

"You live here?" Jimmy croaked.

"I see Lake George has been good for you," Harley held him at arm's length and turned him around. "You've grown into a handsome young man."

"Thanks," he grinned and shuffled his feet.

"It's so good to see you, Mister Harlan!" Evangeline hugged him. "We were all heartbroken when we heard youse was dead."

"Stories of my demise were exaggerated. As you can see, here I am hale and hearty."

"Hey, what about us?" Jamal guffawed.

"Jamal! Keisha! So good to see you both." Harley motioned me forward. "I'd like you to meet my fiancée, Mari."

"Hi," I said shyly. "Harley has regaled me with stories of your adventures traveling with him," I said to Jamal and Keisha. "And with tales of how he tormented you at the lodge when he was young." I faced George and Evangeline. "It's so wonderful to finally put faces to his stories."

I picked up one suitcase. It was quite heavy. "If you'll follow me, I'll show you to your rooms."

I headed down the hall. Flash came out of the kitchen. "I vacated my room. Garrett changed the sheets."

"Thank you, Flash. George, Evangeline, Jamal and Keisha, I'd like you to meet Flash, disc-jockey, and chef extraordinaire. He's prepared all our meals and the food for the picnic. You are in for a treat."

"I made some Jamaican and Cajun dishes for tonight's meal. I'm sure they're not as good as you're used to." Flash smiled.

"Don't sell yourself short, Flash."

"Flash. What an unusual name." Keisha commented.

"Better than being called Fletcher, I think," he replied as he returned to the kitchen.

We turned the corner. I showed our guests the music room and the library. "Feel free to select any reading material you want. Just return it where you got it when you're done." I said as we headed to the elevator. On the second floor, I showed them their rooms. "Someone will bring the rest of your suitcases in a few minutes."

"Where will my kids sleep?" Shauntelle asked.

"On air mattresses in the game room."

"He has a game room?"

"Technically, it's a family room. Harley turned it into a game room with board games, checkers, chess, pinball, and pachinko machines," I replied.

"Really? They will like that." Shauntelle said. "I just hope they won't stay up all night."

"What time do they normally go to bed?" I asked.

"Laila goes to bed at nine. Tyrone at ten. Jimmy and Chantal at eleven."

"Okay, how about Garrett turns off the machines at nine. And for this weekend everyone goes to bed at ten?" I suggested.

"That sounds reasonable."

###

Harley

Dinner that night was a festive affair. Flash had prepared a delectable assortment of food. We had Jerk Chicken, Jamaican Beef Patties, Red Pea Soup made with salted beef, shrimp étouffée, Jambalaya, Boudin, Macque Choux made with corn, bell pepper, and onion braised in stock and seasonings, Dirty Rice, and a variety of fruits and vegetables.

"This is really good," said Keisha as she sampled the beef patties. "Reminds me of home."

"The boudin is excellent," Evangeline said as a smile crept across her face. "Hats off to the chef."

"Thank you," Flash reddened at the compliment. It was the first time I ever saw him blush. "It's not too hot or too bland, is it?"

"I think it's just right," Mari said as she dug into the étouffée.

###

Harley

After dinner the kids, Peg, March, Hixson, Lori, Judy, and Mike went to the game room. Maryanne went to the library, while

Flash, Thomas, Garrett, Mari and I sat with our guests in the living room. Every fifteen or so minutes Flash would get up and go check on the items baking in the oven.

"What are you baking?" Mari asked.

"Let's see…chocolate chip, oatmeal raisin, peanut butter, macaroons, and macadamia chocolate cookies. Walnut Bundt, lemon, strawberry cream, chocolate cream, marble cinnamon swirl cakes. Pecan, shoofly, sugar cream, chocolate cream, peach meringue, apple, cherry, sweet potato, and chestnut pies."

"Wow!" March rubbed his hands in anticipation. "That's some list."

"Where'd you learn to cook, Flash?" Shauntelle asked. "If all your meals are like tonight's, you can come work at my restaurant in Lake George."

I lowered my hand and waggled my fingers to tell her to back off on that idea.

"I think Harley has a secret," Mari laughed.

I shut my eyes and groaned. I just knew everyone except Mari was staring at me. I opened my eyes and saw I was correct.

"You're keeping secrets from us?" Thomas winked at me.

"Not you guys, just Flash." I turned toward Flash. "No worries, it's not bad. I was going to wait until after the picnic, but with tonight's dinner being so delish, I might as well bring it up now. I understand you would like to eventually open your own restaurant. Am I correct?"

"Yes," Flash said warily.

"How about I say pick a location, and I'll fund your restaurant as a silent partner. I will, naturally, receive a portion of the profit. I will offer business guidance, accounting services, and access to my attorneys. While the restaurant will be solely yours, it will be under my umbrella, Davis Enterprises."

"You'd do that for me?"

"You earned it. We can discuss the details of the contract after the picnic. Does that sound like something you'd be interested in?"

"Yes!" Flash leaped up and punched the air with his fist. "But, I also want to work in radio."

"Why not do both? Work in radio part-time and the restaurant full-time."

"All right!"

All too soon it was time to go to bed for all of us except Garrett and Flash.

"We're just going to finish the last round of baking. Flash requested an air mattress be set up in the music room for him." Garrett said.

"On it." Hixson and Mike entered the living room toting two mattresses to be placed in the game room.

"Maryanne asked if she could have a mattress in the library. That leaves two for the living room."

A quick calculation in my head indicated everyone would have a place to sleep. March and Thomas would sleep on the sofas. While Lori and Hixson will share one mattress and Judy and Mike the other. I didn't like it since I practice the law of chastity. At least there wouldn't be any hanky-panky going on with Thomas and March sleeping in the same room.

"Wait up, I'll walk you ladies to your room." I rose and hooked an arm around Mari and Peg.

As we walked to the elevator, I overheard Peg say, "Man, Mari. Your Harley is a keeper. He puts everyone else to shame. What I wouldn't give to have someone like him."

"Don't sell Thomas short. He's pretty cool too. I am so lucky to have Harley in my life. I don't know what I'd do if I ever lost him."

I smiled. At the door to their room, I pulled Mari into my arms for a long, lingering goodnight kiss.

Chapter Thirty-Three

Mari

July

I closed the door and sat on the mattress. I couldn't believe I was going to sleep in Harley's bed. In a few weeks, it will become our bed, and I'd get to sleep surrounded by his scent. When I looked up, I saw Peg staring at me. "What's wrong?"

"Nothing," Peg said as she changed into pajamas. "It's just kind of weird for me to sleep in here. I mean, this is Harley's bed, and soon it'll be yours too. I think I'll join Maryanne in the Library."

Just then, Maryanne rapped on the door and came in. "What about the library and me?"

"I was just telling Mari, I'm going to join you in the library. That way Mari can have the soon to be wedding night bed all to herself." Peg winked at me.

"Oh!" Maryanne turned a princess shade of pink and giggled. She grabbed her sleepwear and hurried into the bathroom. Seconds later, she dashed out. "That's his bathroom…with his stuff in there," she gasped.

"No duh!" Peg chided. "Hurry up and get changed in here."

After they left, I dressed for bed and climbed under the sheets. Harley's unique, intoxicating scent of Old Spice, cinnamon and bay leaves with a hint of pine, and Irish Spring engulfed me. I snuggled with the pillow and burrowed myself in the soft downy comforter. It was luxurious.

###

Harley

The day of the picnic started with an early breakfast followed by setting up tables and chairs. Plastic tablecloths and decorative plants were put in order. Serving dishes and warmers, plastic ware, paper plates, and cups were put on the food tables. Everyone scurried around to make certain all was ready before eleven o'clock.

I felt perturbed at everyone trying to enforce me sitting back and watching instead of participating. I was throwing the picnic. I should be allowed to help set it up.

"Sit down, Harley," Mari said as she gently pressed me back down onto the lounge chair.

"I do not want to sit around doing nothing." I stood, and Mari tried to coax me back down. "MARI! STOP! IT!" I bellowed. "EVERYONE STOP TREATING ME LIKE AN INVALID." I glared at each person.

Mari dropped my arm like it was burning her. She stepped back, turned and ran inside. "Oh jeez," I muttered. "Way to go Harley. Make your fiancée cry." I ran after her, leaving a group of people stunned into silence.

"Mari!" I hurried after her, triggering a leg spasm. "Mari!" I hobbled along inside looking for her. I found her in the music room. "Mari." I approached her.

She swung around to face me. Tears streaked her face. "Ah, Mari." I reached out to wipe the wetness away with my fingers.

"Don't you 'Ah Mari,' me, Harlan Christian Robert Davis!"

Ouch, I winced. Mari used my full name. That couldn't possibly be good. She was holding my Bartók album like she might throw it at me. I sure hope not.

"Don't. You. Ever. Blow. Up. At. Me. Or. Talk. To. Me. In. Public. Like. That. Again." She set the record back in its place. "I'm not a child or property. I'm your fiancée. Your partner."

"I'm sorry. I'll remember and not do that again. I was just frustrated at being treated like some helpless person."

"No one thinks you're helpless, Harley. Don't you know, those people are your friends? We all care about you. We're just looking out for you." She placed her hands on my shoulders.

"I know," I sighed. "I never had many true friends when I was a child. Everyone wanted to be my friend because I was rich."

"Not here, bucko. Has anyone asked you for money?"

"No," I shuffled my feet. "I guess I owe everyone an apology. I'm sorry, Mari."

"I accept your apology, Harley. Now, let's go outside and get this over with."

Just as we headed toward the patio, the doorbell rang.

###

Mari

"You go on. I'll get the door." I hurried into the foyer. I opened the door.

"Dee! I'm so glad you and Frank could make it." I hugged my sister.

"I brought a millionaire pie," Dee said.

"Thank you!" I took a whiff. "Smells great." I took the box from her. "Let me put it out on the dessert table and then I'll show you around."

As I came back inside, I overheard Frank saying, "I feel underdressed, Dee. Maybe we should make our excuses and leave."

"Nonsense. Mari said it was a picnic and to dress casually."

"But, look at the trappings of this house. I bet they have a swimming pool."

"We do have a pool. Dee, did you bring a swimsuit?'

"I did, he didn't."

"And we have a hot tub and a gazebo. Come on, let me show you the house." To your left is the living room, to the right is the family or game room. Straight ahead is a sunroom and an exit to the patio. The stairs lead to the second-floor bedrooms. We won't go there. Turning down this hall to our right is a coat closet and past that is a full bathroom with changing room and shower. To the left is our formal dining room that can double as a ballroom."

"See?" Frank whispered loudly. "A ballroom. Way out of our league, babe."

"Actually, Harley doesn't see people by their wealth or social standing. He doesn't care if you're rich, middle-class, poor, black, white, oriental or any other race," I said. "Continuing onward straight ahead is the kitchen and breakfast nook."

"Wow! It's big enough to cook for a restaurant," Dee exclaimed.

"The room next to the kitchen is the laundry room." We turned another corner. "To your left is the music room." I paused as they looked inside.

"Who plays the piano?"

"Harley does. He plays both the piano and the violin." I walked onward. "The next room is the library."

"Mari! You could spend a lifetime in here. Is that a writing desk?"

"Yes, it is. The next room, we won't look in. It's Harley's home office. Next to the office is the exercise and locker room. At the end of the hall is the elevator."

"Is the artwork on the walls originals?" Frank asked.

"Yes. Some are pieces Harley and Garrett have collected over the years. The rest were done by local artists."

"This house is fabulous. I'm so happy for you, Mari!" Dee hugged me.

Outside, I introduced them to the other guests. Frank introduced himself to Harley. Soon the yard was filled with the staff and their families from Harley's companies. As Flash, Lori, Judy, and Peg worked on food preparation and placement, Harley stood and gave an opening speech.

###

Harley

"First, let me welcome everyone, employees and friends. I am so blessed to have each of you in my life. As most of you know, this past year has been a rough one for me, but I survived. I am so proud of my employees for doing a superior job keeping my companies growing. To that end, I have bonuses and shares in my company to distribute. As I call each name, please come forward. The faster we can do this the quicker we can get to the eating and games. The pool is open to everyone. Children must be supervised and please, do not run near the pool. The hot tub is restricted to adults without a medical condition. The games are for everyone. Garrett, please bring the envelopes." With Garrett handing me each envelope, I proceeded to pass out sizeable bonuses and corporate shares to everyone.

"Keisha, Jamal, and Shauntelle, you now own ninety percent of your businesses." I handed them the legal documents decreeing transfer of ownership with me keeping a minority share of ten percent. I also handed each of them bonus checks for all their employees. Davis Enterprises now employed over five hundred in two states. "Is Stuart's family here?"

"I believe so," Garrett said quietly.

"May Ling, please come forward."

"Yes, Mister Davis?"

"I'm glad your family joined us. I think of Stuart every day. May Ling, you are forever a part of Davis Motors. That being so, I am bequeathing upon you the same bonus and shares as the other employees. Please accept this on Stuart's behalf and know that I have always held him, and will continue to do so, in the highest regards." I handed her an envelope.

"Mister Davis, you no need do this. You already take care of us."

"Hush," I placed a finger to my lips. "A simple Cám ơn, or thank you is fine."

"Cám ơn," she said.

"Không có gì, you're welcome," I replied and hugged her. As she returned to her seat, I pulled out the last envelope. "Flash, please step over here."

"I have the food…"

"This won't take but a moment." I beckoned him over. "Remember what we discussed last night?"

"Yes."

"Here is the contract. Take your time to read it thoroughly. We can discuss and modify the terms when you're ready. There's no rush."

"Tha…thanks," Flash took the legal document with trembling hands and ran inside to put it with his belongings.

"Food's ready," Flash yelled as he returned, bringing out the last dish.

People lined up at the various tables. Plates were piled high. Tyrone was busy at the dessert table.

"Tyrone," I said, "you need to eat a meal before dessert." I took his dessert plate over to where Shauntelle was sitting. "I told Tyrone, he could have dessert after lunch."

"Thank you. These ribs are really good."

"Thank Flash."

Keisha came over and sat down. "Are your employees really veterans?"

"All but a few. Two from my original business in Sagaponack aren't. The rest are. They gave so much to our country. It's time we give back to them."

"That's very honorable."

"Honor has nothing to do with it. It's the right thing to do." I smiled." Now, if you'll excuse me, I need to find Mari."

Mari was carrying a tray laden with food. "Your fiancée is sweet," Evangeline said. "She insisted on bringing us plates."

"And our drinks," George chimed in. "Is it true? Did you chase after her cross country?"

"Sort of," I told them about seeing a vision of her in the hospital after I wrecked my hog in Sagaponack, catching a glimpse of her at the Atlanta Pop Festival which turned out to be another mirage. I told them about the encounters at the Lloyd Center in Portland, Oregon, the café in Chehalis, Washington, the Vintage car ride at the Seattle Space Needle, and the Rink's Department store in Lima, Ohio.

"All those before you really met her in college?" Evangeline sounded incredulous.

"Yep. It was Karma or Destiny. I'm firmly convinced we are meant to be together."

March came up. "Some of us are going swimming. Do any of the kids want to join us? I'm a certified lifeguard if that helps."

"So is Steve," I said. "Looks like he's headed for the pool."

"I wanna go," Laila squealed.

"Me too!" Jimmy chimed in.

"And me!" said Tyrone.

Hixson came by. "We're going to play some of those games. Looks like we're going to have two football teams, four tennis matches, two soccer, and a baseball game. Sure, glad you have a giant yard, Harley. You going to join us?"

"Not now. Might go for a swim later," I said. I swiveled my chair around so I could watch the activities.

The afternoon flew by, and all too soon the picnic came to an end. My employees assured me they had a wonderful time and I announced there would be a Christmas party in December. Everyone was sent home with containers of food enough to feed each family for several days.

Flash had prepared another feast for dinner. He served us a mouthwatering meal of fry bread with red chili, squash, and corn. The rest of the evening was spent playing games and talking.

"So, Mari, what did you think of our Harley when you finally officially met him?" Keisha asked.

"Honestly?" Mari grinned. "I thought he was bad news. I mean, here he was wearing jeans, boots, a leather jacket with chains and he said he didn't bite much."

"What?" Jamal burst out laughing. A spurt of his herbal tea shot from his nose.

"Then he asked me out and wouldn't take no for an answer."

"That I did," I smiled and reached for her hand.

"The date turned in to an overnight visit to Battle Ground, Indiana. We went to Wolf Park and Clegg Gardens. Do you know, he probably knew everyone in every single restaurant there?" Mari asked.

"I'm not surprised," George spoke up. "That boy can sure eat."

"You're telling me," Mari said. "If I ate like he does, I'd weigh four hundred pounds." She turned to me and grinned. "That weekend date sealed my fate. I think I got the best end of the deal." She stared at me with adoration. "Who could ask for a more kind, protective, generous, caring, patient, gentleman than Harley?"

I felt my face turning a brilliant shade of scarlet. "Don't forget, I bite," I growled to the amusement of everyone in the living room.

"According to you, not much," Mari retorted.

"Oh my!" Evangeline laughed. "Sure good to see young people in love."

"You said it," Jamal said. "We plan to attend the wedding."

"So, do Evangeline and me," George commented.

"Count the kids and me in," Shauntelle reached for one of Flash's brownies.

"The WOSL gang are planning to be there too," Flash chimed in.

Peg, Thomas, and Mike promised to drive George, Evangeline, Shauntelle, and kids to the airport. Lori and Judy volunteered to put the air mattresses away and straighten the house up while Garrett, Mari, and I went to church. I was a bit uneasy allowing them to remain in my home when neither Garrett, Mari, nor myself was there but decided I was being overly cautious and needed to trust them.

Thus, the perfect weekend ended. I was surrounded by my loved ones and good friends. Life is good.

Chapter Thirty-Four

Mari

August

If I thought the week leading up to my baptism and the company picnic was hectic, it was a piece of cake, or as Thomas would say, a piece of pie. It was nothing compared to the month before the wedding. To handle everything, I wound up quitting my job at K-Mart.

"Hi, Polly," I said as I walked into her office. "May I speak with you?"

"What is it now, Mari? Need more time off?" Polly swiveled around in her chair to face me. She was painting her fingernails dark red as an accent to her tiny black dress.

"Not exactly," I hesitated and sucked in a deep breath before plunging on. "I have to quit."

"Quit?! But, you just started back last month!" Polly sputtered.

"I know. I'm really sorry. It's just with the wedding and honeymoon planning, plus learning…"

"When?" Polly snapped.

"Today is my last day. I know it's really short notice, but…"

"Short notice?" Polly snorted, "Try no notice. This leaves me in a bind. You will have to forfeit your vacation pay."

"She'll do no such thing," Harley's voice boomed, making both Polly and me jump. I had no idea he had followed me here.

"She will."

"If your corporate policy provides part-time employees vacation time, then you are obligated to pay them for their unused hours. Unless the policy has an exclusion clause, which I doubt it does."

"But…but…"

"No buts. Is there an exclusion clause or not?" Harley demanded.

"No."

"Then, I expect Mari to be paid for all time due her. Do I make myself clear, Polly Workman?"

"She can leave right now. I'll have her check next Wednesday."

"Wrong." Harley had his hands on his hips. He looked every inch like a rough, tough biker with his leather bomber jacket.

"The law dictates you must pay an employee within thirty-six hours of their last working day," he growled.

If I didn't know better I would have been concerned Harley might bite Polly Workman.

"What would you know about it?" Polly snorted.

Harley choked out a laugh. "What would I know?" He winked at me. "I happen to employ over five-hundred people."

"You?" She gulped.

"Yes. How many work here under you? Fifty?"

"Less." She hung her head. "I'll write out a check right now. Naturally, I must withhold taxes."

"I wouldn't expect any less." He hooked his arm around me, "C'mon, we'll wait outside her office."

A few minutes later she came out with a check."

"Are we still invited to the wedding?" Polly asked with a meekness unlike herself.

"Of course," I said and glanced at Harley. He nodded in agreement.

Harley put me on his payroll as a manager trainee. Learning the corporate structure and operations of Davis Enterprises was a shock.

Never in my life would I have guessed how much effort he put into it. I knew he attended a lot of meetings with clients and staff. How he managed to have the time to take classes and date me, I'll never know.

What I did come to appreciate was his need to ride his Hog. He explained it as being free of everything except the ride. It helped him clear his head and enjoy the call of the open road.

"Mari," Harley said quietly as he prepared to ride. "The open road calls me. It's like a balm to my soul. While riding, there's just me, the road, and my Hog. It's freedom."

"From responsibility?" I asked.

"In a manner, yes."

"From me?" My heart felt heavy.

"No, Mari, never from you. My love, you are the other that can soothe the devil in me." Harley pulled me into his arms.

He ran one hand through my hair while his other held me close. "I might answer the call of the road, the wind, and solitude, but I'll always come back to you." He caressed my cheek.

"Don't you know by now; my home is just a place to rest my physical body? It's a sanctuary. But, you, Mari, is where my soul is at peace," he murmured, kissing me lightly.

"In your arms is where I will always belong. Even when I'm gone, if you need me, I will know, and I'll come right back to you." His words of endearment put a soothing balm on my heart.

"Okay," I sniffled. I'm not much for crying, but Harley always seemed to bring out the tears in me, and the laughter, love, and joy. "Go on. Please be careful."

"Always my love. I won't be gone long. Until then, I leave you in the capable hands of Edward. He'll guide you through the meeting with my accountants and lawyers."

"Accountants? Lawyers?" I gulped. "As in plural? More than one?" I could feel the panic setting in. I was not good at anything having to do with mathematics."

"Yes," he chuckled. "I have a team coming in to go over the books and explain the entire system to you. It is more than just paying the bills. It's payroll, accounts receivables, payables, corporate and employee taxes, benefits, and much more."

My head felt like it was spinning.

"Time to get your feet wet, Mari," he smiled and laughed.

"I know," I sighed. Disappointment welled up inside, and it was hard to keep it out of my voice.

"What is it, my love?" Harley gently cupped my chin.

"It's just," I hiccupped. "I miss riding behind you, holding onto your body. It's been a long time."

Harley glanced down at his watch. "How about a short ride. Can I drop you off at your sister's?"

"I'll check." I ran into the house.

I came running back a few minutes later carrying a bag with my business suit, and my helmet. "She said yes."

"Will she drop you off at Davis Enterprises around twelve-thirty?"

"I'm pretty sure she will. We're going to have an early lunch. Then she can drop me off before she runs errands and picks up Frank from work."

I climbed onto the Hog and put my helmet on. I placed my feet like he had shown me when I first rode with him.

Harley jump-started the motorcycle. My arms circled around his torso and I lightly rested my cheek against his back. That old familiar feeling felt so good.

I inhaled his scent like I couldn't get enough. I never grew tired of smelling, or holding him. It was like coming home. Harley made me feel safe, secure, beautiful, and most of all loved. What middle-class girl like me could ask for more?

In no time we pulled up to my sister's home. Dee came out. "You ready?" she asked me as Harley wheeled around and took off down the road.

"Yes."

"Where do you want to go eat? I'm hungry." She unlocked the doors to her car.

"How about the Ponderosa?" I folded myself into the passenger seat. How Frank ever got into this tin can, I didn't know. I'm only five-foot six-inches, and he was at least six feet tall.

"Why do you have to be at his office by twelve-thirty?" Dee casually glanced in the mirror.

With her dark brown hair and slightly olive complexion, she got the beauty and the brains genes.

Me? I got the creative ones, writing, sketching, and photography.

Dee was naturally graceful while I always felt inept at best. Maybe that's why I tormented her.

"Earth to Mari. Come in Mari," Dee nudged me.

"Huh?" I snapped out of my introspection

"We're here."

"Okay," I laughed. "Lunch is on me."

###

Harley

Seeing Mari look so happy as she approached my bike made me re-think my assessment not to teach her how to ride. I could tell, it was now in her blood much like it was in mine. Between now and our wedding, I vowed to teach her how to properly and safely ride a motorcycle and help her get her license.

She's much smaller than I am so, I'd have to get her a Harley-Davidson that would fit her. After dropping her off, I swung by my shop in Delphos.

"Mister Davis," Edward greeted, "Always a pleasure to see you."

"I see you're making the rounds before the meeting at our home office."

"Yes, sir."

"Mari will be attending the meeting. As my Vice President of Operations, I expect you to show her the ropes."

"It'd be an honor."

"Now, I want to discuss something personal. I'd like to get Mari a Hog like mine, only smaller in terms of length, but keeping with the same or close to the same size engine and gas tank. Think you can do it? It needs to be ready before the wedding."

"Absolutely. You can count on me." Edward turned and gave instructions to Adams about the new bike.

"Thanks, man." I clapped him on the back. "It's my wedding present to her."

"Any time, Mister Davis."

There are no words that can adequately express how a biker feels riding. There's just me, the open road, and my Hog. Freedom.

How sweet it feels.

The road is like a river flowing on forever through countryside, towns, and eventually to the oceans if you ride long enough.

Sometimes you ride alone, others you come across a fellow biker and travel together.

The one thing you can count on is the brotherhood of bikers. If you belong to a club, your allegiance is to the members and affiliated groups.

If you're a loner, like me, you are still part of the brotherhood. Bikers have a creed that is basically a moral code of conduct.

Your word is your bond so keep your word at all times.

If you give respect, you get it in return.

Never mistake kindness for weakness.

Do not leave other riders stranded by the side of the road. If they see you pulled over, they will stop and ask how they can help.

They will defend their right to live the 'biker's lifestyle,' so do not try to change them.

Most bikers are law-abiding. Only a tiny minority are outlaws, also known as one-percenter because ninety-nine percent are your average rider and the remaining one percent live outside the law.

It's like all motorcyclists are family. Family that you get to choose.

Kuttes or Cuts as they are called are worn because they protect your skin, and keep your core body temperature warm, but also are more visible.

The idea, to my thinking, is visibility is important. The more visible you are to a cager, a car driver, the less likely they will accidentally hit you.

Still, a dark colored one does little to improve your visibility. I usually wear a black or brown Kutte. I like the vintage aviator look.

The insignia on the back is usually, but not always, colorful. The name of the club and jurisdiction are depicted in what is known as colors.

I have two Kuttes. I have one that I wear when riding for myself. The top rocker on the back says Davis and the bottom rocker says Ohio. The one I wear for business says Davis Motors on the top and USA on the bottom.

Ever since there were motorcycles, there were songs about the lure of the open road. One of the most famous is by Steppenwolf, 'Born to be Wild.'

Others made popular in the counterculture include 'Ballad of Easy Rider' by the Byrds and Roger McGuinn, 'Motorcycle Mama' by Sailcat, 'Midnight Rider' by The Allman Brothers, 'Bat Out of Hell' by Meatloaf, and 'Ezy Ryder' by Jimi Hendrix.

I cued these tracks on my helmet headset prototype. I ramped them up loud enough to be enjoyable but not so much that I couldn't hear the traffic approaching me.

The solitude, good music, countryside scenery, and the open road tug at a man's soul. The song of the ride resides in a biker's heart and pulls until he simply must get on his motorcycle and go.

I rode for hours, reveling in the feel of the wind plucking at my jeans and jacket, the whine of the engine's roar, and the freedom of spirit.

###

Mari

All too soon lunch was over. I changed into a dark green business pantsuit. Dee looked askance at me. "Harley has me meeting with Davis Enterprises's accountants," I said.

"Whatever on earth for?" Dee asked.

"He wants me to learn his business." I shrugged, trying to act more nonchalant than I felt. Truthfully, my stomach was doing flip-flops and felt like it was full of butterflies.

"Thanks for lunch," she said as we pulled into the parking space reserved for me.

"I enjoyed it. We'll have to do it again before the wedding."

"That'd be great."

I watched her leave. For several long minutes, I stood in the parking lot lost in thought. Edward came out.

"Not thinking about ditching, are you?"

"Huh?" I blinked. "No. I was just marveling at having my very own reserved parking space. Even has my name on it. Mari Forrester Davis." I pointed.

"I know," Edward chuckled. "C'mon, we'd better get inside before they get here. I have some things to go over with you."

We walked in. Miss Langford greeted me with an ice cold can of Vernors. "Good afternoon Miss Forrester."

"Hello, Miss Langford. Thank you for the soda."

"Please call me Edna." She winked. "My husband teases me when I'm called Miss, don't you Roger?"

Roger was a stout older man charged with keeping the shop and office machines running.

"Yes, dear," he continued tinkering with a control panel on the wall.

"Come along, Miss Mari," Edward gently tugged on my arm. We walked down the hall toward Harley's office. We stopped two rooms before reaching Harley's office. "This is your office. I hope it's to your liking."

Inside the office was a wall-to-wall and floor-to-ceiling cherrywood bookcase that matched a large ornate desk. On the desk were an ink blotter, notebooks, a daily diary also known as a bound day planner embossed with Mari Forrester Davis.

There was a pen and pencil set and a vintage brass desk lamp with a multi-faceted green glass shade.

Behind the desk was a brown leather high backed executive chair. In front of the desk were two matching Captain's chairs and a glass end table between them.

In the far corner were a matching oval management table and chairs for four.

The walls boasted a series of framed modern art. The paintings were tastefully done in golds, browns, and yellows, creating a warm and welcoming environment.

The office looked out over the production floor. I could watch everyone building custom Hogs. In one corner was a door leading into a closet.

On the opposite wall was another door. This one went into the boardroom, which also adjoined Harley's office.

"My office," I said, "it wasn't here the last time I was here. Wasn't it a big storeroom?"

"Yes. We built a storeroom onto the ground floor production area to make your office." He beamed proudly at me. "We did all the work in-house."

"You did?" I was astounded. "Job well done!"

I picked up one of the notebooks and thumbed through it as he explained their contents.

"Each book is an operation manual for a division of Davis Enterprises. The one in your hand is for Davis Motors. There's one for Davis Vintage Car Restoration and Sales, Davis Auto Shop, Jamal Vintage Cars, Just Like Home Lodge, Shauntelle's Kitchen, and Davis Enterprises, the corporate umbrella. There's also a manual being developed for Flash's restaurant," Edward explained.

"Wow! Seven businesses all under Davis Enterprises. Poor Edna!"

Edward laughed. "Edna is Mister Davis's personal secretary, office manager, and in charge of the employment department. She was manning the reception desk while Cynthia took a break.

Cynthia served as a nurse during the Vietnam conflict. On the other side of this building are the secretarial pool and the employment department. They are also all veterans. They served during World War II, the Korean War, or Vietnam."

"What is the percentage of veterans to non-veterans?" I asked. I thought about how hard my Dad had it the first few years after he retired from the Marine Corps.

"Ninety-eight to ninety-nine percent."

"That's really good."

"Now, let's go into the boardroom, shall we?"

The boardroom consisted of a large mahogany table and a dozen Captain's chairs, a sideboard the width of the room, and a blackboard.

An information packet for each expected attendee was placed around the table. All seven businesses were represented.

Flash arrived looking as nervous as I felt. One person came representing the Lake George outfits. Edward was representing the three companies here.

"Who is representing Davis Enterprises?" I asked.

"You are with me assisting," Edward and Edna replied.

I gulped, "I think I'm going to be ill. Then, I'm going to kill Harley for doing this to me."

"Relax, Miss Forrester," Edna laughed.

"If they ask you anything just defer the question to Edward or me. Whatever you do, and that includes you, Fletcher Elliott, if the accountants are silent do not speak unless you are asked a direct question." Edna looked pointedly at each of us.

"Their silence is an old ploy to trap you into saying something that will give them a reason to do an internal audit."

"Please call me Flash."

"Mister or Chef Elliott would be more appropriate," Edna said.

"Now, I'm going to be sick along with Mari," Flash joked weakly.

"Want to join me in clobbering Harley after this meeting?" I asked.

Edna had catered an assortment of finger sandwiches, fresh vegetable, fruit, and cheese trays, soup, Swedish meatballs with gravy, bread, and pastries. Beverages included grape, orange and apple juice, herbal tea both hot and cold, ginger ale, root beer, and water. The other representatives filled their plates and sat down. They talked quietly among themselves.

"Miss Mari, since you are representing Mister Davis, you need to sit at the head of the table. I will sit to your right, and Miss Langford will sit to your left. Flash, you sit next to Miss Langford so she can guide you through this since she knows the ins and outs of your contract."

"Very well," he sighed with relief.

Me, on the other hand, felt like I had a giant bulls-eye painted on my front and back.

As soon as we sat down four men dressed in varying shades of gray suits walked through the door. The accountants were followed by Harley's corporate legal team. Both groups carried themselves with military precision. There was no need to speculate if they were veterans.

Each person helped themselves to the refreshments and settled into their seats. We went around the table introducing ourselves and a little of our history with the corporation.

Edward launched into an overview of the corporate structure. I was certain he did this for Flash and my benefit since the managers and accountants had been with the company for years. Then each manager presented a state of their operation report.

This was followed by the accountants launching into their reports. One handled the restaurants, another the vintage cars and automobile shops, the third did the motorcycle outfit and the last one handled the corporate umbrella.

They also talked about philanthropic endeavors funding charities, hospitals, nursing homes, soup kitchens, environmental efforts, job retraining for disenfranchised people who lost they jobs due to economic downturns, wildlife sanctuary funding, and the list went on endlessly.

The bottom line was a shocker. Even with the economy drifting into recession, if not outright recession, Davis Enterprises was clearing a hefty profit. Through earnings and wise investments, the corporation was still on target to clear a billion dollars in profit by the end of the year.

There was an attorney for each division and the corporation. They numbered eight. Each talked about upcoming employment law changes and the potential impact on the umbrella. A summary of legal briefs filed on behalf of the corporation was discussed. This included a couple of lawsuits, and a few filings seeking punitive damages.

The number of employees working in some part of Davis Enterprises was now well over five-hundred and nearing six-hundred.

I left that meeting with a whole new appreciation for Harley's business acumen. He didn't need a degree in business administration, he could teach it. My bad boy Steppenwolf loving biker was an astutely brilliant man in business dealings.

I always knew he customized motorcycles for law enforcement locally within a tri-state area. I never guessed his reach was from coast to coast and north to south, including Canada and Mexico. Even with all that going on, he still managed to funnel several million dollars yearly into his parent's accounts.

"How did it go, babe?" Harley greeted me in the reception area.

"My head is swimming with all the facts and figures and legal dealings. Now, I can fully appreciate you wanting to go for a ride alone. You head up quite a business, Harlan Christian Robert Davis. I will never fault you going off for a few hours alone. Never again."

"Awe, shucks, ma'am." He shuffled his feet.

"I'm serious, Harley. My head is still spinning. I didn't know you exported to Canada and Mexico too."

"And soon to some European countries. I just inked a deal with Spain, France, England, and Japan. Each country has specific requirements that have to be met to begin exporting and manufacturing." Harley spoke matter of factly.

"Japan was the hardest to get into. I had to agree to use Japanese motorcycles such as Honda, Suzuki Yamaha, and Kawasaki. He twiddled with his helmet.

"All employees have to be Japanese, including management. That's not a problem. Our staff here will be trainers and have oversight authority." Harley cocked his head and grinned. "Intimidated?"

"To put it mildly," I replied.

"Relax. You'll get the hang of corporate life." Harley said before outlining the rest of his planned expansion.

"Next year, we'll be opening facilities in each of those countries. I just put a team in place for each country to begin building facilities and hiring staff."

"How will you have time to do that and go on a honeymoon?" I asked.

"It's not an issue. Each country is where we have honeymoon plans. We can spare a day or two to meet with them."

"What if I don't want to share you with business ventures while on our honeymoon?" I asked to see his reaction.

"Then I won't meet with them." Harley shrugged. "My wife is more important."

"I wasn't serious. Of course, we can meet with the management team during our honeymoon."

"I knew it." Harley pulled me into his arms for a brief kiss.

He pulled back, gazed into my eyes, and lowered his face for another kiss. He deepened the kiss and pulled me against him to the whistles and hoots of the employees.

"Seriously, Harley. How do you do it?" I asked. "I mean, I don't need much sleep, but you, you must get even less than I do."

"How much do you sleep, Mari? I hear you pounding away on your typewriter at two in the morning, and you're up at seven."

"I need about five to six hours. I can get by with four."

"I get by with two but normally try to sleep three hours."

"I guess that makes us the most sleep deprived couple in the world."

"Our church says we must take care of our bodies as though they are temples. We are to sleep as long as we need it, eat foods that provide nourishment and study the scriptures for our souls. If you need five- or six-hours sleep, that's what you should get."

"Then, I guess we're okay."

"I'd say so. How about we go home and spend a couple of hours planning for our wedding and honeymoon? We'll enjoy a leisurely dinner with Garrett and then spend some time relaxing." Harley draped his arm around me and waved at his staff with his other.

"Sounds good to me." I replied.

"I'd really like a simple, yet elegant wedding like we talked about. I think I picked out the perfect gown. I can show you a picture of something that comes close to what I'd like. Sister Sheila said she could make the gown and veil and customize it for me. You just can't see the real thing." I winked at him.

"Bad luck, huh?"

"Something like that."

We spent the next several hours picking out the final items. The invitations had come in, and Garrett took it upon himself to address each one. His handwriting is the epitome of old-world elegance.

We worked on the wedding plans after a scrumptious dinner. We put on alternating Steppenwolf, Gordon Lightfoot and Shubert albums to listen to while we worked. It was a most relaxing and enjoyable evening.

Chapter Thirty-Five

Harley

August

The week before the wedding was a whirlwind of activity. Outside of four hours a day at the office and one hour during my lunch break where I focused on teaching Mari how to ride, I barely saw her. She and her bridesmaids and matrons of honor were swamped with fittings and driving Flash nuts with menu selections for the rehearsal dinner. They poured over his suggestions for the main foods for the reception. Sampled the potential wedding and groom cakes Flash provided.

Three days before the wedding I took Mari for her motorcycle test and license. Two days before the wedding, out of town guests began arriving. Late in the afternoon the day before the wedding Mari's parents arrived.

Mari insisted on putting them in her room. I gave my room to George and Evangeline and slept in the living room along with Mari, Flash, and March. Thomas slept in the library.

Garrett slept in the music room on a lounge. His room was being used by Keisha and Jamal. Shauntelle and Chantal shared a guest room.

Peg and Maryanne shared the other. Shauntelle's kids again had the game room. I put Hixson, Mike, Lori, and Judy up in a hotel.

The night before the wedding a bachelor's party was held for me at a local establishment. We took the minibus with Hixson, March, Flash, Thomas, Frank, Mike, Garrett, George, Jamal, Mari's Dad, Jimmie, Tyrone, and some guys from church.

It turned out the local establishment was the back room of Thomas's parent's bar and grill. Streamers hung from the rafters, balloons were tied to the serving tables laden with finger sandwiches, chips, dips, and desserts. Shackles, chains, and handcuffs were placed strategically. Tables were laden with finger foods and boxes of pizza from Zaganos Pizzeria. There was a keg of beer in one corner.

I leaned over and asked Thomas, “There isn’t a stripper is there?”

“Why, yes there is. She’s due in an hour.” Thomas poured a glass of beer and offered it to me.

I shook my head. “I’m Mormon and so are half the guys here. We don’t drink beer. Remember?”

Thomas slapped his forehead. “How could I forget? Well, there’s tea and soda.”

“Herbal tea and root beer or ginger ale?”

“Caffeine! Oh no!” Thomas started to rush from the room but turned back. “No stripper, right?”

“Right,” I said dryly.

“Right. I’ll be back.”

I heard him hollering for his Dad. “Dad! They don’t drink beer or caffeine. Do you have any herbal tea? Root beer? Ginger ale? What? Yes, we’ll keep the other stuff for the rest of us.”

He returned with several wait staff in tow. They quickly added the other drinks.

“Did you call the stripper?” I asked, amused.

“No! I’ll do it now!” Thomas yelped.

“Too late,” I snickered and nodded in the direction of the door.

“Anyone call for a priest?” The stripper had plugged in the cassette player.

“Oh, no! Guess it’s too late. You’ll live through it,” Thomas cringed.

“Actually, you will. No stripper is going to sit on me and do a lap dance.”

“Don’t tell me,” Thomas whined. “It goes against one of the Mormon teachings.”

“Modesty and chastity.”

“Who’s the lucky man?” The stripper asked.

“He is,” I pointed to Thomas.

“Mister Davis,” Thomas’s mother, stood in the doorway. “There’s a call for you. She says her name is Mari.”

“Thank you. I’ll be right there.” Turning, I laughed at Thomas’s bright red face. “Enjoy,” I snickered when he stuck out his tongue at me.

Members of my church laughed at my good-natured teasing of Thomas. The more I teased him, the more embarrassed he got.

Thomas's mother led me behind the bar. "Thank you," I said as I put the phone to my ear and turned my back to the bar.

"Harley!" She gasped into the phone.

"Yes?" It was so noisy in here I had to cup a hand around my ear just to hear what Mari was saying.

"Did your family say they were coming?" Mari sounded panicked.

"No. I even called, and my parents never returned my calls. Why?" I asked.

"Because they're here!"

"I'll take care of it. I'll book them rooms at the same hotel Hixson is staying in. Have Peg take them there."

A deep sense of foreboding overcame me. I'd have to get to the church early and talk with the Bishop. I wanted to see if we could skip the part about asking if there was anyone who objected to the marriage. I wouldn't put it past my Father to come just to do something like that.

In the meantime, I'd better send one of the guys over to assist if needed.

###

Mari

A bridal shower, hosted by Dee, was held at our home and included our Mom, Peg, Judy, Lori, Maryanne, Karen, Susan, Polly, Keisha, Evangeline, Shauntelle, Chantal, Laila, Wanda, Jennifer, a friend from high school, Sheila, and some of the Sisters from church.

The living room was festooned with party favors, streamers made from crepe paper, origami, and plants. Thankfully, there were no balloons. I've hated balloons since the second grade when boys took great delight in tormenting me by popping those nasty things behind my back.

Flash and Garrett had made an assortment of ladyfingers, sandwiches, sushi, fruit, veggies, and desserts to go with chips and dips. Dee had brought Vernors, root beer, and there was a pitcher of herbal tea in the refrigerator.

Gifts were piled onto the coffee table. Dee had made flash cards for games to be played. Creedence Clearwater Revival's 'Cosmos Factory" album was on the turntable when the doorbell rang.

"I'll get it," Peg said.

She returned in minutes. "We might have a problem."

"What?"

"Harley's parents are here. They brought guests."

I shot to my feet and hurried to the door." This is unexpected," I blurted.

"Why? That the parents of the groom would come to his wedding?" Harley's father asked. "Please get his servant to show us to our rooms and bring our luggage."

Panic set in. "I'll be right back." I hurried down the hall to Harley's office.

"Harley!" I gasped. "Did your family say they were coming?"

"No. I even called, and they never returned my calls. Why?" Harley sounded like he was talking through a wall of noise.

"Well, they're here. Your Mother, Father, Elizabeth, and the Vickmans including Ashley. What do I do, Harley?"

"I'll book them into the same hotel as Hixson, Mike, Lori, and Judy. See if Peg will drive them there."

"Okay."

"Thanks, love," Harley said as he disconnected the call.

I explained to Peg what was going to happen.

"I'm not sure that's going to work." She looked doubtful. "I get the impression they think they're staying here."

"They can't. There isn't any room."

"And she mentioned a celebratory gala."

"Boy, is she in for a shock. Harley's getting them rooms at the hotel where Hixson is staying."

"They are going to be upset."

"It's a nice hotel. Not the Ritz-Carlton, but nice," I said and sighed. Who was I kidding? Peg was right.

Hixson and March walked in. "The cavalry has arrived," March announced and did a mock bow. "We're here to take you to your digs for this weekend."

"Digs?" Mister Davis turned red.

"Your, ah, shall we say, accommodations." March tried to affect a stiff upper British attitude and failed.

"We want to stay for the bridal shower," Mistress Davis said and fanned her face.

"And I want to go to the stag party." Mister Davis declared.

"Peg?" I said.

"Yeah, I'll drive the girls to the hotel after the party."

"And I'll take Mister Davis after the bachelor party," March said.

Ashley and Elizabeth spent the evening trying to make us all miserable. "Who came up with these lame games."

"My sister did, and I love them. No one said you had to play."

"When does the male stripper get here?"

"There isn't one. I'm Mormon," I said, gritting my teeth.

"Mormons don't have fun? Good clean fun? After all, you guys have polygamy."

"No, we don't. That practice went out over a hundred years ago. Strippers are not part of our moral code. It's sexual in nature. Mormons engage in sexual activity only with their marital partner."

"Well, Lawdy-dee-dawdy," Elizabeth said. "Aren't you high and mighty marrying into Harley's money."

"You no talk that way to my daughter. Maru is not a gold digger," Mom jumped into the fray and poked Elizabeth.

"Your mother is a yellowbelly chink."

"I Japanese, not Chinese," Mom retorted.

"Even better, a slant-eyed Jap."

"That's not nice," I said.

"Who made these?" Mistress Davis asked. She had a pig in a blanket on her plate. "They're quite tasty."

"That honor belongs to my sister, Dee."

"Please pass on my compliments." She seemed out of it. I wondered if she had taken any anxiety medication.

"I will."

"Now, if you don't mind, I think it's time we went to our hotel. What time shall we be here tomorrow?"

"Around nine should be good," I replied as I helped carry their luggage to the waiting vehicles.

The day of the wedding was a madhouse. Both Harley's parents demanded to be in the wedding.

"Your mother should be Matron of Honor," His father insisted.

"I'm sorry," Harley said. "If you had bothered to tell us you were going to attend, we might have been able to accommodate your request. Since we were not informed, we made other plans. I am not going to ask Mari to rearrange things at the last minute at the risk of usurping her family."

It was such a relief to have Harley handle that problem. Last night was bad enough with them arriving unexpectedly and acting put out because no one met them at the airport. How was Harley and I supposed to know their plans when they didn't bother to rsvp, to begin with?

"Miss Forrester," Harley's mother, followed me into Harley's bedroom where I was packing bags for our honeymoon at the Condor Pass Resort.

"Yes, Mistress Davis?" I paused and glanced at her.

"I am assuming there will be a gala tonight after the wedding. Why isn't it set up already? I adore balls and could finish that task if you would provide me with the details."

"Gala?" I questioned. Did she really think we were going to have a ball after the reception? "I'm sorry. There is no gala planned. Harley and I are leaving soon after the reception."

"Well, I never attended a wedding that didn't have a formal dinner and dance afterward." She huffed.

"We wanted a simple ceremony followed by a reception. The only formal dinner was the rehearsal one a few nights ago. Now, if you don't mind, I have a ton of stuff to do before the ceremony."

"Aren't you being a bit high and mighty?" She snapped.

"No, ma'am, I'm just stating the facts. Now, if you'll excuse me, I need to finish packing. The hairdresser will be here shortly. If you're hungry, I'm sure Garrett has some refreshments ready."

I turned my focus back on the task at hand. I looked at the checklist Harley had provided me to pack for our honeymoon. The list for him was short. That man could travel light. He had a few changes of clothes, one suit, pajamas, undergarments, swimwear, a change of shoes, and his toiletries. I tried to pack my bag like his. Unfortunately, I had to have more than he did. Being a girl has its disadvantages such as needing slips to match dresses, bras that complemented outfits, shoes for each outfit and so on. Thankfully, petticoats were no longer popular, or I'd have to have a big trunk!

The hairdressers arrived. There was one for each member of my wedding party and myself. Each of us also had manicures and pedicures. Some wanted their nails painted. Then came the makeup. Finally, we were ready to head to the church where we would meet up with Sheila and change into our gowns.

The wedding was scheduled for noon in the Chapel. And the reception was to follow immediately after in the Cultural Hall. After the reception, Harley and I were headed out to the Condor Pass Resort in Arizona.

Harley arranged to have me and my parents arrive at the church in the limousine. Dee and Frank had their own transportation. Garrett drove Harley, Thomas, and Flash. Hixson drove the minibus with Keisha, Jamal, Shauntelle, the children, Maryanne, Peg, Lori, Judy, Elizabeth, and Ashley. It was a good thing the bus could hold fifteen passengers. Mike drove the Bentley with George and Evangeline. March drove the Mercedes with Harley's parents and the Vickmans. I felt sorry for March. He'd have to put up with their boorish behavior.

Somehow, everyone made it there without killing anyone. When we arrived, Harley dashed from the car he was in and went straight to the Bishop's office.

The men went toward the Chapel where they greeted our guests and seated them. The women went into the Relief Society room. Sheila had made an elegant off-white wedding gown.

The long sleeves were embroidered lace that came up over the shoulders. The dress swept down to my ankles and had a white rose at my waist. The veil matched the sleeves and bodice. Hints of gold coloring were woven into the fabric to complement the naturally golden highlights in my hair. It was so perfect I felt like a fairytale princess.

The bridesmaids had long gowns with splashes of color to match their eyes or hair coloring. Dee's dress had shades of auburn woven in that really brought out her coloring and emphasized her eyes.

"Look at you!" I gushed. "You are so beautiful!"

"Mari," Dee fingered my gown. "This gown is exquisite."

"Don't you love it? Sister Sheila made it. And, well, you know, she made all the dresses."

I was about to put the dress on when someone knocked on the door. I draped a robe around me and answered it.

"Mari," Thomas said, "Harley said the Bishop wants to meet with the congregation in the Chapel."

"Is there a problem?"

"Nope, he just wants to ask the congregation if they approve of this wedding. Harley said it's an unusual request he made of the Bishopric to avoid a potential conflict with his parents."

"Oh!" I wasn't surprised.

Thomas whispered to me, "I think the entire congregation turned out for this wedding. Over one hundred members of the church are here."

"Wow! Now, I'm scared."

"Don't be. It'll be a piece of pie."

"You mean a piece of cake," I giggled.

"Piece of cake, a walk in the dark, whatever."

"A walk in the park," I laughed.

"There you go, that's my girl."

"I need to get back into my street clothes. They can't see me in a robe!" I ran back into the Relief Society room and threw on a pair of jeans and a shirt. "Okay, now I'm ready."

"Let's go," Thomas hooked his arm through mine.

Harley's father stood at the door to the chapel." I fail to see why I can't go inside. I'm the father of the groom."

"This is for members of the church only, sir," one of the priests explained as he held the door open for Thomas and me.

"He's not a member of the church!" Mister Davis pointed at Thomas.

"I'm just walking Mari inside. I'll be right back," Thomas steered me through the door. He walked me up the aisle to stand beside Harley. Once I was in position, Thomas left, pulling the chapel doors closed.

"Brothers and Sisters, we have a unique request from Brother Harley. He has asked us to have the congregation give their approval for the marriage between Harlan Christian Robert Davis and Mari Marie Forrester. Is there anyone here who knows of any reason these two individuals should not be united in holy matrimony?"

The Bishop waited several minutes before continuing. "Seeing none, all those who find this couple worthy of marriage please indicate with a show of their right hand."

Every hand went up. "Anyone opposed, please express disapproval by a show of their right hand."

Not a single hand went up.

"Then by the power vested in me, in the name of Jesus Christ, our heavenly father, and the holy ghost, I pronounce this couple worthy of marriage in the eyes of the church. Thank you. The ceremony will begin shortly. Until then, please avail yourselves of the fabulous refreshments."

The Bishop left the podium and came over to us. "I think that will take care of the problem, Harley."

"I am most grateful, Bishop. I just know my parents will do anything to prevent our marriage. When I was in the hospital and requested the Bishop or priest visits there, they stopped the visits by declaring they were my medical power of attorney. Garrett went behind their backs and arranged for visitations while they were away from the hospital. I assure you, my parents were not my DPA. Garrett was given that honor, but he thought I was dead." Harley explained.

"Dead? How did that happen?" Bishop asked.

"I suffered a major relapse just before I was to return to Lima for three months. I had a code blue. While I was unconscious they told Garrett, I had died. Being Garrett, the kind of man he is, he thought he should tell Mari and Thomas in person." Harley frowned. His voice hitched at the painful memory.

"He flew home after making funeral arrangements, not knowing I had been moved into intensive care. They changed my listing to no information may be given out. While Garrett was in Lima, I was transferred to another hospital. They fired him when he returned." Harley pulled out a handkerchief and blotted his face.

"And they dislike Mormons." I chimed in.

"Yes. My parents refused to come to my baptism near Lake George." Harley said in agreement. "Father proclaimed no son of his was going to become a Non-Christian Mormon."

"Now, I understand," Bishop chuckled. "Not to worry. They will not stop this wedding."

"Thank you, Bishop," I said and glanced at the clock on the wall. "Please excuse me. I need to finish getting ready."

###

Harley

I was glad that was over. When the music changed, I took my place at the altar with both Garrett and Thomas beside me. The groomsmen stood in the back ready to escort the bridesmaids.

The traditional wedding march began with Sister Carla on the organ and Sister Diana directing.

Sister Sheila's two-year-old son, Brandon, was given the rings on a gold leaf embroidered pillow. Brother John's three-year-old daughter, Amanda had the rose petals.

Brandon was supposed to go first followed by Amanda, but they wound up walking together. They were adorable. Brandon in his suit and Amanda wore a mainly white dress with shades of pink. I could envision someday having kids like that with Mari.

The groomsmen, in turn, held out an arm to escort the ladies. As the Matron of the Bride, Dee came first with March escorting her. Then came Susan as the Matron of Honor with Brother Luke, Peg as Maid of Honor escorted by Brother Peter. Then came Hixson and Lori, Mike and Judy, Brother Nick escorted Karen, and Flash with Maryanne brought up the rear.

Mister Forrester proudly held his arm out to his daughter. My breath caught in my throat. Mari was stunning. She radiated joy and love and was easily the most beautiful lady in the room. Pure, unadulterated happiness filled my entire being. I had eyes only for her.

Her father handed her to me and stepped back to stand with his wife.

###

Mari

I watched the wedding procession proceed down the aisle but have no clear memory of it. Dad gently took my arm and tucked it in his. He led me down the aisle. The only thing I remember is seeing the most handsome man standing at the altar. I hadn't noticed before, but Harley was dressed in a dark gray tuxedo, white shirt, and black bow tie. When did he get his hair trimmed?

He stood looking directly at me. Suddenly, it was as though we were the only two people in the room. When Dad guided me to Harley's side, I saw sparkles in Harley's blue-gray eyes. Were they tears? Or was his love shining through? He grasped both my hands and whispered, "You are so beautiful."

"I love you so much," I whispered back.

###

Harley

The music stopped, and the Bishop cleared his throat. We turned to face him.

"Brothers, Sisters, family and friends, we come together on this day August 19, 1978, to celebrate the joining of Brother Harlan Christian Robert Davis and Sister Mari Marie Forrester in holy matrimony. I am going to perform a modified ceremony at the request of Brother Harlan and Sister Mari. Shall we get started?" Bishop looked around the room and saw nods of approval

"Brother Harlan, and Sister Mari, please join the patriarchal grip or sure sign of the nail."

"Hold on there!" Mister Davis bellowed. "What happened to asking if there was any reason they should not marry?"

"And, sir, you are?" Bishop asked.

"His father."

"Mister Davis, I am pleased to inform you, the congregation and the church have found this couple worthy of marriage. May I remind all non-members, you are here at the behest of the couple to be married. Now, if we may continue without further interruption." Bishop looked around the Chapel.

I breathed a sigh of relief as did Mari.

"Who gives the hand of Mari in marriage?"

"Her mother and I do," Mari's father stood up and beckoned to her mother to do so also. "We are honored to gift Mari's hand in marriage to Harlan."

"Who gives the hand of Harlan in marriage?"

"I do," Garrett stepped forward, "As his adopted father, I am honored to gift Harlan's hand in marriage to Mari."

I can count on one hand the number of times Garrett called me Harlan instead of Master Harley.

"His adopted father?" My biological father fumed. "What nonsense is this?"

"I'm sorry, Mister Davis, with all due respect, one more outburst and I will ask you to leave," Bishop said calmly. "Today is about Harley and Mari."

"Thank you, Brother Garrett, for your response," Bishop said. "Brother Harley, do you take Sister Mari by the right hand and receive her unto yourself as your lawful and wedded wife in sickness and in health, for richer or poorer until death do you part? Do you with a covenant promise you will observe and keep the laws, rites, and ordinances of this holy order of matrimony? Do you promise this covenant in the presence of Heavenly Father, and the witnesses here today of your own free will?"

"Yes, I do." I held her right hand. With my left hand, I slipped her engagement ring off, put on the wedding band and then replaced the engagement ring.

"Sister Mari, do you take Brother Harlan by the right hand and give yourself to him to be his lawful and wedded wife? Do you with a covenant take him to be your lawful and wedded husband in sickness and in health, for richer or poorer until death do you part? Do you promise you will observe and keep the laws, rites, and ordinances of this holy order of matrimony? Do you promise this covenant in the presence of Heavenly Father, and the witnesses here today of your own free will?"

"Yes," She took my right hand. "I do." She slipped a wedding band onto my left ring finger.

"By virtue of the holy priesthood and the authority vested in me by our Heavenly Father and the State of Ohio, I hereby pronounce you husband and wife. Amen."

"Brother Harlan you may now kiss the bride."

I gently pulled her into my arms and kissed her. It was such a sweet agonizing kiss. I wanted so much more but would have to wait until tonight.

We followed the recessional out of the Chapel and into the Cultural Hall where we received congratulations on our marriage. "We get to repeat this in a year with a temple ceremony where we'll be sealed together for eternity," I said to Mari.

"I can't wait. I'm so glad you talked with Bishop and stopped your father's hijinks."

Once all the greetings were done, Mari tossed her bouquet to baby Amanda who squealed in delight. We then had our first dance as a married couple. I had selected 'Love Theme' aka 'Speak Softly Love,' from the Godfather. It was also the song we were serenaded with during our first date. We spent a few hours at the reception, enjoyed the food, conversation, posing for official wedding photographs and then made our excuses. Mari made certain we spent some time with her family.

As we were headed to the Relief Society room, Mother stopped me. "Okay, I understand there isn't going to be a gala. What about a dinner tonight with your father, me, Elizabeth, the Vickmans, Ashley, Mari's sister Dee and her husband, and her parents?"

"I'm sorry, Mother, but Mari and I have a plane to catch. Garrett and the WOSL gang are taking Mari's family to dinner. If you want, I can ask if you can join them."

I made the arrangements with Garrett, made sure the dinner was charged to me and asked him to make Mari's family comfortable.

Mari came out of the Relief Society room wearing dark green pants and a matching shirt. "Ready?"

"Yes, Sister Sheila is driving us to the airport."

"Our families?" She lifted a brow at me.

"My mother wanted to participate. Don't worry, Garrett. Thomas, Flash and the WOSL gang will keep things in hand, even if they have to toss my family out of the restaurant."

"I hope it doesn't come to that."

"Me too."

"By the way, I upped what we're paying Sheila for the gowns and everything else she's done. I also left a sizeable check for my sister to cover her expenses for food and the bridal shower. They can sure use it. I just learned Frank's company laid off half the staff."

"Maybe Edward can use him in the warehouse. I'll call him from the airport, or when we get to the resort."

"You are so wonderful," Mari said.

"You folks ready? Sorry, I'm a little late. I had to change Brandon before I handed him over to his daddy."

"Not a problem. We have three hours before the plane takes off."

"Sheila," Mari said, "I want to thank you so much for all you've done. Garrett will have your check for the dresses and my beautiful gown in the morning. You can get it from him any time."

"It was my pleasure."

She pulled out of the parking lot, and we headed to the airport.

Chapter Thirty-Six

Mari

August

I kept looking at my ring finger. My wedding band was an exquisite mix of gold and silver intertwined with small diamond chips along the band and anchored by a black opal that sparkled with hues of green, pink, and blue.

"It matches your engagement ring," Harley leaned over and looked at it.

"It's beautiful."

We arrived in Dayton ninety minutes early. "Sheila, would you mind taking us to a Chinese restaurant I know of around here?" Harley asked.

"Just tell me where."

He gave her directions to the place we'd dined at before. "We're treating you to dinner. I hope you like authentic Chinese cuisine." I said.

"I love Chinese food, but you don't have to do this."

"Yes, we do," Harley said. "You did such a lovely job with the gowns on short notice. It's the least we can do."

We spent a fun hour eating dim sum with Harley explaining each dish. Sheila had never eaten a true dim sum meal and was suitably impressed.

"Where in China did Dim Sum originate?" Sheila speared Gohk Char Siu Bao, a baked pork bun.

"The kind served here began in Hong Kong." Harley sipped his water before digging into Garlic Pea Sprouts.

"You did missionary work in Bolivia?" I asked as I nibbled a savory steamed shrimp noodle roll called Har Cheung.

"It was the best two years," Sheila commented.

Soon it was time to go to the airport. I was nervous we were going to miss our flight. We bade Sheila goodbye and headed into the terminal.

"There's something I should tell you," Harley shuffled his feet.

"What's our flight number? And airline?" I asked as I scanned the list of departures. "Are we flying into Phoenix?"

"I bought two jets," Harley said in a rush. "We're flying into Flagstaff. From there, we're driving to Page."

"Wait a minute," I spun around and faced him. "You bought two jets? Why two?"

"Yes. If I'm going to go international, I need the planes to transport my teams.

"When did you buy them?" Mari sounded surprised.

"It was before you returned to Lima."

"Then what am I doing looking at the boards?"

"I don't know, love," Harley laughed. "C'mon, our plane awaits us."

The interior of the airplane was plush. It had a kitchen, dining area, a decent sized bathroom, and bedroom in addition to the spacious seating area. "Welcome aboard, Mister and Mistress Davis." A stewardess greeted us. "Here, let me stow your luggage. Mister Davis, I'm going to secure your cane overhead also. As soon as the pilot gets clearance, we will be on our way."

"Thank you," Harley said as he surrendered his walking stick.

"We should arrive in Flagstaff around six mountain standard time. Your transportation will be waiting. You should arrive in Page around eight o'clock."

"Very good." Harley nodded. "Thank you."

###

Garrett

What an onerous task I had, taking the Davises and the Vickmans to dinner. I tasked Hixson with driving Elizabeth and Ashley in the minibus with the WOSL group, and Shauntelle's children. March drove George, Evangeline, Keisha, and Jamal in the Bentley. Mike drove Shauntelle and the Forresters in the Mercedes. Several church members volunteered to take anyone else needing a ride. I was pleased to learn several of Harley's employees would also attend.

Dinner was at the Western Steakhouse. Master Harley had booked the entire restaurant for the occasion. When we arrived, I held the limousine door open and assisted my passengers out.

Mistress Davis stood staring at the building. "Is this where we're having dinner?"

"Yes ma'am, it is," I replied.

"Why…it's…it's a dump!" Mistress Davis exclaimed. Her hand fluttered to her chest.

"I assure you the food here is quite good." I hurried to open the restaurant doors. I was gratified to see March and Mike assisting their passengers out of the car.

Inside, I thought Mistress Davis was going to have the vapors over the western motif. She was absolutely appalled. Mister Davis thought the place was beneath him. The Forresters liked it.

"Honey, doesn't this place remind you of the Ponderosa over by the K-Mart?" Mari's dad commented.

Harley's employees sat with the Forresters. "Let me guess," Edward said. "Marine Corps?"

"Yes. Retired."

"A Marine can always tell. Semper Fi." Edward shook Mister Forrester's hand.

"Semper Fi."

The wait staff took our beverage orders. Naturally, Master Harley's family requested champagne.

"I'm sorry, but we do not have champagne. We have tap beer, bottled beer, and wine, red or white," The waitress said. "May, I suggest a red wine?"

"Oh, all right," Mister Davis grumbled. "Some of us are celebrating a marriage. I am lamenting the foolish decision my son made to marry a harlot."

"Mister Davis!" I bellowed, "I canna allow you to speak disrespectfully of Mister Harlan Davis nor of his dear wife, Miss Mari."

"Did I hear him call my daughter a harlot?" Mister Forrester rose out of his seat.

His diminutive wife placed a hand on his arm and urged him to sit down. To my surprise, she stood up and shoved her finger into

Mister Davis's chest. "You are bad man. You talk ugly about Maru."

I cringed. I was always under the impression the Japanese were meek, mild, and ultra-polite.

"My Maru is a decent girl. You no talk bad about her or I punch you."

"Honey," Mister Forrester tried to placate his wife.

"No. He nasty man. Talk bad about Maru and his own son. He should be ashamed of himself. He brings shame to both families."

Ah, ha! I thought. It's about saving face. Now I understood.

"Oh, please," Mistress Davis said fanning herself as though she might faint. "What do you know about honor? You're just a Chinee."

"I am Japanese. Japanese are honorable." Mistress Forrester balled her hands into a fist and swung.

Before she could connect with Mistress Davis's face, Mister Forrester wrapped his arms around her in a giant bear hug. "Honey. Show them we are better than they are. Make polite conversation." He gently urged her back into her seat.

"Okay. I still not like them."

"Well, now that was exciting," Mistress Vickman spoke up. "Almost had ringside seats to the fight of the century."

Ashley and Elizabeth sat with the WOSL group. They took great delight in tormenting everyone at the table.

"And who made those awful dishes at the reception?" Elizabeth asked.

"Members of the church and me," Flash bristled.

"It was simply horrid," Ashley contributed. The people at the tables surrounding them stopped talking.

"Well, excuse me. You seemed to make quite a pig of yourselves at the reception," Hixson commented.

Peg followed suit by eliciting appropriate pig noises, and Maryanne snorted.

"I think, I'm going to take myself and my horrid cooking abilities to another table." Flash stood, gathered his plate and drink and went to sit with the congregation.

One by one the rest of the WOSL staff did likewise until only Ashley and Elizabeth remained at their table.

"What'd we say?" Elizabeth asked.

"We don't fraternize with boorish people," Flash said, affecting a bored English accent.

"We aren't boring," Ashley said.

"Okay, then, we do not care to eat beside mean-spirited people," March responded in that laid-back hippie manner of his.

"You're just some dumb hippie," Ashley huffed.

"Okay, but at least I'm a well-liked dumb hippie who has a popular radio show. What do you do? Sit around all day getting your nails and hair done? Bad mouthing people? What a sorry life you have." March countered.

"Bravo, March!" Mike pounded him on his back.

"Now, shall we regale these good people at our table with tales from WOSL radio?" Hixson chuckled.

"Oh, no!" Judy exclaimed. "We should all run while we have a brain cell left in our heads!"

I was never so glad when dinner ended, and I could drop the Vickmans and Davises at the hotel. When I arrived home, the WOSL group were in the game room with the kids. The adults were in the living room eating scones and sipping herbal tea. Mistress Forrester was refilling cups.

"Mister Garou," she beckoned me. "Come. Have tea."

"Why thank you, ma'am," I settled on the love seat and accepted the cup she proffered.

"I bet you are glad tonight is over," Jamal commented.

"Aye, that I am," I sighed.

"Did I hear correctly? Harley adopted you?" George asked. "Mistress Forrester, this tea is excellent."

"Domo Arigatou."

"Yes, he did," I responded. Once again, I found tears welling up in my eyes. "I am a most fortunate man."

"You know, a few years ago, I was surprised when he called me and asked permission to date Mari," Mister Forrester said. "Most young men don't do that anymore."

"Aye," I nodded. "He is always about being proper."

"I was surprised when he explained it would be an overnight date, that nothing would happen, and they would have separate rooms."

"The Law of Chastity," I again nodded.

"That's what he said. I didn't know until recently that he's Mormon."

"As am I, and now Miss Mari."

"I'm Baptist, and my wife is Buddhist. I suppose it really doesn't matter as long as we believe in God."

I was glad when I could finally go to sleep on the sofa in the living room.

Chapter Thirty-Seven

Harley

August

We sipped sparkling cider and nibbled on assorted cheeses and fruit during our flight. I have never been so happy as I was today. My angel was now my wife. I cannot adequately describe the joy, the pride, and the love I was feeling. I kept stealing glances at my beloved. How Mari could be both excited and serene at the same time, I'll never know. She sat beside me writing in her journal and nibbling snacks.

When she looked at me, she smiled. "What?" she asked.

"Nothing," I grinned. "I'm just enjoying the view."

"What view?" She looked out the window. "I see clouds."

"You, silly," I laughed and grasped her hand. I raised it to my lips and kissed each finger before kissing her palm. "I think I'm going to try to take a nap." I unsnapped my seat belt. "Care to join me?"

"I'm too excited to sleep, but you go ahead."

"You sure?" I winked lasciviously at her.

"I'm sure." She smiled sweetly.

Oh my! She was such an innocent. It endeared her to me even more. "Okay. I'll see you soon."

"Enjoy your rest, my love."

"I'll try." I just knew I was going to have to take a cold shower once in the bedroom.

I lay on the bed and thought about all the times we'd had, both good and bad. The great times far outweighed the horrible stuff. I was so fortunate she believed me when she thought I was dead. I shivered at the thought of everything I put her and Garrett through. One of the worst things I did was my run-in with an outlaw motorcycle club. Still, Mari stood by me.

I smiled thinking about how persistent I was chasing after her. I just knew Mari was the one for me. She could soothe the devil in me when no one else could. She made me feel loved. Indeed, I am a lucky man. I now have Garrett and Mari who love me unconditionally. I have good, close friends who are there for me and dedicated employees. Life is good.

I can't wait to see Mari's face when she sees her wedding gift. It was a miracle I was able to keep it a secret, let alone ship it to Flagstaff, Arizona.

###

Mari

I settled into my luxurious seat with my journal. I wanted to record every second of this glorious day. It still feels like a fantasy dream come true. Sitting beside me is my husband, my best friend, my anchor in rough seas, and my soul mate. Not many people are so lucky as I am.

I kept stealing glances at him. I loved the way his feather brown lashes kissed his cheeks when he closed his eyes. The startling blue-gray of his eyes made him look simultaneously like a naughty child and a sexy man. My Harley was so handsome and oblivious to the effect he had on other women. He had just enough devil in him to be exciting, and yet still remained kind, caring, and generous.

"I think I'm going to try to take a nap." Harley unsnapped his seat belt. "Care to join me?"

"I'm too excited to sleep, but you go ahead," I replied.

"Are you sure?"

I looked up to find him grinning at me. He looked wicked. "I'm sure," I replied and smiled.

"You will be pleased to note, we are arriving in Flagstaff an hour early," the pilot said. "Please fasten your belts."

Harley returned to his seat shortly after the pilot announced we were approaching Flagstaff. He looked freshly showered.

I wondered if I should have taken one too. I surreptitiously smelled my armpits only to hear Harley gag.

"What?" I was mortified. "Do I smell that badly?"

He burst into peals of laughter. “Only if you think you do. I showered to…um...calm my libido down.”

“To what?” I felt a blush coming on.

“You aroused me. Not wanting to be crude, I took a shower…a cold one.” He smirked.

“Oh!” Now my face was bright red.

“Oh my, you are an innocent,” Harley chuckled and leaned over to kiss me. “I rescheduled my checkup for the middle of September. That way we can see some of Europe next. I’d like Garrett to go to Scotland with us after my checkup. He hasn’t been back since I was born. Is that okay? If not, I’ll change things back.”

“Sounds good to me.” I cinched my seatbelt. “Buckle up.”

“Oh, right,” He hastened to pull his seatbelt across his lap.

When we got off the plane, I looked at the rental car agencies. “Are we driving or flying to Page, right?”

“Driving. Come with me.”

We walked past the rental cars and went to claims. “I’m Harlan Davis. I believe you have two vehicles stored here for me.”

“Yes sir, we do. I’ll have someone bring them out to the pickup lane for you.” The attendant said.

I turned to Harley, “You had two vehicles sent here?” I was flummoxed. We headed to the exit.

“Ah…” He waggled a finger at me. “Not just any vehicles, but two Davis Motors originals.”

“We’re riding a motorcycle?” I turned to face him.

“Two motorcycles. I had one built and customized for you. It’s a smaller version of mine. Happy wedding day, my love.” He pointed at the flatbed pulling up. The two men unloaded the bikes. Harley tipped them generously before they left.

In front of us were gleaming black and chrome Hogs with tags that read Davis Motors 1 and Davis Motors 2. I squealed so loudly he clapped his hands over his ears and laughed.

“Here’s your key.”

I opened the hard case saddle bag to put my luggage inside. “No wonder you insisted on duffle bags. Will my extra bag fit on the back?” I pulled my jacket and helmet out from the large case on the rear.

"Sure. We just secure it like this." Harley took my larger bag and hooked it to the back He secured it, and then he placed my smaller items inside the hard cases.

At first, I was timid handling this powerful machine. However, I had to overcome that in a hurry if I wanted to keep up with Harley. We sped down I-17 North to US 89 and arrived at the Condor Pass Resort just outside Page, Arizona.

Located along Lake Powell, the resort was a mixture of adobe and marble tiles. Rose bushes and stone trellises surrounded an elegant fountain and stone benches. The driveway was to the side and unobtrusive for guests sitting along the fountains. It had an old-world mystical feel that was warm and inviting. Canyons dotted the horizon.

The interior was stone, adobe, and marble. A giant fireplace with gorgeous seating enhanced a Native American motif in the reception area. Navajo blankets festooned the walls as tapestries interspersed with paintings of canyons and the lake. A dark wood counter polished to a high sheen served as the registration desk.

"May I help you?" The beautiful Navajo woman asked.

"We're Mister and Mistress Davis. I believe we have a suite."

"Oh yes," She leafed through a book. "Here you are. Your rooms are on the top floor." She handed us two keys. "You may take the private elevator. It's the third one and is operated by your keys. It opens into your suite. Inside the suite, there is also an emergency stair exit. I hope you enjoy your stay with us."

"Thank you. I'm sure we will." Harley smiled.

Our suite was stupendous. The elevator opened into a spacious hall tastefully decorated with a continuation of the Navajo motif. Paintings of canyons and condors adorned the walls. Handmade pottery perched on strategically placed tables.

The living room held luxuriously comfortable leather armchairs and a sofa with a glass table. It looked out through floor to ceiling doors onto a balcony. From the balcony, you could see the canyons and glimpses of Lake Powell.

Off from the living room was a full kitchen and dining nook. The kitchen equipment was stainless steel. The table and chairs were made of wood. On the table was a woven basket filled with a variety of fruit, chocolate, juice, breadsticks, a dip, roasted pine nuts, and water.

The bedroom hosted a roughhewn bed frame with a king-sized mattress draped in Navajo blankets. At the foot of the bed was a wooden chest for storing valuables. A padlock secured the contents. The Armoires were handmade and matched the bedframe. From the bed, you could enjoy the same view as from the living room. The windows were floor to ceiling without drapes to obscure the scenery.

The bathroom had his and her dressing areas, two sets of sinks, a glass-enclosed shower, and a sunken tub.

Everything screamed elegance, comfort, serenity, and a hint of the mystic. There was a feeling of reverence in the décor that spoke volumes to the soul. “This place is absolutely fantastic!” I lay back on the bed.

“Isn’t it?” Harley sat next to me. “When we were checking in, I saw a small sign saying this place is for sale. I’d like to check into buying it. What do you think?”

“That would be great, depending on why it’s being sold.” I sat up.

“I’m hungry,” Harley said. “Care to go down and get a bite to eat?”

“I could use something light,” I replied.

###

Harley

We could have ordered room service, but I wanted to see what the on-site restaurant was like. I also wanted to talk to the manager about the for-sale sign.

The restaurant served a delectable assortment of meals ranging from American, Mexican, to Navajo. I selected the fry bread with red chili and asked them for hot sauce. Mari chose a Navajo taco.

The portions were huge. Mari made it a fourth of the way through her meal, while I managed to eat half of mine. We had the wait staff pack the leftovers so we could eat them later.

We walked over to the reception counter. "May I help you?" The desk clerk asked.

"I'd like to speak to the manager about the for-sale sign."

"The manager is the owner. I'll ring him for you," she smiled.

Within minutes a distinguished gentleman arrived. The clerk directed him to us.

"Hello. I'm Jameson Whitaker. I understand you're inquiring about the for-sale sign?"

"Yes, sir," I responded.

"Let me guess. You want to know why anyone would want to sell this fine establishment. Am I correct?"

"Yes."

"I don't really. My wife and I love it here. The problem is, my wife's health is declining, and she can no longer withstand the heat. We're hoping to relocate to Florida."

"I see." I studied his face for any signs of treachery.

"Perhaps we should discuss this matter in my office."

He led us down the hall to a well-appointed office. He sat behind the desk and beckoned us to sit. "Mister Davis, at the risk of sounding rude, are you seriously thinking about making an offer for this placc?"

"I am," I steepled my fingers and continued to gaze at him.

"The price might be a bit steep for someone your age."

"The selling price is?" I asked.

"Ten million."

"May I take a look at the books?" I continued to study him.

"Mister Davis, with all due respect, you might wish to have an accountant do that."

"I'm perfectly capable of assessing the worth of a business, Mister Whitaker."

"I'm sure you are," he backtracked. "If I may be so bold, you are a bit young. What business experience do you have?"

"I owned two businesses when I turned sixteen. I now own three businesses outright, and I'm part owner of four additional companies under my umbrella, Davis Enterprises. One is a resort in Lake George, New York. Two are restaurants of which one is in Lake George, and the other is in Ohio. The other three are motor vehicle companies. I'm getting ready to go international. I think that should explain my business experience."

"Yes, sir. When would you like to look at the books?"

"In a couple of days. Right now, I want to spend some time with my bride."

"Very good, sir. I will make sure everything is in order."

"Thank you," I stood and shook his hand.

Mari was silent during the entire exchange. From the expression on her face, I knew my mogul side, as she calls it, had put in an appearance.

Inside the elevator, I turned to her. "Mister Whitaker overinflated the selling price. As beautiful as this resort is with all the amenities, there is no way it is valued at ten million."

"What do you think it's worth?" She twirled a strand of hair around her finger,

"I'd say about four million." We stepped out of the elevator and into our suite. "Now enough business. Would you like a nice long soak in the tub?" I asked as I put our leftovers into the refrigerator.

"That sounds heavenly." She entered the bathroom. Soon I heard the water running. I waited until it stopped before I entered the bathroom.

###

Mari

The water was steaming hot and felt so good as I sunk into the bubbles. I was lathering myself with a wonderfully scented soap when I heard the door open.

"Mind if I join you?" Harley's voice sounded unusually husky as he stepped into the tub and sat behind me. "Here, let me soap your back."

I was both mortified and happy. Harley gently ran a wash towel over my skin, eliciting the most sensual feelings of delight. I was mortified because I was sitting naked in a tub with him.

"Are you embarrassed?" He whispered in my ear.

I could only nod.

"Don't be," He inhaled deeply. "You are the most beautiful woman I've ever known. I love everything about you."

"But…but…we're naked!" I sputtered.

Harley burst out laughing. "I should hope so. I don't know anyone who would sit in the tub fully clothed." He leaned forward and nuzzled my neck sending shivers of delight down my spine. "I want you, mi amore." He reached around me and pulled the plug, letting the water drain before refilling the tub so we could rinse the soap off.

Harley stepped out and wrapped a large towel around his midriff. He held a bath towel out for me. He held it high enough that he couldn't see me. Harley was thoughtful in that way, not wanting to cause me further embarrassment. I climbed out of the tub, and he pulled the cloth around me.

He took my hand and led me to the bed. "Don't be afraid. I know you're a virgin. I promise to be gentle. Sometimes the first time for a woman can be a little painful. I will do my best not to hurt you."

Harley turned the sheet and cover down. He lifted me into his arms and softly deposited me on the bed. He settled beside me and removed my towel.

I attempted to pull the sheets up around me.

"No," he whispered. "Let me see you." He shifted the sheet away and gazed at me. "So lovely."

He kissed me tenderly and then deepened the kiss. He gathered me in his arms and stretched out beside me. I could feel the silkiness of his skin against mine. He felt so delicious.

Harley went so slowly and gently I felt no pain, only ripples of sensation. He was tender and obviously experienced. I lost all track of time as we made love well into the night, eventually drifting off to sleep in each other's arms.

Chapter Thirty-Eight

Harley

August

I woke up before sunrise eager to head out to Marble Canyon and Navajo Bridge. I let Mari sleep while I hopped into the shower. I hope she wouldn't be sore from last night. When I came out, she was stirring.

"Good morning, sunshine." I covered her in kisses.

"Um…hmm…," she stretched and kissed me back. "What's the plan for today?"

"If we can get there by sunrise, we might be able to see some condors."

She sat up, pulling the sheet to her chin, eliciting a laugh from me. "Really?" I chortled. "After last night?"

"Where are they?"

"Navajo Bridge near Marble Canyon. I asked room service to make a fruit and bread basket for us to take along."

"Do, I have time for a quick shower?"

"Don't take too long," I looked down. Suddenly, I was completely aware of every part of my body.

"Give me fifteen minutes!" Mari hopped out of bed and raced to the bathroom, leaving the sheet behind her.

I'm afraid the devil in me made an appearance. I wolf whistled and chased her, stripping as I went. I jumped into the shower with her.

"Harley!" She gasped.

"What" I feigned innocence. "We're married. It's okay for a husband to take a shower with his wife." I began soaping her back, arms, and legs.

"Um…Harley…" Mari groaned.

"Hmm…?" I continued my ministrations.

"Oh…" she moaned. "We're never going to leave this suite if you keep doing this to me."

"That wouldn't be so bad," I murmured into her ear.

"It is if you want to see the condors."

"Condors. Right." I got out, dried off and got dressed. "Party pooper," I muttered.

Back in the living room, I dialed my attorneys and accountants and planned for them to fly from Dayton to here. My flight team was then notified of the arrangements.

Room service arrived, and I tipped them generously. Mari came out dressed in jeans and a shirt. We grabbed our helmets and jackets and headed down to the lobby.

The ride took an hour and was quite scenic with vistas filled with canyons, desert, and the Colorado River. Reds, blues, greens, yellows, browns, and tan colors splashed the landscape like a paint palette gone awry. I had leg cramps that I tried to keep hidden from Mari. I didn't want her worrying about me on our honeymoon. I attributed the muscle spasms to the long ride on my Hog from the day before and this morning. I wasn't used to sitting on my bike as I once was.

"Are you okay?" Mari asked when she caught me rubbing my calf.

"Yeah," I replied. "It's just a charley horse."

"Are you sure? We can find someplace to sit."

"I'm sure," I said and straightened up.

"You'd tell me if you weren't okay. Right?" She continued to eyeball me.

"I'm fine, love." To prove my point, I headed toward the bridge.

We stopped at the historic Navajo Bridge and walked to the center. It spanned the Colorado River. It was originally named the Grand Canyon Bridge in 1929 and was later renamed the Navajo Bridge in 1934. It is 834 feet in length and rises 467 feet above the river.

It had magnificent views of the canyon. After drinking our fill, we found a location and settled down to watch for the condors. As the sun continued to rise we were visited by mule deer, a coyote, and a raccoon. Wrens, peregrine falcons, turkey vultures flitted in and out making for a stupendous aerial circus.

Then they appeared. The magnificent California Condor flew overhead. First came one, then two, and finally four of them. These birds are massive, look intimidating, and are terribly ugly, but so graceful in flight. However, due to their weight, they often have trouble becoming airborne and will run downhill or leap off the edge of a cliff. Once in flight, they soar for hours, dipping and weaving while searching for carrion.

Mari and I sat watching in companionable silence for hours. Occasionally, we nibbled on the fruit and bread from the basket. With great reluctance, we left and headed over to the visitor center. We shopped the local vendors.

Mari bought me a book on the history of the Navajo Bridge and the condors. She also bought us matching turquoise bracelets. We then drove the scenic route back to Page and stopped at a restaurant serving Mexican food for a mid-afternoon lunch.

"Mari, let's go back to the resort and pay Mister Whitaker a surprise visit. I want to see his reaction when I ask to see the books now."

"Why? Do you think something isn't right?"

"I just want to make sure he's not cooking the books."

"Do you want me to be there?"

"I'd like that, but it's not necessary. It shouldn't take much time to take a cursory look. Our legal and accounting teams will join us tomorrow. I booked them a couple of cabins here."

"Okay. I'll go take a nap. You wore me out last night," Mari giggled as we entered the lobby.

"You might want to get used to it. There's more where that came from. Lots more." I acted like I was going to chase her.

Mari danced away from me toward the elevator. I caught her, spun her around and pulled her up against me. I lowered my face and devoured her lips in a hungry, yet sweet kiss. I just couldn't get enough of this girl. My hand reached up and stroked her hair. This woman made my life complete.

Reluctantly, I let go and stepped back. "I'll see you in a bit. Te Amo, I love you."

"I love you," Mari stepped into the elevator and blew me a kiss before the door closed.

I stared at the door for several long minutes. There was nothing I wanted more than to join Mari in our room. With a sigh, I turned and headed to the reception desk where I asked to see Mister Whitaker.

He came striding down the hall with a frown on his face. "Mister Davis. To what do I owe this pleasure?"

"I'd like to take a quick look at the accounts, if I may." I held out my hand to shake his.

"This is not the most opportune time," Whitaker grumbled.

"Maybe not, but I hardly think you want to alienate a potential buyer."

"Very well."

I followed him to a conference room. "I would like to see your current balance sheet, profit and loss statements, tax returns, most recent audit, and a list of debtors. My team will want a more detailed examination tomorrow."

"Tomorrow? I can't possibly be ready tomorrow!" Whitaker thundered.

"Why is that?"

"That's not enough time."

"I see." I leaned back and sat silently.

"These things take time," he yammered.

I remained quiet. I noticed Whitaker was fidgeting in his seat. That could be a sign of nervousness or something more nefarious.

"I'm a busy man." Whitaker protested.

I uttered not a word, nor did I make a gesture.

Sweat beaded on his forehead. Soon there was a trickle running down his face.

"Okay, I'll have the documents brought in here and secured.

"Tell me, Mister Whitaker," I continued to stare at him. "Are you always this nervous when someone wants to audit your books?"

"Yes," he replied, looking at me directly in the eyes.

"Is there something I should know?"

"No. Nothing unethical or illegal."

"Good to know. Now, if I may take a quick look?"

"Absolutely. I'll be right back."

I spent the next two hours looking at the accounting. At a glance, everything seemed to be in order.

"How did it go?" Mari asked. She must have gone shopping. She was attired in a blue dress. "There's a dinner and dance tonight. I thought we'd go if that's okay with you." She motioned to the bed where a black suit was laid out. "I took the liberty of buying you a suit for tonight."

"Thank you. I removed my jacket and proceeded to get dressed for dinner.

The meal was fabulous. We met some lovely people who had been coming to the resort every year for vacation. Afterward, we went back to our suite to dress for the dance.

"I want to go look at something. Will it be okay if I met you at the fountain?" I asked as I put the finishing touches on my tie.

Mari wore a cream evening gown that accentuated her coloring. She looked ravishing. "You are so beautiful," I murmured and leaned in for a kiss.

"Thank you. You look pretty dashing yourself," She kissed me in return. "I'll see you there," Mari said gaily.

###

Mari

I sat quietly on the stone bench. If I listened, I could just make out the lapping of waves from Lake Powell. The night amplified the sounds creating a cacophony that was music to my soul. There was a rock fireplace nearby with a beautiful blaze reaching heavenward. I sat with my back to the fire and watched for Harley.

Moonlight wafted past the rose bushes, dark now in the night-time hours; climbing silently, it shimmered gently across the stone trellis and crept softly over the marble tiles. Lifting my head, I gazed into the starry sky. So many stars twinkled overhead oblivious to the hammering of my heart as I listened to the soft strains of a waltz playing in the distance. Harley could not have picked a more perfect place for our honeymoon to begin.

I could feel his presence closing the distance with each passing minute. My pulse quickened with anticipation. I could almost see him standing high upon the cliffs regale in all his biker glory, a specter, ghost-like wraith, unseen, unnoticed by those inside. The silver turquoise trinkets I had given him glistened in the ever-encroaching gloom. Shadows threadbare, thin, spelling out their doom as his sultry voice drifted over the wind and gently caressed my face.

"Mari." He said.

In the pale moonlight, Harley approached, holding out his hand. A necklace dangled between his fingers. Silver and turquoise with hints of gold entwined, it was an exquisite piece of Navajo workmanship. He bent and fastened it around my neck and then held his hand out to me.

"Dance with me," Harley's voice was a silky whisper against my ear.

In silence, I rose off the cold bench and glided into the sureness of his arms. Harley's right hand possessively traveled up my back to my neck as his fingers stroked my skin through the silken fabric of my gown and finally cupped my face.

Effortlessly my warrior drew me against his lean, muscular body until we seemed to meld into one as he guided me in the soft sway of a slow dance. Drugged by his hypnotic gaze, I rested my head against his shoulder and listened in a dreamy swoon to the thumping of his heart.

Chapter Thirty-Nine

Harley

August

My team arrived the night before and was ready to go over the books at seven o'clock in the morning. Mister Whitaker was not amused. I introduced them to him and left him in their capable hands. I arranged for refreshments and meals to be provided.

Then it was off to visit Rainbow Bridge on Lake Powell in southern Utah. Being the middle of August, it was sweltering hot. The day was sunny, and by ten o'clock the temperature had climbed into the low 80's with a projected high of around 95 degrees. I made sure we each had a thermos full of water and a few snacks.

The bridge is a natural wonder known by the Navajo as Nonnoshoshi or rainbow turned to stone. It is one of the largest natural bridges in the world and is almost as tall as the Statue of Liberty. This structure is comprised of two types of sedimentary rock. The first is known as Navajo Sandstone. It reminded me of pictures of the Sahara Desert. The parabolic curve of the bridge was made of Navajo Sandstone. The other is Kayenta Sandstone which formed the foundation of the bridge. Kayenta Sandstone is typically below a layer of Navajo Sandstone and is thinner and darker. It usually has broken ledges.

There is a footprint of a Dilophosaurus about fifteen yards from the trail on the right. We also saw a petroglyph about fifty yards to the left of the trail.

This entire area felt reverential; sacred. We spoke in hushed voices. Mari, while taking pictures of the Navajo Bridge and the Condor Pass Resort, took the most photos at Rainbow Bridge.

"It's so gorgeous and peaceful here." Mari took a deep breath while gazing at the landscape. "I can see why the Navajo hold this place in deep regard. It calls to the soul, you know?"

I looked around. Everywhere there was a mix of colors that brought feelings of serenity. Even the waters of Lake Powell evoked the mystical sense of timelessness.

All too soon, it was time to return to Page. We spent a couple hours looking for trinkets in the local shops. Mari bought a small pottery vase while I purchased a handwoven Navajo blanket.

When we arrived back at the resort, I met with my legal and accounting teams.

"How's it looking?" I asked, Richard Beardsley, head of my accounting team.

"The accounting system is remarkably simple. I place the valuation at around four million. I'd start by offering three million and go no higher than five."

"That's what I was thinking," I nodded. "Let's wait a couple of days before making the offer."

I turned to Benjamin Steele, "Can you draw up the necessary paperwork before then?"

"Can do. Under Davis Enterprises?"

"Yes, but I want Davis Enterprises as the umbrella. I want the resort in Mari's name." I looked at her sitting beside me. Mari's expression rapidly turned from complacent to surprise and then shock.

"I want this wrapped up by the end of the week."

"We'll get right on it, Mister Davis," replied both team leaders.

"Thank you." We rose to leave. "If you'll excuse us, my bride and I are going to lounge by the pool.

"Harley!" Mari gasped once we were in the elevator. "You're putting this place in my name?"

"Yes," I winked at her. "You love Anthropology and aboriginal culture. What better way to indulge your passion than ownership of the Condor Pass Resort in the heart of Navajo lands?"

"Will we keep the staff?"

We entered our suite and dug out our swimwear.

"If you wish."

"I'd like to see more Navajo people hired, and a bonus system similar to what Davis Enterprises has in place." Mari tugged on her swimsuit. “I know! Maybe, we can hire Navajo Veterans!” She sounded so enthusiastic it made me smile.

The pool was located behind the main resort. Cabins lined each side of the main building. Regardless of where we reclined, we had stupendous views of either the gardens, a gazebo, canyons in the distance, or hints of Lake Powell. I can honestly say I could stay here for eternity and be perfectly content.

Thursday, I made my offer.

“Three million is too small. I’ll take eight.” Mister Whitaker countered.

“Mister Whitaker,” I placed my fingers in a steeple pose. It’s a habit I have during negotiations and other periods of contemplation. “With all due respect, this fine establishment is nowhere near an eight-million-dollar valuation.”

“I won’t go below seven,” he offered.

I remained silent, watching his body and facial language. The longer I stayed quiet, the more agitated he became.

“Will you take six?”

“I’ll go four million, not a dollar more.”

“But…but…but…” Whitaker stammered.

My chief attorney, Benjamin Steele, and my head accountant, Richard Beardsley, whispered in my ear. “Mister Whitaker, my offer stands firm at four million.”

I continued to gaze at him. Mari swiveled her head from me to my attorneys, accountants, Mister Whitaker and back. Her movements reminded me of a bobblehead dashboard dog.

As the minutes dragged on, I employed the age-old tactic of drumming my fingers lightly on the table.

“Gentlemen,” I started to rise. “Time is up.”

My acquisitions team began shuffling their papers together in preparation to leave the room.

“Wait!” Whitaker called out. “I accept your terms.”

Everyone sat back down. My legal team handed out the contracts outlining the terms of the purchase. They went over it in detail, making sure everyone understood and agreed.

The financial group then explained how they reached the valuation they assigned, the profits, funding needed to provide some necessary upgrades, and taxation.

Once everyone agreed, the contracts were signed. I wrote a check for the entire purchase amount and obtained the legal bill of sale and receipt.

Mari kept looking at the paper in her hand. “This place is really ours?”

“Yours,” I smiled. “You are the principal owner. Our team will file the necessary forms here and back home as needed. Now, let’s go enjoy our last remaining day here.”

Friday came too soon. We were flying from Page to Angkor Wat before meeting Garrett in New York City for my medical checkup.

Chapter Forty

1978 Sweden is the first country to ban the sale of aerosol sprays. Inflation was at 7.62 percent although some states were still seeing much higher rates. Egypt and Israel sign the Camp David Accords to try to secure peace between the two countries. NASA announced the first women astronauts, which included Sally Ride. The Double Eagle II balloon became the first balloon to complete a transatlantic flight. Naomi Uemura of Japan completed the first solo expedition to the North Pole. The comic strip, Garfield, makes its first appearance.

Harley

August

We flew from Page, Arizona to Los Angeles where we stopped to refuel and then headed on to Bangkok. The total flight time took almost twenty-six hours. We checked into a luxurious hotel and spent several days sightseeing and partaking of the local cuisine.

Once we were acclimated, we traveled on to Cambodia and Siem Reap, a major city in the northwest. We had rooms at the Grand Hotel d'Angkor located approximately three miles from Angkor Wat. Siem Reap means the total defeat of Siam. The history of Siem Reap is tainted with tales of the brutal regime of the Khmer Rouge.

The temple was built by King Suryavarman the Second. His name means Shield of the Sun. Archaeologist Charles Higham claimed Suryavarman wasn't just a man, but a demigod. All depictions of the King show him as a large muscular man surrounded by his court.

Angkor Wat is an extremely large three-tier pyramid built to resemble Mount Meru, the mythical sacred home of the gods in Hindu mythology. There are other similar structures throughout the world which gives rise to the legends of the ancient gods from other worlds.

Angkor Wat is also known as a celestial temple. It was constructed using a series of mathematical equations that bring the temple into harmony with the universe. The temple is supposedly riddled with hidden rooms that are still in use. It was once considered to be lost to the world. Periodically rumors popped up about its existence. In truth, it was never lost.

Carved into monolithic structures are sensuously alive statues depicting Garudas, Bodhisattvas, and the Naga. The Naga is a snake king and the protector of the Angkor empire. Still, other tales have the temple being a portal to other places on earth and an interstellar port.

Both Mari and I found ourselves so completely engrossed in Angkor and the Angkor Wat temple we often lost track of time. The place had a reverential, spiritual essence I have never felt in other historical sites. It truly felt as though everything within its boundaries was ethereal, rising out of the fog like ether to point the world in the right direction.

"This place," Mari whispered. "It's like it knows us from the inside out."

"I think it does," I whispered back. "I think it calls to our innermost being."

I peered at the carvings on the outer wall. There were eight panels containing scenes depicted from the Hindu sacred book, Mahabharata. The detail in these carvings was astonishing. The temple also held more than 1,796 portraits of women who are supposedly goddesses. Are they symbolic? If so, of what?

Mari appeared fascinated by the elaborate statues throughout the temple." I think there's an astronomical use of this temple. It all seems to be too precise for it to be anything else."

"Maybe it points to other portals?" I suggested. "You know like Daiken Alba suggested in his lecture. He said these temples and the Nazca Lines point to other locations on earth. When they are correlated, they point to an unknown location in the constellations."

"I remember," Mari said. "I wondered if he was mentally unbalanced. What if everything he said was true?"

"That'd sure turn the world on its ear."

Sadly, our week came to an end, and we had to leave for Japan before returning to America. I've visited Angkor Wat several times. Sometimes it was for a week, other times I stayed a month. No matter how long I visited, it always felt like I didn't have enough time. So much to view, to study, and to learn.

We left Cambodia on September 4th headed for Japan. We were going to visit Tokyo, Buddhist temples, and gardens. I got to practice my Japanese. I enjoyed interpreting for Mari and taking her to my favorite places. We planned to spend a week there.

I met her Aunt Kiku. Kiku means chrysanthemum. According to Japanese custom, we brought gifts for each member of the family and treated them to dinner. Every time we ventured out of our hotel, Mari tensed as though she was frightened.

"Is something wrong?" I asked.

"No." She sounded miserable. "It's just, there are so many people, and I hate feeling trapped in an ocean of people."

"Tokyo is vibrant." I watched her expression.

"It's garish."

"Hold onto me. I won't let anything happen to us." I tucked her arm into mine and pulled her close. "Do you want to cut our visit here short?"

"Can we? We've been here four days." Mari said relief was evident in her voice.

"Sure. How about we head to New York tomorrow?" I suggested.

"Thank you. That'd be great."

After Japan, we headed to New York where we would meet up with Garrett. It was time for my follow up cancer check and possibly a round of treatment. I slept through most of the flight. Traveling made me uncharacteristically tired.

Garrett met us at the airport and took us to the penthouse near the Cancer Institute of New York. We had a few days to rest before my scheduled appointment.

###

Mari

I can honestly say I dreaded this medical appointment. It came in the middle of our honeymoon and only days from Harley's birthday. I could not sleep during the entire flight from Japan to New York.

We had to go through customs and declare the souvenirs we had purchased in Cambodia, Bangkok, and Tokyo. It seemed to take forever. Garrett met us as we left the customs area.

"How did you like the resort?" Garrett asked as he took the luggage from Harley.

"We loved it! Harley bought it!" I enthused. "Garrett, it was so beautiful there and serene."

"I'm glad you enjoyed it, Miss Mari. And how was Angkor Wat? Japan?"

"Angkor Wat lived up to its reputation. It was very mysterious. Japan was too crowded for me," I replied.

Harley remained silent as we walked toward the exit. I could only imagine his thoughts must be focused on the upcoming medical examination. Garrett took us to the penthouse he had purchased when he rescued Harley from the Davis's. We rested for a few days and then headed to the hospital for the dreaded checkup.

The exterior of the Cancer Institute of New York resembled an old gothic revival building. Inside, it was completely modern. The reception area and waiting rooms looked like a living room. All the patient rooms were private. No roommates. These looked sterile. It was up to family and friends to decorate. Harley was given a gray gown to wear.

For the next three days, this place was his home. Garrett and I spent as much time as possible with him.

"Garrett, when I get out of here, we're going to Scotland. Will you come with us? You can show us the sights."

"Master Harley, this is your honeymoon. I don't believe it would be appropriate…"

"Balderdash!" Harley exclaimed.

"We'd love you to go with us to Scotland," I interjected. "Please? Please? Please, come with us!"

"Garrett," Harley said. "We want to see Scotland through your eyes. I want to see the places you had your adventures. You know, the ones you used to tell me about when I was little. I'd like to see Loch Lomond, the highlands, Loch Ness, and Inbhir Theorsa. I believe you called the town Thurso."

"Aye, you'd be correct." Garrett had a faraway look in his eyes as though he was remembering his old hometown. "It'd be nice to see the old place again."

"Then, you'll come with us?" I asked.

"Aye, Miss Mari. I'll join you."

"Are you ready, Mister Davis?" A nurse and orderly entered the room. "The phlebotomist is here to take samples. Then we'll take you down to radiology for some imaging studies."

"I guess." Harley sounded depressed.

How he must hate this place. My heart hurt for him. I reached out and gently squeezed his hand. "It'll be okay. Garrett and I will wait right here for you." I leaned forward and tenderly kissed his lips.

Harley offered a wan smile in return. "I can't help but wonder if the Rhabdomyoscarcoma is back." His voice cracked. He watched as they drew six vials of blood from his veins.

"Hush, don't think it. Nothing good can come of thoughts like those," I stroked his brow. "Think positive thoughts."

"I'm trying, Mari. I don't mind admitting, I am scared."

"I know you are, love," I murmured.

"Okay, Mister Davis," the orderly said. "Can you get onto the gurney, or do you need help?"

"I can do it." Harley swung his legs over the edge of the bed, stood and then climbed onto the gurney.

I walked beside him, holding his hand until we got to radiology. "Garrett and I will be waiting for you in your room."

I watched them wheel him into the room. The nurse came back out within a few minutes.

"Hi, I'm Ellen. I'll be his day nurse while he's here." She walked beside me.

"Hi, Ellen. I'm Mari Davis."

"How are you related to Mister Davis?"

"I'm his wife." I still marveled at calling myself Harley's wife.

"Oh! I didn't know he was married."

"We're newlyweds."

"You are very lucky. Harley's a wonderful person." Ellen pushed the door to Harley's room open.

"Don't I know it." I turned to her. "What kind of tests are they going to perform?"

"X-rays, bone scans, PET scans, and ultrasound. Depending on the findings these may be followed up with a biopsy."

"A biopsy?"

"Yes. It's a surgical procedure where a piece of suspicious tissue is removed and examined. Depending on the results of the biopsy treatment may or may not be needed. Don't worry, Misses Davis, he is in good hands here."

"Thank you." I felt as though a giant lump was lodged in my throat. I looked at Garrett. He seemed to feel the same as I did. Fear gripped us both.

The time passed at a snail's pace. Finally, the door opened, and Harley was wheeled in. He looked haggard as though the imaging studies sapped his strength.

A food tray with chicken soup was brought in. Garrett helped him raise the head of the bed, so he was sitting upright and fluffed his pillows. I perched on the edge of the bed and spooned soup into his mouth.

He closed his eyes, savoring the flavor. "Thank you." He shook his head after three spoonfuls. "I can't eat anymore. My appetite is gone."

"Just a few more. You need to keep up your strength." Garrett said.

"I'm not hungry."

We stayed until visiting hours were over. "We'll be here first thing in the morning." I kissed him. "Sleep well. Call if you need me."

"I will. Goodnight."

I looked back at him as we left. He looked so forlorn and young. I could picture him as a small child wishing for his mother to tuck him in. I rushed back into the room. "I'll stay here tonight, my love." I looked at Garrett, "Please go on to the penthouse and get some rest, Garrett. I'll call you if anything comes up. Otherwise, we'll see you in the morning."

"Master Harley?" Garrett asked.

"What she said, Garrett. I'll be okay."

"Very well. I'll see you both in the morning."

I pulled the recliner to the opposite side of his IV pole. I tucked the blanket around him. "Go to sleep, love. I'll be right here."

An hour later, I went to the restroom. When I came back out, there was a sandwich on the lap table. "I asked for it when they took my dinner tray away. You had gone to the vending machine for a root beer."

"Shall, I feed you?" I asked and unwrapped the sandwich."

"It's for you. You haven't eaten, have you?"

'I had a little lunch while you were in radiology."

"But no dinner."

"No dinner." I agreed.

"Then eat," Harley beckoned.

"I will if you'll share it with me." I picked up the knife on his table and cut the food in half, handing Harley the bigger piece.

It wasn't long after he finished his morsel when he drifted into sleep. I stepped out and asked for a blanket. While at the nurse's station I informed them, I was staying the night at his side.

Shortly after Garrett arrived the next morning bringing bagels and cream cheese, the doctor came in.

"Well, Mister Davis, I have the results of your imaging studies."

Harley watched him warily. "You found something." He stated.

"Let's just say there is an area of concern. It is near the original location of the primary tumor. I don't think it's anything but scar tissue. Still, to be safe, I have scheduled a biopsy for today and a round of preventive treatment. Chances are, you'll leave here with a clean bill of health."

An hour later the orderlies came to take him into surgery. “You guys sure don’t waste any time, do you?”

“Not where cancer is concerned. The quicker a diagnosis is made, and treatment started the better the chances of survival are.”

Once again, I held his hand and walked with him. This time it was to the operating room. Garrett walked stolidly beside us.

Two hours later the surgeon came into the waiting room. “Davis family?”

“Over here,” Garrett responded.

The surgeon walked over to us and knelt down. “He came through just fine and is in recovery. In a few minutes, you can go in and be with him. Naturally, we need to wait for the biopsy results, but from what I saw, it appears to be scar tissue. I removed it and, in a few days, he should be able to travel back home.”

Scar tissue! I felt like a huge boulder had been lifted off my shoulders. “Will he need any treatment?”

“Not that I can see, but that’ll be up to his doctor.”

Harley was released two days later with instructions to return in three months for another follow up. He was told to get plenty of rest. No travel for a week. He was given an antibiotic prescription to be filled before we left for Scotland. Garrett flew home to pack his bags and returned.

Chapter Forty-One

Harley

September

We left New York exactly five days after I was discharged from the Cancer Institute of New York. It was two days earlier than the doctor recommended. The flight from New York to Inverness, Scotland took sixteen hours. In retrospect, I should have rested two additional days before traveling to Scotland. My left leg felt extremely sore by the time we arrived at the airport in Inverness. I used my cane.

"Are you okay?" Mari asked with concern.

"Yes. I'm just tired," I sighed as we walked to the rental car agency.

"Master Harley," Garrett took my bag from me. "I suggest we rest for a day before going toThurso."

We checked in to a hotel. "Rest, my love," Mari said. "I'm going to go downstairs and take a look at a few shops with Garrett. I won't be gone long."

The next day we headed to Inbhir Theorsa, Thurso. It was my birthday. From whispered conversations between Mari and Garrett, I assumed they had something planned. I hoped it wasn't anything elaborate. My leg still ached.

The drive from Inverness to Thurso took almost three hours. We went past Inverness Castle. Scenic Scotland lived up to its reputation. It was moody, beautiful, mysterious, wild, fiercely loyal, brooding, and simple. I got the impression it was a secret kept hidden from the world in plain sight.

###

Mari

I noticed Harley kept rubbing his calf. Once we got into our room, I insisted he let me and Garrett take a look. The area he was rubbing turned out to be the incision from the biopsy. It looked puckered and red.

"What do you think?" I asked Garrett.

"Looks like it's healing. We probably should have stayed in New York a few extra days. Let's start him on the antibiotics just in case."

I got the bottle of pills and handed them to Garrett while I went to get a glass of water. Soon after taking the medication, Harley fell asleep. He woke up long enough to eat dinner and went back to sleep.

The next morning, he was fine. The redness on his leg had faded. He ate a hearty breakfast of yogurt, fruit, porridge, and toast. This was followed by half a tomato broiled with cheese on top, a rasher of bacon, a tattie, scone, bangers, sautéed mushrooms, baked beans, egg, and black pudding. I found the black pudding to be revolting. It is made with pig's blood, fat, oats and spices stuffed into a length of intestine.

After breakfast, we got in the car and drove fourteen miles to Loch Ness. Harley regaled us with the absurd plans he and Thomas had concocted on capturing Nessie.

"Me and Thomas figured we could lasso Nessie and ride on her back to shore."

"Uh…Have you ever lassoed anything?" I asked. I could just picture the two of them trying to throw a rope around a dinosaur's neck much less climbing onto its back and riding it.

We took a boat ride. Harley peered intently through binoculars Garrett had purchased for his birthday. His entire body tensed and he pointed to a spot on the Loch near Urquhart Castle.

"Look!" He excitedly handed me the binoculars. "What do you see?"

"Something huge rising up from the water," I spoke in hushed tones.

"Do you see a long neck?" Harley was bouncing from foot to foot.

"Could be. Here, Garrett, take a look."

Garrett took the device with a bemused expression on his face. "Well, Póg Mo Thóin, kiss my arse!" Garrett exclaimed. "Looks like old Nessie is showing off for us."

"How cool is that?!" Harley crowed. The look of excitement, joy, and fun on his face made the little excursion worthwhile.

Then we headed back to Inverness for lunch before traveling another three hours to Thurso. Harley spent the entire drive from Inverness to Thurso talking about Loch Ness and Nessie. He knew all the folklore surrounding the sea serpent.

Our hotel in Thurso was quaint. We were housed in a cabin that had two bedrooms, one bathroom, and living space. On the porch outside were two rocking chairs and a bench swing.

"So, you planned the visit to Loch Ness? I mean, it was in the opposite direction from Thurso." Harley asked.

"For your birthday. We were going to head there yesterday but your leg was sore, and you looked exhausted." I said. "So, we decided to do it today."

"It lived up to my expectations." Harley clasped his hands together. "It was fabulous. And then to see something that could be Nessie…I sure hope the pictures turn out."

"Don't hold your breath. If they show anything at all, it'll be a tiny speck. We were too far away," I laughed.

"Even a tiny dot will do."

Once in our cabin, Garrett insisted Harley take a nap. He went out and purchased dinner. We sat outside and enjoyed an authentic repast while watching the sunset.

I gave Harley a photo book about Loch Ness and its famous inhabitant, and a book about the old St. Peter's Church. "Happy birthday, love."

Garrett handed him a tartan, a skean dhu known as a single-edged knife, kilt hose, and garters. "You are now an honorary Scotsman under my name, Geddes."

"Oh wow!" Harley fingered the garment. "I'm honored," he smiled. "Thank you!"

"What birthday would be complete without a pastry, eh?" Garrett went inside and came out bearing a cake. "It's Scottish ginger cake with lemon frosting and ginger crystals. I loved this cake when I was growing up."

"This is the best birthday celebration I've ever had. My two most favorite people beside me, seeing Nessie, eating cake, what guy could ask for more?"

The next day we toured the ruins of old St. Peter's Church, and then the Castle and Gardens of Mey where we enjoyed the food at the onsite tearoom. The gardens were beautiful. We took a leisurely stroll. Both Garrett and I were so engrossed in the scenery, we failed to notice Harley was lagging behind and using his cane.

###

Harley

The day started out fine, but as it wore on, I felt increasingly tired and weak. I knew in my bones something wasn't right. I chocked it up to jet lag and all the walking we've been doing. By the time we finished touring the Castle of Mey and gardens, I wanted nothing more than to return to our cabin and rest.

When we got back, Garrett suggested going to the museums. "You go ahead. I want to take a nap." I yawned.

Both Garrett and Mari stared at me. "Are you okay?"

"Yeah. I think I traveled too soon after the biopsy, I still have some jet lag, and all the walking has tired me out. A nap will do wonders."

"We'll stay here too," Mari said.

"Master Harley, let me take another gander at your leg." Garrett knelt and began rolling up my pant leg. "Looks good."

"Garrett, please go enjoy the museums," Mari said. "I'll stay here with Harley.

"Very well, Miss Mari." I'll check with you in a couple hours."

Mari curled up beside me and we both napped.

I woke up an hour later feeling refreshed. I gently turned onto my side and began placing kisses on Mari.

"Umm," she stretched. "How are you?"

"I feel great," I continued teasing her lips. "I want you." My voice dropped to a husky whisper.

We spent the remainder of the afternoon making sweet tender love. I couldn't get enough of her.

We were sitting in bed with the sheets draped around us when Garrett burst into the room. "You ready for dinner?" He glanced at us and then did a double look. His face reddened. "I'm…I'm sorry, I guess you aren't," he stuttered.

Mari and I burst into gales of laughter. "Give us a few minutes."

I never saw Garrett backpedal out of a room so quickly.

Dinner was a simple affair at one of the places Garrett frequented when he was a young man. The setting was family style with groups of people all sitting at the same table. There was no menu. Food was passed around, and everyone took what they wanted. The conversation was lively and at times boisterous or jovial.

We retired to our cabin early. Garrett settled in his room with a book he had purchased. I indulged in my new favorite pastime, making love with Mari.

The next day we visited Dunnet Head, the most northern point in Scotland. It was a very beautiful but isolated location. Our next stop was Holburn Head Lighthouse near Scrabster. The cliffs are stupendous with blow holes in the rocks. There are sheer drop-offs with no fencing, so we took extra care when climbing the cliffs.

Mari scrambled up the cliffs with ease. Garrett took a more leisurely pace, while I brought up the rear much further behind them. By the time I got to the top, I felt winded. I rarely get breathless, so I knew something was seriously wrong.

"Are you okay?" Mari grasped my arm. "Where's your cane?"

"I dropped it on the path." I pointed to it.

Garrett lifted me and took me to a rock to sit on. Mari scampered downhill and retrieved my cane.

We sat there for a long time. Each of us lost in our thoughts. Finally, I let the elephant out of its pen. "I don't feel well. Can we go back to the hotel?"

"Of course, we can." Mari and Garrett stood to each side of me.

###

Mari

Halfway down the trail, Harley stumbled. I was terrified he was going to fall over the edge of the sheer cliff.

"Harley!" I cried out.

Garrett and I hoisted him back onto his feet. A few steps further, he collapsed. Garrett gathered him into his arms and slowly carried him down from the cliffs and to the car.

We took him to a local doctor. "Given his medical history," the doctor peered at his clipboard.

"I suggest he be taken to the hospital in Inverness. I can arrange an ambulance service there." The doctor looked up with a grim expression. "I won't lie. I suspect his cancer may have returned."

"But…but…he was just given a clean bill of health about a week ago!" I cried.

"Funny thing cancer is. You can be clear one day and sick two days later. Newlyweds, eh?" He looked kindly at me.

I nodded, "Just over a month."

"I wish the best for you and your husband."

Garrett hurried from the room. I guessed he was in tears and may have gone to sign us out of our hotel. He was back an hour later. "I put our flight crew on notice." His voice was bleak, devoid of emotion.

How hard it must be on him. He'd lost newborn son thirty-two years ago, and now his adopted son might not survive. My heart went out to this lovely man.

At the hospital in Inverness, Harley was admitted. While waiting for test results, Harley told us the plans he had made. "Mari, I did as you wished except for one thing. The Condor Pass Resort is one hundred percent yours. Garrett, I have made generous provisions for everyone. I want you to hand Davis Enterprises over to my employees. I have made certain you will be taken care of with the bulk of my funds under your control."

"That should fall to Miss Mari." Garrett wrung his hands in distress.

"Mari wanted it this way."

"Please, Master Harley, let's not talk of such depressing matters."

"You're talking like you're going to die." I hiccupped.

"I'm being realistic, Mari. Something is seriously wrong with me. I just want you to be prepared."

"For what? Your death? How can anyone be prepared for the death of a person they love?"

The doctor came in. "I have the preliminary results. I'll be honest. It doesn't look good. Unfortunately, we do not have sufficient experience with this rare form of cancer. Your best option is to return to New York and the hospital that treated him, to begin with. I'm having him discharged immediately. I suggest you make flight arrangements as quickly as possible."

"You're certain it's back?" I asked, desperately wishing he was just taking precautionary measures.

"Yes, ma'am. The tests, while not conclusive, seem to indicate that is the situation."

We headed to the airport and turned in the rental car before boarding our plane. Once again Garrett carried him. After placing him in his seat, Garrett sat a few rows away. Occasionally, I could hear him sniffling.

I tucked a blanket around Harley and strapped him into his seat. I couldn't talk. It felt like my world was crashing around me.

Harley tried to lighten our moods by talking about all the crazy memories we had made. How he pranked Garrett with pink flamingoes and ugly garden gnomes. The exploding Valentine's day dinner, the horrible home cooked meal meant to prank me and almost got Garrett. How Garrett and Flash pranked the WOSL gang, Harley and me during Halloween by reenacting a scene from the 'Haunting of Hill House.'

"Mari," Harley croaked. "Spill no tears for me. I have lived a wonderful life made richer with you in it. If I should pass from this physical plane, I am not gone. I will have merely stepped behind the veil into the celestial where I will watch over you. Love means…"

"Never saying goodbye," I whispered as I spooned ice chips into his mouth.

"I will wait for you just as you will wait for me. Have our marriage sealed posthumously. When the time is right, we will be reunited for our love is for eternity."

I kissed him tenderly. It was so unfair. Harley was a great guy, so caring, kind, protective and generous. Why is it the best people seem to die so young?

He reached up and ran his thumb over my cheeks. "Sweet Mari, do not cry for me."

"I love you so much, Harley," I sobbed.

"Hush…" he kissed me back. "I know you do. And I love you. We were meant to meet and to marry. Now, it's time to move forward. I will be with you for eternity."

He gently held my hand. We sat that way for hours. Somewhere over the Atlantic, Harley slipped the bounds of earth to ride with the angels.

Epilogue

Mari

An angel once whispered softly in my ear. He wrapped me in his arms and held my fears at bay, and taught me to be a motorcycle mama loving the open road.

Harley had a reason for loving me and used to talk about how I was his soul mate. He always said he felt at home in my arms. He said holding me closely soothed his bedeviled wandering soul.

His was a warm and tender love. He always looked out for me even when he was a bit of a devil. He showed his affection not so much in words, but in deeds.

The gentle touch of his hand on my arm as he led me around a puddle, the way he cocked his head and gazed into my eyes, and the sheer joy that spread across his face when he saw me waiting for him in the parking lot.

He watched over me by trying to keep me safe when I did something foolish, but he never suffocated me. He gave me freedom and wings to fly high and experience life in all its glory.

I know it's not possible, but I still long for his kisses, and I still want the future we had dreamed about. I swiped at the dampness on my cheeks as a tear leaked from my eye. I will always miss having his arms around me, feeling his sweet breath as he whispered in my ear.

Dixie's restaurant has become one of my favorite places. It is often frequented by bikers. It reminds me of the old diner Harley loved in Lafayette with booths lining one wall and a counter with stools on the other side. Antique tabletop jukeboxes sit in each booth. I flipped through the selection until I found 'Another's Lifetime' by Steppenwolf.

Having made my choice, I perused the menu. A turkey sandwich and a long tall glass of Born Wild, a juice concoction of cranberry, grape, strawberry, and lemons, looked good.

My thoughts turned back to those halcyon days and the WOSL-Lima gang. What crazy, fun times we had. How I wished I could roll back time to do it all again, to hold and love Harley just one more time.

Having made my choices, I sat back with my eyes closed and listened to the growling voice of John Kay.

During all the treatments that stole time from him, he never cried out. When he was going through so much pain and misery, he never complained; not even once because he knew what awaited him on the other side.

There were many nights when I awakened certain I heard his beloved voice calling my name.

"Mari."

I lay there listening, hoping to hear him once again before sleep overcame me. It seems I always heard him when the time was blackest. His voice was like a guide bringing me from the brink of darkness into the light. Oh, how I miss him, even now. I lost him way too soon; a little over a month after we married.

After returning to the USA, I had him cremated and carry his ashes in an urn until I find the perfect spot. I suspect it will be at the Condor Pass Resort.

Harley taught me how to love unconditionally. Kindness and generosity can lift up those people less fortunate and will earn you respect. Spirituality is important for the soul, and living life without regret is essential to happiness.

There's no one looking over my shoulder or giving me a hug; no one to take away my fears; no angel whispering softly of love. It's so peaceful and so lonely. And should he find me some morning, my thoughts will have taken me far, far away from here back to the time when he still lived.

There comes a time when you feel the want to leave, to see the world, indeed, the universe, outside of here. And should he see me as the sun sets, he will look deep into my face and see the longing to know and visit the places he has been and held so dear. He will see a desire to have those adventures we had dreamed of but have only read about.

Oh, how I wish I could go to the places he had, to see the sights as he viewed them. It would bring a calming influence to my soul to know that I walked along the same paths, trails, and markets where he once trod. What joy I would experience just knowing I sampled the same foods, cultures, and environs he loved.

"Hey, love," the rich tones of a familiar baritone voice caressed me as I listened to the music.

With eyes closed, I could almost picture Harley standing beside me like he did so many years ago at Zagano's Pizzeria. "You're a hard person to keep up with."

Harley's voice came softly through the strains of the music. "May I sit here?"

I opened my eyes and stared into the face I thought I'd never see again. Harley looked much like he did back then. "It's not possible," I shook my head.

"When you died, a part of me went with you." A tear leaked from my eye. "I had us sealed in the temple posthumously."

"I know," Harley said gently. "I was there."

Harley reached out and took my hand, "Mari, not everything you read in the paper about death is the truth." His hair was a deeper shade of sandy and dark brown and now had streaks of silver.

He had a silver beard. He looked so much older in the two years that have passed. He wore a black leather jacket, black shirt, and jeans, and carried a motorcycle helmet in his hands. He flipped the aviator glasses up on his head. I stared into the wildly innocent eyes that have haunted me these past few years.

"I went through a lot with cancer treatments, some of them I told you about when we talked on the telephone late at night. Others, I didn't care to rehash, they were so brutally draining. I never called you after those days, but I dreamed about being with you. Eventually, they found the right combination. That's when I learned you had gone to Texas. I was overjoyed when you returned, and we got married. I really thought we had a lifetime to live. Then cancer returned, and I moved to the celestial world. I've been looking after you ever since."

I cried, and he slid beside me in the booth. It felt as though time had stopped and rolled back to 1975 and the Lafayette diner where our first date began.

"Trying to live life without you is the hardest thing I've ever had to do, Harley. I miss you so much. Not a day goes by that I don't wish you are here with me to kiss away my fears, to protect me, teach me, and to love me."

"Even though I wasn't physically with you these past few years, I never went away Mari. I'll be here forever, watching over you, loving you."

I tried to hold back the mist gathering in my eyes and keep the quiver in my voice unheard as I whispered, "I miss you so much."

He gathered me into his arms, and my angel whispered, "I told you we would find each other again because love means never saying goodbye. Go to the Condor Pass Resort. I'll be there. I will wait for you, my love."

Author's Notes

Most of the music mentioned in this novel can be found online. Unless otherwise noted, the music can be purchased at:

Amazon.com:
https://www.amazon.com

Steppenwolf:
http://steppenwolf.com

- Just for Tonight on Hour of the Wolf
- Another's Lifetime on Hour of the Wolf
- Tenderness on Steppenwolf Gold and on For Ladies Only
- Rock and Roll Song on Skullduggery
- Jupiter's Child on At Your Birthday Party
- Jeraboah on Slow Flux
- In Hope of a Garden on For Ladies Only
- Skullduggery on Skullduggery
- Hippo Stomp on 7
- Foggy Mental Breakdown on 7
- Ride with Me on For Ladies Only
- Rock Me on At Your Birthday Party
- Screaming Night Hog on Steppenwolf Gold: Their Greatest Hits, 1970
- Drift Away on John Kay's solo album My Sportin' Life 1973
- Desperation on Steppenwolf 1968
- Disappointment Number on Steppenwolf The Second 1968
- Lost and Found by Trial and Error on Steppenwolf The Second 1968
- Hodge, Podge, Strained Through a Leslie on Steppenwolf The Second 1968
- Resurrection on Steppenwolf The Second 1968
- Berry Rides Again on Monster 1969
- Howling' For My Darlin' on Early Steppenwolf 1969

- I'm Going Up Stairs on Early Steppenwolf 1969
- Born To Be Wild on Steppenwolf 1968

Meatloaf
- Two Out of Three Ain't Bad
- Bat Out of Hell 1977

The Godfather
- Love Theme, aka Speak Softly Love

Jimi Hendrix
- Ezy Ryder on The Cry For Love released posthumously 1971

Kris Kristofferson
- Help Me Make It Through the Night

The Byrds and also Roger McGuinn
- Ballad of Easy Rider

Sailcat
- Motorcycle Mama 1974

Creedence Clearwater Revival
- Cosmos Factory album

Harry Nilsson You 1970/Bad Finger 1970/Shirley Bassey 1972/Heart 1978/Air Supply 1991
- Can't Live if Living is Without You also known as Without You

Bob Seger
- Tryin' to Live My Life Without You on Bob Seger and the Silver Bullet Band Greatest Hits 2
- Gates of Eden on Ride Out

Tom Wait

- Hold On on Mule Variations

The Band
- The Weight

The Allman Brothers
- Midnight Rider on Idlewild South 1970

Peter Hollens
- Loch Lomond on Legendary Folk Songs (this version was not available in the 1970's but is an excellent representation of the song)

Bartók

Shubert

Mormon Hymns
- I Need Thee Every Hour
- Lead Me into Life Eternal
- All Creatures of our God and King

Books:

- Jesus Christ Latter-Day Saints: Gospel Truth, 2 vols Salt Lake City, Zion's Bookstore 1957 1:30
- President Spencer W. Kimball statement made in 1976 later published in Teachings of Spencer W. Kimball, edited by Edward L. Kimball, Salt Lake City: Bookcraft, 1982, page 187.
- Elder Bruce R. McConkie, formerly of the Quorum of the Twelve. Mormon Doctrine, Salt Lake City: Bookcraft, 1966, page 771

- Harley's Redemption: The Search for True Love; book one in the Ride With Harley series.

- Harley & Me: Love Means Never saying Goodbye; book two in the Ride With Harley series.

Movies:

- Foul Play July 14, 1978, Goldy Hawn, Chevy Chase; comedy
- Convoy June 28, 1978, Kris Kristofferson, Ali MacGraw; action
- Heaven Can Wait June 28, 1978, Warren Beatty, Julie Christie; comedy

- The Haunting of Hill House, Julie Harris, Claire Bloom, horror

Places:

Piatt Castles:
Mac-A-Cheek Castle
1051 Townsend Road 47
West Liberty, Ohio 43357
Mac-O-Cheek Castle
2319 State Route 287
West Liberty, Ohio 43357

P.O. Box 497
West Liberty, Ohio 43357
937-465-2821
937-844-3480

Good' N Plenty
150 Eastbrook Rd (Route 896)
Smoketown, PA 17576
717-394-7111

Zaganos Pizzeria (closed)

The Tudor Arms Hotel Cleveland
Double Tree by Hilton
10660 Carnegie Avenue
Cleveland, Ohio 44106
216-455-1260

Navajo Bridge Marble Canyon, Arizona
Lakeview Cemetery
12316 Euclid Ave.
Cleveland, Ohio 44106-4393
216-421-2665

Rainbow Bridge National Monument
c/o Glen Canyon National Recreation Area
PO Box 1507
691 Scenic View Dr.
Page, Arizona 86040
928-608-6200

Grand Hotel d'Angkor
Siem Reap, Cambodia

Angkor Wat
Siem Reap, Cambodia

Inverness Castle
Inverness, Scotland, uk

Loch Ness
Loch Ness, Scotland, uk

Old St. Peter's Church (ruins)
Thurso, Scotland, uk

The Castle and Gardens of Mey (with tearoom)
Thurso, Scotland, uk

Dunnet Head
Thurso, Scotland, uk

Holburn Head Lighthouse
Scrabster, Scotland, uk

Visit Wolfpark.org at http://wolfpark.org/
They are a very worthy organization, and I hope you will consider donating to them.

Wolf Park
4004 East 800 North
Battle Ground, Indiana 97920
765-567-2265

Houston Intercontinental Airport is now Bush Intercontinental Airport

Church of Jesus Christ of Latter-Day Saints
1195 Brower Road
Lima, Ohio 45801
419-227-2537
https://www.lds.org

I love hearing from my readers. Please feel free to email me at:
cassandraparker753@gmail.com

Visit my Amazon page at:
https://www.amazon.com/-/e/B019CT2XMW

Facebook:
https://www.facebook.com/CassandraParker/

Copy and paste the links in the above pages into your email client or web browser.

An honest review is appreciated.

Made in the USA
Columbia, SC
04 October 2018